Omahia Heat

The Protecting Love Series

Michelle Donn

Omaha Heat

First Edition

Copyright © 2022 Michelle Donn

All rights reserved.

This book is a work of fiction. The names, characters, places and incidents are products of the writer's imagination or have been used fictitiously and are not to be construed as real. Any resemblance to persons, living or dead, actual events, locales or organizations is entirely coincidental.

Editing by Mistress Editing

Proofreading by Tiff Writes Romance

Contents

One

RICK HUNG HIS HEAD and pressed a hand to the shower wall as the scorching hot water beat down. The regular rhythm of the spray matched the pounding in his skull.

The meeting with his boss replayed behind his eyelids.

It had been a formality. Rick knew he wasn't ready to get back in the field before he sat down across from his boss. Shit, the walk from the parking lot to the office kicked his ass. He'd been shaky and out of breath by the time he made it there. And he had to wipe the sweat off his forehead before he knocked on the office door.

An FBI field agent had to rely on his body. Since getting shot, the only thing Rick could rely on his body to do was hurt. All the damn time.

But there was a massive difference between logically knowing his body was damaged and being on medical leave from the bureau. The only way he got his gun and badge back was to pass the FBI's physical and mental evaluations. His boss had tried to cushion the blow with the offer of additional healing time and the promise of a desk job if he never got back to normal.

He pounded the cold tile wall with his fist. The movement sent pain radiating from his shoulder, causing him to wince.

Normal. What a crock of shit. He'd never been normal. He'd been one of the best agents in the Miami field office. Nothing stood in his way when he worked a case. Not shitty judges who tossed out evidence for no good reason. Not a boss who was more concerned with bureaucracy than justice. Or FBI policies that left him frustrated at every turn.

Despite it all, Rick did his job—he closed cases. Until he got shot closing his last investigation.

Everything about the fake Vermeer painting case had been a shit show. His boss saw a chance for a headline-grabbing bust and overrode a number of Rick's concerns. And ultimately, Rick paid the price. Two 9mm bullets fired at close range into his chest.

He twisted the faucet and turned off the water. He carefully stepped out of the shower. Fast movements and slick tile weren't his friends. Little old ladies were safer in a bathroom than he was.

He rubbed a towel down his body and looped it around his hips one-handed. The thick layer of steam on the mirror couldn't hide the hideous sight of his wounds.

He wiped the condensation off the mirror and stared at his reflection. He traced the long white scar that slashed down the center of his chest and then curved under his right pectoral muscle. The skin felt alien under his fingertip, its texture strange. The damaged nerves didn't register sensation correctly, and the oddity of seeing himself touch his chest but not feel it made him vaguely nauseous. Lower down his side, a pucker of skin was all that remained where the chest tube had been inserted.

He pinched the healed-over bullet hole between his thumb and forefinger. A few inches up or down, left or right, he would have died.

Beyond the scars, his body was withering. The abdominal and chest muscles he'd carved with almost daily workouts in the FBI gym were atrophying. He tugged away the towel. Even his thighs that had been hard as granite from long runs along the beach seemed diminished. He pulled his towel back in place.

"Yeah, I'm so fucking lucky," he told his reflection. His sharp, cynical laugh echoed in the small apartment bathroom. He swiped a bottle of pain pills off the counter and popped two in his mouth. He hadn't taken any before seeing his boss and was feeling it now. He shouldn't have abstained; the Vicodin might have made the meeting a bit more bearable.

He was sick of people telling him he was lucky. What he was looking at in the mirror wasn't the body of a lucky man. A lucky man didn't get shot in the first place. Or would have been wearing a vest. Or would have taken a hit in his shoulder. A lucky man didn't have his chest cracked open in the emergency room like a fucking piñata.

Lucky to be alive was the dumbest thing he'd ever heard. Luck was bullshit.

When they discharged him from the hospital five weeks ago, he was weak as a kitten. They'd told him he shouldn't lift anything heavier than a half-gallon of milk. He wasn't doing much better now. Between lack of use and scar tissue formation, his right shoulder was all but frozen. His endurance was at an all-time low. And the hours he spent in a pain pill-induced haze pretending to watch cooking shows on TV wasn't helping.

He flipped on the cooking channel as he walked past the TV in the bedroom but clicked mute on the remote. He didn't need to hear the host's voice. Silence was about his speed today.

He sat on the edge of his bed. He should get dressed and go outside. His physical therapist said he should walk more to start building endurance.

His cell phone rang. He picked it up off the bedside table and looked at the screen. It was his mother. With his finger over the ignore option, he hesitated. If he didn't talk to her now, she'd call back. She always called back. His brother Michael was the same. His friends, on the other hand... most of them had given up.

He pushed ignore. Again.

He'd call her later when he took his walk. That was a lie. He wasn't going to call his mother or take a walk. Hell, he probably wasn't even going to get dressed. Just crawl back into bed and zone out for the rest of the day.

As he reached over to put the phone back on the table, it buzzed with a text message. His mother wanted to know if he was coming to family dinner tomorrow. Everyone would be there.

He could see it now: twenty of his happy relatives all jostling for the best position in the buffet line around his mother's dining room table while asking him if he was feeling better yet.

Yeah, no, he wasn't doing that either.

He put the phone face down on top of a letter that he hadn't bothered to open. It was from his late grandmother's lawyer. Mona, his favorite grandmother, had died back in February, and he missed her. A kid probably shouldn't have a favorite grandparent, but by the time he was old enough to learn that, it was too late. He and Mona had bonded.

He pulled the letter from Jacob Hansen out from under the phone. He was sure it was about Mona's house, which he'd inherited when she passed. She had moved home to Omaha to live with her older sister in the family homestead after her husband's death. The house was another responsibility he'd been ignoring. But in all fairness, he'd been ignoring the house since well before he was shot. He didn't want to do anything with that old house. It was a museum to Mona's memory.

He ripped open the flap on the envelope and scanned the letter. Hansen wanted him to know that like much of the country, Omaha was experiencing a real estate boom. And Mona's house was in one of the hottest neighborhoods in the city. If he wanted to capitalize on this once-in-a-lifetime opportunity, he should come to Omaha, oversee some minor renovations on the house, and get a real estate agent working for him. Selling the house would deliver a windfall of profits and create a lasting legacy for him and his future like Mona had always dreamed.

Legacy. Rick snorted. Who was this guy?

He lay back on the mattress, feet on the floor, the wet towel still under his ass. He'd spent quite a bit of time in that house. As a kid, his family often vacationed in Omaha to escape the oppressive heat of Florida summers. As he got older, trips to Mona's house were a way to recharge. She was a quiet, contemplative woman at heart. And always quick to offer comfort food and a sympathetic ear. She'd helped him pick a major in college, then decide to join the bureau. And she'd talked him through his first and last broken heart when a girlfriend left for grad school.

She was gone, and her passing left a hole that he couldn't imagine ever filling.

His life was in the shitter. He was contemplating filing for permanent disability before his fortieth birthday. Damn, that thought made him squirm. If that was his fate, maybe the windfall from the sale of Mona's house would be the money that kept a roof over his head for the rest of his miserable life. The reality was that unless he got a lot better, he wouldn't ever be a field agent again, and even a desk job might be beyond his capabilities.

What a bleak fucking life. But if he had a nest egg to rely on, it would help cushion the blow.

His cell phone buzzed again. Without checking, he knew it was his mother.

Omaha could be just what he needed. There were too many expectations here in Miami. And way too much family pressuring him to get better. A change of scenery might be good for him.

He was sure no one in Omaha would tell him he was a lucky guy.

Two

"WE ARE SO, SO going to be late." Maggie pointed her car toward the highway exit for Evan's school. Her boss would be pissed if she interrupted the meeting by arriving late.

"Mom, it'll be fine. It's always fine. I think you like freaking out in the mornings."

"Thank you, voice of reason. No, it's a big deal today."

"Whatever."

For a nine-year-old, her son was way too calm. Then again, she stressed enough for both of them. Today, she and her boss at the Omaha convention center would be meeting with the US Diamond and Fine Jewelry Show organizers. The show was huge, massive, and amazing. It usually was held in Houston, Texas, but a hurricane had damaged the convention center there, and Omaha was the only venue that met all the show's security requirements and had open dates.

She turned a corner and could see the backup of high-end cars waiting to drop off at Evan's private school. She eased her ten-year-old Honda behind a sparkling new Range Rover, joining the line of cars creeping toward the drop-off zone. Her car's brakes or transmission or something squealed in protest every time she lifted her foot to roll forward. She sank down in her seat, totally embarrassed when one of the faculty members on the sidewalk shot her some side-eye.

"Told you, Mom. Tons of time." Her son continued filling her in on all the end-of-school-year happenings: a class party, summer reading lists, and speculation on who would be the new fifth-grade teacher. Evan might be brilliant, but right now, he sounded like any other kid excited for summer vacation that started next week.

"Do you think he has a gun?"

"Who?" The random change in subject confused her. She glanced at Evan, trying to follow the conversation. He was getting big, another growth spurt starting. Great, he'd need a whole new wardrobe of summer clothes, and then new school uniforms come fall. Oh well, it's just money. Fuck.

"Mona's grandson. I heard you and Mr. Hansen talking about him. He's an FBI agent. Mona told me cool stories about how brave he is and how he helps people."

"I guess he'll have a gun. I've never met an FBI agent in real life."

Rick Cabrera, Mona's grandson, had been the hot topic at last week's front porch party in the neighborhood. Apparently, he was finally coming to "deal" with the house he'd inherited back in February when wonderful, sweet Mona Cabrera passed away. She missed her landlord and surrogate grandmother.

"What about a badge? He'll have to have one of those, right?"

"On TV, all the FBI agents do."

She wasn't as excited to see Rick Cabrera as Evan. Rick was a favorite of Mona's, but he'd not once come to visit his grandmother in all the time Maggie had been renting the basement apartment at Mona's house. It rubbed her the wrong way. Mona was almost ninety when she died, and her favorite grandson should have made an effort.

"That's so cool. Think he'll show it to me?"

"You'll have to ask. Politely." She shouldn't think badly of Rick. They'd been friends as kids before her family moved across town to live closer to her father's new parish. Rick had been just enough older that she'd idolized him when he came to visit. She had a vivid memory of him at the big public pool jumping off the high dive when all the rest of the neighborhood kids chickened out. They must have been around Evan's age at the time.

"Yes, Mother. I know." For a nine-year-old, her kid had exasperation down to an art.

Maggie's phone rang, and she twisted, fumbling for her purse in the back seat. Her fingers wrapped around her phone, her foot slipped off the brake pedal, and the car lurched forward. A hideous crunch followed. She'd hit the back bumper of the SUV in front of her.

Shit. An accident in the carpool lane—only her. She quickly told her boss she had to call him back and opened her car door. "Stay here. I'll deal with this." Her son didn't need to witness her mortification.

Evan's eyes were wide and fixed on the chunk of her Honda's front bumper that was dangling off the hitch on the back of the Rover. It swung back and forth a few times before falling to the ground. She was ninety percent sure he was about to laugh.

It was only a tap. How the hell did it rip off her bumper? She crossed her fingers, hoping the pricey SUV wasn't damaged.

The driver of the Range Rover hopped out to meet Maggie on the curb. It was the new news reporter from the local TV station. She was all blonde perfect television hair and makeup. Her baby pink tracksuit clung to a to-die-for hourglass figure. Even her sneakers were sparkly.

Maggie bent down and scooped up her bumper. "I'm so, so sorry about this. I was late, and my phone was in the back. My foot slipped. I don't even know how it happened."

The reporter shrugged. "The school drop-off lane is a dangerous place." She squatted down and inspected her car. "I don't think my tank sustained any damage." She smoothed a nicely manicured hand over the pristine paint.

"Oh, good."

"Is the family you work for going to be upset about all this? I mean, I would never want to cost someone a job over something silly like this."

"The family—" Maggie trailed off. The reporter thought she was a nanny. Then again, no other parent at the school drove a ten-year-old car. Who was she to correct a news reporter? "No, they're cool."

"Awesome. I'm Cheryl from channel seven." She held out a hand to shake.

"Yes, I recognized you. I'm Maggie."

"Okay, Maggie. Can I have your info in case something comes up when I have the dealer check her out?"

The dealer? Shit, that sounded expensive. She dug in her purse for a card. She always kept a few at the bottom.

"Mom! I'm going to be late." Evan jumped out of her Honda and kissed her on the cheek before bolting toward the school entrance. Cheryl's daughter clambered down from the tall SUV and followed, taking Evan's hand.

"Oh, my God, I'm so embarrassed." Cheryl pressed a hand to her chest and looked ready to beg Maggie's forgiveness. "You're a parent. I just assumed."

"It's so not a big deal. At all." She squeezed Cheryl's arm reassuringly before giving her a big smile and a careless shrug.

"What grade is your son?" Cheryl pointed at their kids, walking hand in hand.

"Fourth. Your daughter?"

"Same. She started after spring break. Do you know anything about the new fifth-grade teacher? I hear the rumors are flying that another class is going to lose their teacher."

"The drama, right. I don't have the inside track. I wish I did. My son wants to know."

"I feel you. These extra-smart kids don't roll with the punches like we did, right?"

Maggie laughed. The expression on Cheryl's face spoke to something deep inside her own heart. Having a genius for a kid was an experience. Sometimes good, sometimes bad. But it always kept you on your toes.

"Promise not to tell anyone?" Cheryl looked around and lowered her voice. "But her homework scares me."

"Same. The math he's doing is so far over my head. I let him explain it to me while I sip a glass of wine and nod."

"Me, too. I'm still not sure how my DNA and my idiot ex's DNA created her. She's so next level. I need a friend that understands. We have to meet up. Start a support group for normal humans raising little Einsteins. I'll bring the chardonnay."

"I've got the cheese and crackers. We can compare smart kids and stupid ex-husbands."

"Maggie, I would love that. Other parents just don't get it." Cheryl's impulsive and exuberant hug almost knocked her over.

A horn blared from behind them. They were totally messing up the drop-off system.

Cheryl looked at the card Maggie had given her and did a double-take, ignoring the horns. "You're Lone Tree Botanicals?"

"Yes, that's me." When she wasn't working at the convention center or trying to be Supermom, she was Lone Tree's only employee.

"Forget cheese and wine. I must have a trunk full of your beauty products. Last summer, when I came to interview at the station, I stopped at the green market and bought some of your lip balm. That stuff is heaven in a tube."

"Yes, we can do it all—the wine and the lip balm. But we better move our cars before someone gets homicidal." Maggie chucked the bumper scrap in her trunk and jumped behind the wheel. She waved at Cheryl as she peeled out of the school roundabout.

She would need to break every traffic law in the state of Nebraska if she was going to make it to work on time. Because while she loved making and selling her beauty products every summer to pay for her son's private school tuition, her convention center job paid rent, provided health insurance, and fed her and Evan.

As she floored it, a smile curved her lips. She loved meeting new people, and strangely, that was the second time in her life she had turned a fender bender into a happy accident.

Three

EVERYTHING HURT. HIS HEAD pounded; his shoulder burned. Even his back and neck hurt.

Rick shifted in the rental car seat, looking for a modicum of relief, but until he could stretch out in a bed, lay flat, and pop a few pain pills, it wasn't going to improve. He hadn't considered how hard sitting in coach on an airplane would be on his body.

The GPS in the car chimed and told him his final destination was five hundred feet ahead on the right. He took his foot off the gas and let the car coast slowly down the block. The street had a row of homes on one side, a city park on the other. As a kid, he played in that park, climbed the trees, and rode a bike down the paths. Now, a sign pointed visitors toward a dog park.

A lot had changed, but a lot stayed the same. It had been six or seven years since he'd visited. He should have made time. He'd been too busy, and now he regretted it. He wasn't surprised by the ache growing in his chest as he looked at the familiar street.

He rolled to a stop in front of his grandmother's house. It looked every day of its hundred and thirty years old. The bright white paint was dull and peeling in places, an upper window was missing a decorative shutter, and the elaborate Victorian gingerbread on the turret was missing. It was a depressing version of the house he remembered.

The yard was a total contrast. It was more meticulously maintained than the city park across the street. A riot of plants surrounded the lavender bushes that flanked the front steps. On the front porch, large planters overflowed with small herbs. And in place of the lawn on either side of the front walk, beds of small, daisy-like flowers grew. There wasn't a single weed in sight.

All this must be Maggie's, the tenant who rented the basement apartment. The memory of a ragamuffin little girl with dirty blond hair and beat-up Chuck Taylors floated through his mind. As a kid, she'd always wanted to tag along with the older boys no matter what trouble they were planning on getting into. He had a hard time reconciling that image with the stories of a divorced single mom his grandmother shared in their weekly phone calls.

Looking at her beloved house, the reality that Mona was gone hit him hard. He hadn't been able to attend her funeral back in February because he had to testify in the federal trial that sent the former mayor of Miami to jail. He should have come anyway. The mayor would have gone to jail without his testimony.

He rubbed his jaw; the pain of Mona's loss still felt fresh even though it had been months. She had been the odd woman out in Miami. The Cabrera family was a big, loud Cuban clan. Mona, a reserved Midwesterner with family ties back to the pioneer days, had been an anomaly. She was his island of calm amid the chaos. And Rick had loved her for it.

The memories of Mona sat heavy on his shoulders. Maybe this wasn't the best idea. This house might bury him in the past instead of offering him a path forward. His trip wasn't about the house. It was about the money it could bring when sold.

He turned the wheel and maneuvered the car down the short drive alongside the house toward the old barn. He had forgotten how big this lot was. It must be almost two acres. No wonder Jacob Hansen wanted him to get on the hot real estate market. It would be a rare find.

The backyard, like the front, was missing its lawn. Rows of plants and bushes he couldn't name filled every inch. The old peach trees were still there. The row of trees produced the most incredible fruit. He could almost taste Mona's cobbler thinking about it. Her sister would overnight the ripe fruit to Mona when she still lived in Miami to bake with it. He grew up on the decadent but simple dessert.

He parked the car in front of the small barn's double doors. Mona and her sister Polly had always parked their vehicles in the building but stubbornly refused to install an automatic opener. He heaved his wretched body out of the car and groaned. He tried to stretch and loosen up, but his body wasn't cooperating.

He dropped his good shoulder against one of the doors and leaned. The door glided open so easily he almost face-planted in the dirt. When he regained his footing, he was astonished at the sight that greeted him. He would not be parking his car in the barn.

The inside of the barn housed a factory, a distillery, a something... What the hell?

And the smell overwhelmed him. It was reminiscent of those stores in the mall that sell scented candles. A jumble of fragrances so mingled together he couldn't identify a single one.

In the center of the barn, a large butcher block worktable had a row of small empty bottles lined up across it. He picked up one and turned it to read the label: Lone Tree Botanicals – Mint Face Scrub, all-natural and made in Omaha.

The plants, the bottles, it all clicked into place. Maggie had a side hustle of epic proportions and was running it from his late grandmother's barn. He tapped the empty bottle on the tabletop. A twinge of concern wormed its way into his brain. He couldn't help but wonder if Maggie might have overstepped and taken advantage of Mona's kindness.

He put the bottle down and closed the barn doors. He killed the engine in the car and wrestled his bag out of the trunk. Every movement was an effort, pulling at the scar tissue that banded his chest and reminding him that his physical endurance was zero.

He needed a bed and a pill—everything else he'd worry about tomorrow.

At the front door, he propped his rolling suitcase against the clapboard siding and fished out the keys Hansen had sent him. While opening the envelope, he glanced at the raised planter bed next to the door. Mint. He'd drank enough mojitos in Miami to know the herb on sight.

He plucked a leaf from one of the plants and rolled it between his fingers. The herbaceous scent transported him back to nights out in South Beach. Gorgeous, barely dressed women, flashing strobe lights, and DJs whipping the crowd into a frenzy. That was his past. He dropped the leaf like it burned, but the smell lingered.

The house was a time capsule. Every knickknack and hand-crocheted doily had been there since he was a kid. And the smell of Mona's rosewater perfume lingered in the air.

The gracious staircase with its long, curved banner might be the death of him. But with a herculean effort, he and his bag made it to the top. Without conscious thought, he found the guest room he'd always slept in. The full-size bed was the most beautiful thing he'd seen all day.

Zombie-like, he stripped to his briefs, found the little brown bottle of pain pills, and dry swallowed two. He flopped forward onto the bed, willing the drugs to kick in. After a few hours of oblivion, he could deal with all of this.

Four

"RICK, IT'S BEEN TOO long." Maggie smiled brightly at Rick through Mona's screen door. She was a hugger and wanted to lean in for a friendly embrace, but he didn't move to open the door. She stopped short, a little offended. It might have been twenty years, but a little hug...? Come on, man. A hug never hurt anyone.

She waited. Nothing. "You remember me, right? Maggie Stewart."

"Ah, yeah. Good to see you." His words were welcoming, but his tone was flat and eyes dull. His arms stayed crossed over his chest.

She laughed to fill the awkward pause. "It's good to see you too."

She knew he was a nice man, a good guy, and according to Mona the life of every party. But she didn't see any of that reflected in the figure before her. He was withdrawn and cold. Jacob Hansen said something about an injury in the line of duty delaying his trip to Omaha. Maybe that could explain the lukewarm reunion.

She pulled open the door with one hand and held out the cake she made with the other. "It's Mona's recipe. I saw the rental car in the driveway yesterday and wanted to welcome you properly." She stayed up late last night and baked for him. He should be a little more excited, damn it.

Reflexively, he took the cake plate. His slow, deliberate movements reminded her of a robot. The screen door started to swing closed, and she caught it with her foot. The door thwacked hard against her favorite pair of red Chuck Taylors. He looked down at her shoes, and an inkling of a smile flirted with his lips.

They were nice lips, full and smooth, almost too lush for a man. And a glaring contrast to the lines on his forehead and the dark circles under his eyes.

Rick was good-looking. Tall with broad shoulders, thick sable hair, and rich brown eyes. But he wasn't at his best. He was gaunt. His oversized and wrinkled shirt hung loose on his large frame. Instead of a Florida tan, his olive skin was ashen like he needed a dose of vitamin-D-filled sunshine and a good night's sleep.

She had Rick at a disadvantage. She'd already known what he looked like all grown up. Mona often shared family photos of him. And he'd been front and center during the press conferences on CNN when the mayor of Miami was arrested. She knew he was handsome and distinctly remembered telling Mona that.

He cleared his throat. "I see you've taken over the barn with your hobby, er...business."

"Business." She pulled the screen door all the way open and stepped into the foyer. "Let's go inside and talk like civilized people. I'll slice the cake."

She headed for the kitchen. He silently trailed behind her.

The familiar house felt strangely empty. Maggie hadn't been inside since she helped Jacob Hansen and a cousin of Polly's set the house to rights after Mona passed. Part of her expected to see Mona in the kitchen when she turned the corner.

She flipped the kitchen faucet to wash her hands and glanced at the lavender bushes outside the window. They had been the start of Lone Tree.

She asked Mona and Polly if she could cut some to make scented bath salts, and the rest was, as they say, history.

She reached for a towel and caught Rick running his fingers over the worn recipe book in the center of the scarred kitchen table. It was propped up by a Fiestaware napkin holder on one side and a set of cow salt and pepper shakers on the other. For as long as Maggie could remember, the salt cow had had a chipped tail.

"It feels like she should still be here, doesn't it?" she asked.

He nodded. "Yeah, I woke up in the same room I've always stayed in when I visit. Part of me wanted to stay in bed until the smell of bacon and her biscuits wafted up the stairs."

"Mona's biscuits were legendary. The recipe's in there." She nodded at the worn cookbook under Rick's hand. "Sit. Want coffee or tea? I can make it."

"No. I'm fine." He sat slowly, carefully.

She found plates and the ornate cake server that Mona always used for company and sliced two generous pieces for them. "The cake smelled so good baking in the oven that I dreamed about it last night."

She slid his plate over the wood table to him, and he took a small bite. He chewed and shook his head and then pushed the plate away.

"That bad?"

"No, it's good, just like I remember." He cleared his throat and in a husky voice added, "I'm just not hungry."

Maybe making one of Mona's signature cakes was a bad idea. Rick wasn't ready to burst into tears, but she could tell she'd hit him with a sucker punch on his first day back in Omaha. But the hint he was a loving grandson warmed her heart.

She took a bite, and a million memories flooded through her: Mona, this kitchen, holiday parties. All triggered by the flavor of the spice cake. The power of foods and scents to awaken memories was something she had always loved. They were a one-way ticket to the past.

"Mom?" a young boy shouted from the foyer. The thunder of small feet on hardwood floors followed the slamming of the screen door.

Rick turned in his chair to see a boy, maybe about ten, fly into the kitchen. Had to be Maggie's son. He had her same dirty blond hair.

"Evan, slow down," she said.

"Okay, Mom." Evan turned and looked at Rick. "You're him! The real FBI agent. Just like on TV."

Rick nodded.

"That's so cool. You're going to live here, fight crime, and catch bad guys. Can I help?"

Evan didn't pause long enough for Rick to answer; instead, he clasped his hands together and made a gun with his index fingers. He hid along the side of the refrigerator and mimed clearing the room of bad guys. "Pew-pew. FBI, freeze."

"Evan, how about you get some cake? And then, I'll introduce you to Rick properly."

Rick was grateful for the moment to collect himself. He hadn't expected to get emotional over a bite of fucking cake. And the kid jumping around with finger guns and asking about the FBI prodded at an entirely different set of uncomfortable feelings. This was precisely why he stayed home in bed and watched marathons of the British Baking Show—on mute.

Evan held out a paper towel for his mother to put his slice of cake in. "Thank you," he told her and kissed her cheek.

"Rick, if you hadn't guessed, this is my son, Evan."

"Nice to meet you, Evan." Rick offered a fist bump.

"You too, Rick." Evan tapped his knuckles against Rick's and spun to talk to his mother. Apparently, the novelty of his status as an FBI agent had already evaporated. "Mom, can I go to James's house?"

"Home before dark."

"Yep, got it."

And as quickly as he came, hurricane Evan bolted from the house. Rick could practically see Mona patting the young boy on the head and laughing at his antics.

"A mother's work is never done." Maggie took another bite of her cake.

"I think we were talking about your business before Evan descended on us."

"Sure, what do you want to know?"

He wanted to know how long it would take her to move her shit out and make the yard back into a yard. People buying houses didn't want a semi-commercial mini-farm and a beauty lab. They wanted grassy lawns and a place to park their cars.

He was sure his grandmother had never once said no to Maggie as her side hustle took over the property. Now it was up to him to be the asshole and rein it in.

"It's quite an operation. You've kind of taken over the place."

"Are you accusing me of taking advantage of Mona Cabrera?" She snort-laughed at him. He could not remember the last time a woman had intentionally done that in front of him. "I promise you no one took advantage of Mona. She and I had a deal. All the paperwork is with Jacob Hansen, her lawyer. You can look it over as soon as he gets home from his cruise."

"Cruise?"

"Yeah, two weeks in Alaska. It's one of the first sailings of the summer. I bet he's freezing his ass off. So, what's your plan for the house?"

"Fix it up and sell it." Evict you, the adorable single mom, and your equally cute kid.

"Ha, you and everyone else in Omaha. A few guys I know from work bought a fixer-upper a few blocks over. This neighborhood is hot, but they can't get the work done."

"Why?"

"You know that old saying? You can get it fast, you can get it cheap, or you can get it right?" She pointed her fork at him to emphasize each option.

"Sure."

"Well, in Omaha, if you're remodeling, it doesn't apply. Right now, it's all expensive and slow, the quality of the work—" She shrugged and took another bite of cake, somehow managing to chew and smile at the same time.

He couldn't help but notice that Maggie was girl-next-door pretty. Her looks screamed down to earth, from her worn sneakers to her oversized gray T-shirt and messy bun. There was even a rip in the knee of her jeans, and not the strategically placed kind of hole South Beach girls paid extra for when they shopped at Bal Harbour mall. Hers was purely organic.

"I'll figure it out," he said. "I want you to understand that I'm planning on selling. Cause... you know?" He rubbed a hand over his face. He was going to have to spell it out.

"Know what?"

Was she trying to make this harder?

"Well, the yard, and the lab, er, workshop thing. They have to go back to normal. And..." Fuck. He felt like a dick, but that wasn't going to stop him. "You'll have to move when it sells."

"I need the plants and the workshop for the summer." She looked at him, and he could see a flash of something in her eyes that made his resolve to be an asshole waver. "After the first frost, I'll get some people to help me, and we'll make all of Lone Tree Botanicals disappear."

"You just told me there are no people to get."

"No, there's no one to hire. But friends that owe Mona a favor...there's a million of those." Her tone implied that she could make a few calls, and half the county would show up in honor of his grandma. That sounded about right; Mona was a force.

"I want the house up for sale in a few weeks."

"You're dreaming. You can't even get cabinets in a few weeks."

He swore under his breath. He had a plan. Get out here. Get the house cleaned up. And get it sold. While in Omaha, he'd work with his new highly recommended physical therapist. And by the Fourth of July, he would be home in Miami. Ready to try and pass his physical assessment so he could get his badge back.

"You know, it's not bad here in the summer—no hurricanes. And you liked it when you visited as a kid. It could be worse." She picked the last few crumbs off her plate with the back of her fork. He watched her lick the tines. Her pink tongue held him transfixed. With effort, he pulled his gaze away from her distractingly pretty mouth.

If she was right, his ambitious plan was dead in the water. And all he had to look forward to this summer was a lack of hurricanes. Fuck.

Five

"I'LL TRADE COFFEE FOR details on your sexy new landlord." Lena held up a paper cup with the Omaha convention center logo. Maggie could smell the delicious, caffeinated bribe from her seat at her desk.

"I'll trade you my spleen for that mocha latte." She held out her hand and beckoned Lena closer.

"Nope, not interested in harvesting organs before noon. I want to hear all about mister FBI agent. Is he as hot in person as he was on CNN? Damn, he could fill out a suit." Lena growled and clawed the air with her long nails.

"Easy, tigress. He's not what I expected. Jacob mentioned that he'd been injured. I think whatever happened, he's still recovering." Maggie snagged the coffee off the edge of the desk where Lena had set it. Bliss in a cup.

"You could play naughty nurse. How long since you got some action? And not the self-administered, takes-three-double-A batteries kind of action."

"Ugh, too long." Maggie thought back. She'd have to use her fingers and maybe a few toes to count how many months it had been since her last overnight date. As a single mom, dating was low on her priority list. It sat just above learning another language. Both items sounded like something she should do, but she didn't have time to devote to either.

"Rick is your chance. Dating, but you don't even have to leave the house."

"I'm pretty sure that's called hooking up."

"You say tomato. I say *tomahto*." Lena shrugged.

"Well, if he gets his way, he's not going to be in Omaha long enough for me to tomato or *tomahto* him. He wants to sell the house as soon as possible."

"Sell Mona's house. Damn, that's the best house. Hasn't it been in his family for like a hundred years?"

"Longer. Her family built it in the late 1800s."

"He's an idiot."

"No, let's not go that far. He lives in Miami. Mona knew it when she left him the house. So he isn't going against her wishes or anything. He plans on fixing up the place before he lists it, so that works in my favor. The house needs almost everything upgraded. The historic homes in that neighborhood only bring top dollar after renovation, and that will take time." Unless Rick had hidden Bob Vila tendencies, he had a long and expensive road ahead of him.

"Yeah, I'd guess the house will take all summer." Lena perched one hip on Maggie's desk.

"Exactly. There is plenty of time for me to harvest everything growing in the yard and get it sold. So I can pay Evan's tuition."

Great. Another item for her overloaded to-do list: looking for a new place. The odds of getting a situation like she had now was zero unless she moved way out of town. Damn, she hated the thought of a commute.

"So back to the man. Hot or not?"

"Hot. But reserved and nothing like Mona described or I remember when we were kids. I don't think he smiled once."

"That's a bummer. We're getting too old to put up with moody even if they are hot."

Maggie laughed. "I thought in our mid-thirties our options were limited. Shouldn't we be keeping more men in the pool?"

"You have it backward. Our options are limited because our standards are high."

Lena raised her coffee cup, and Maggie bonked it with hers, a toast for all the mid-thirties single ladies and their impeccable taste in men.

"I don't need to date him, but it would be nice if he wasn't a bear to be around. I'll be running into him all the time. A smile or a friendly greeting would be nice. Last night he tried to carry on our conversation through the screen door."

"If anyone can get him to change his tune, it's you. Everyone loves you. A few homemade desserts and a couple of hugs, and you'll have him eating out of your hand in no time."

Lena might have a point. Working to get on Rick's good side could only benefit her. At the least she'd have a good relationship with her landlord. And if his attitude was from his injury, cheering him up was like banking good karma points. With all the changes flying toward her at light speed, some good karma might be the difference between having to shut down Lone Tree Botanicals and not.

"Okay, so that's my mission, make friends with Rick Cabrera. I'll start by giving him a sample of the new arnica and chamomile muscle balm I've been working on."

"Now that all that is sorted. Have you seen the newest email from the jewelry show people?"

Maggie scrolled to the unopened email and clicked. The number of exhibitors had grown to sixty-five, and there was a new security concern. Because millions in art and jewelry weren't enough of a headache. She'd be happy to see this event return to Houston next year.

"A five-million-dollar violin?"

"Actually, a five-point-two-million-dollar violin."

"And someone is going to play it at the closing party. Shit, I'd be scared to pick it up."

"To these people, a Stradivarius is just a musical instrument." Lena sipped her coffee.

"And they don't like the design for the event billboards?"

"Yes, the billboards that go up in two weeks aren't chic enough. I don't think we can make them happy. They aren't feeling the love for anything in Nebraska."

"Can we send them back to Houston and book a few nice, normal conventions in their place?"

"I'm going to remind you of that next time a medical or technology convention opens and you complain it's boring."

The doorbell at Mona's, er his, house sounded like church bells. The gentle bong-bong washed over him as he lay sprawled in the old recliner. His burst of motivation had gotten him to Omaha. And then it fled, probably back to Miami.

He managed to call a few home remodeling people he found online during the last week. They echoed Maggie's view. He had one hell of a long project in front of him. The real estate agent he talked to encouraged him to keep looking for a qualified contractor if he wanted the best price for the house. She wanted the project done before they spoke.

His major accomplishment toward his goal: he switched from cooking shows to home remodeling ones.

And flushed the Vicodin. But since then, good sleep had been elusive.

He didn't live through getting shot to end up an addict. The way he needed a pill when he got off the plane the other day had scared the shit out of him.

The doorbell song restarted, prodding him into action. He heaved himself out of the recliner he had been dozing in most of the day. The broken-down chair had to be twenty years old, but it was ridiculously comfortable.

He ran a hand through his hair. He was pretty sure he'd showered that morning. Oh well, too late now. He glanced down at his gray sweatpants and old college shirt. Looked clean enough. He staggered to the foyer and opened the front door. Maggie's son had his finger on the bell and was leaning into the button with all his weight.

"You're slower than Mona," Evan said.

"That's not polite." Maggie bumped her son with her hip.

"I just woke up," Rick said through the screen door looking between mother and son.

The kid tilted his head, confused. Rick didn't blame him. It was early evening. Not exactly prime napping time.

"Hi. I made you some chicken and dumplings." Maggie lifted the large casserole pan up, potholders over her hands, and the smell wafted toward him. His mouth instantly started watering.

Her smile was bright and reached all the way to her eyes, so genuine—so real. Not the strange half-smiles that many of the women in South Florida flashed at him, their foreheads frozen from too much Botox. It was refreshing.

"Evan, get the screen door for me." Her son opened the door, and Rick reached for the pan. But she pulled it away.

"No, it's still hot. I'll carry it into the kitchen." She wiggled past him through the open door before he could invite her inside, Evan right behind her. He followed the smell of the food like one of those cartoon characters floating a few inches off the ground, pulled along by the delicious aroma.

"This is my grandmother's chicken and dumpling recipe. Not Mona's. After the cake, I thought I'd switch it up." She arranged the hot pan on a cutting board next to the old cast iron sink. "My granny has been gone a long time. But one taste of this and it's like she's giving me a big hug. You know?"

Rick nodded, but he wasn't listening. He wanted a bite.

"There's fresh thyme in the dumplings and sage in the chicken broth, both from the yard. But the secret is that I roll out the dumplings on granny's old marble slab."

Maggie kept talking about her love of home cooking and having fresh herbs to use while he rummaged in a few drawers to find a spoon. By the time his spoon crunched through the golden top of a dumpling and dipped into the beautiful rich broth underneath, he was drooling. He leaned over the sink and blew on the piping hot bite until he dared to shovel it in his mouth.

Heaven.

It was the best thing he'd tasted since getting shot. He went back for another bite, then another. He knew it was rude to keep his back to Maggie and Evan, but he couldn't help it. The flavors were so bright and rich. He shoved his spoon back in and pulled out a chunk of tender chicken dripping with broth. The texture was perfect. It melted in his mouth.

He wanted to bathe in this chickeny perfection.

Maggie leaned her butt against the counter next to him, that same smile he'd noticed earlier on her lips. "I guess you're hungry tonight."

He finished chewing and wiped his face with a dishtowel. "Yeah, it's really good."

She crossed her arms and nodded once.

"Mom, can I ask him?"

"Sure."

Rick braced himself for more FBI questions. The food he'd just inhaled sat heavy in his stomach.

"Can I borrow one of Mona's books now that you're here?"

"Mona's books?" There were bookshelves all over the house, some filled with books, others with small knickknacks and trinkets.

"Mona had a set of children's fairy tales. They're bound in black leather, and they're the old stories right from the brothers Grimm. Hideously violent and nasty. He loves them. I'm sure other parents would be horrified I let him read them."

"I know those books." He'd read them a hundred times if he read them once. "Evan, can you show me where they are?"

Evan rushed from the room, and Rick followed him to the formal living room. Low on a bookshelf behind an uncomfortable looking settee, Evan plopped to his knees. The shelf held the same tattered books Rick read as a kid.

"Open the third book to the front page."

Evan carefully pulled the old book from the shelf and opened the cover. Rick watched the boy run his fingers over Rick's name. "Did you write in Mrs. Mona's book?" His voice was a hundred percent damming accusation.

Rick nodded. "I was practicing my cursive."

Evan shook his head in disappointment.

"He's never going to forgive you for that," Maggie said from the doorway.

A bark of laughter escaped from his throat, so unexpected it even startled him.

"Come on, Evan, pick one. We should get back to our dinner before it gets cold."

Evan ran his fingers over the old black leather spines, considering his options. He selected one and stood up. "Okay, I'm ready."

"I'll walk you guys out." Rick motioned for them to lead the way.

Maggie let Evan go ahead of her, and she fell into step with Rick. Their shoulders bumped as they walked down the narrow hall leading to the foyer.

"I have something else for you." She pulled a small tube out of her back pocket. "It's a new product I'm developing. Arnica and chamomile muscle balm. I have to order the arnica gel, but the chamomile comes from the front yard. Try it. I can see you're a bit sore. It can't hurt."

"I'm more than a bit sore," he mumbled as he took the tube.

She and Evan jogged down the front porch steps and headed for the entrance to the basement apartment around the corner of the house. Evan stopped to wave before he stepped out of sight.

Back in the kitchen, Rick savored a few more bites of the casserole. God, he forgot how good food could taste. Next to the dish was a sheet of foil with a note stuck to it. It had Maggie's cell number written in purple pen.

He stared at the number for a few moments before he reached for his phone. He never thanked her for the food or the muscle cream. Shit. When did he become this big of a dick? His mother and Mona both would have smacked him in the back of his head for such poor manners. He texted her a simple thank you and instantly felt better.

He took one last bite of the chicken and dumplings before covering it and putting it in the empty fridge. If he had to remind himself to do something as basic as saying thank you, it was time he pulled his head out of his ass and rejoined the world.

Six

RICK HATED HOSPITALS EVEN before he spent a few weeks in the ICU. The smells, the constant beeping, the harsh fluorescent overhead lights. Nothing about a hospital was designed to make a person feel better. No matter how fancy the lobby was, it still smelled like antiseptic. He stared at his phone, ignoring the doctors in white coats standing with him while he waited for the elevator.

The ride up to the administration floor of the university hospital felt like it took forever. He couldn't wait to get out of the claustrophobic box filled with doctors chatting about procedures and patients. The atmosphere on this floor felt more like an office building, and he was grateful for it. According to the sign on the wall, his new physical therapist's office was to the left.

His doctor back in Miami had recommended Hector Cruz based on his expertise working with patients who had survived severe physical trauma. Like getting shot twice at close range. Rick had almost rescheduled the appointment. Then a text from Maggie popped up on his phone. All it said was, *you're welcome*. But damn if that wasn't enough to renew his determination to rejoin the world.

Rejoining the world meant getting better. And as much as he hated to admit it, laying on his ass watching TV wasn't getting it done. This Cruz guy better be as good as advertised.

Rick took a deep breath before he knocked on the door.

"Come in."

Cruz stood up from behind his simple glass and chrome desk. He was younger than Rick expected. No gray hair or paunchy belly like all the medical guys back in Miami. He was in fighting shape. Sports memorabilia, mostly Yankees stuff, decorated the office. And a large lithograph of the New York skyline hung behind his head.

"Hector Cruz, nice to meet you." Cruz held out a hand as he rounded his desk.

"Rick Cabrera."

Cruz had a firm handshake and a friendly if appraising gaze.

"Have a seat. I've read your medical file. You're one lucky guy."

"Ah, yeah, I guess." Rick looked away from Cruz. His hope that his new physical therapist would be different from the rest dissolved. He wanted to shout he wasn't fucking lucky. He was a hot mess.

"What happened right then?" Cruz leaned a hip on his desk.

Rick shrugged and shot a glance at the door behind him. Escape.

"No, you shut down. Why?"

He cleared his suddenly tight throat. "I'm not fucking lucky." The words came out choked and ugly.

"You survived two gunshots to the torso and a resuscitative thoracotomy—only about twelve percent of people that require that procedure live. So in my book, you're lucky. The alternative outcome is pretty grim."

"It's not luck. It was a doctor's skill." Unexpected anger flooded his body. Who was this asshole?

"Ah, okay. You're not lucky, and you're not dead. Then what are you?"

Rick didn't have a ready answer. Before, he might have said an FBI agent. After a long pause, he spat out one word. "Alive."

Cruz began to pace the office, hands in his pockets. "Just alive? What would make it better? Change just alive to living?"

"I don't know." His new physical therapist sounded like a shrink. And he hated it.

"Bullshit. You need a goal."

"I want to get better." He clenched the arms of the chair to keep from bolting or trying to take a swing at Cruz.

"Nope, that's a stupid goal." Cruz stopped in front of Rick, his hands on his hips. "It's vague and nebulous. I want a tangible thing." His stare pinned Rick to the chair.

Rick's breath rushed in and out of his burning lungs. Anger, rage, and hope all fought inside him. An epic battle waged in moments. And deep down in his gut, he knew what he wanted. He knew it to the marrow of his bones. To the deepest recesses of his racing heart.

"I want to run ten miles again." He wanted it so bad he could taste the mix of sweat and ocean spray that coated his face whenever he ran along South Beach. The warmth of the Florida sun on his unscarred chest and the sound of the waves breaking at his feet felt real but were only an illusion... a delusion.

Hector slammed his fist down on the desk, making a picture frame tip over. "That's what I'm talking about. That's a fucking goal." Eyes glittering with passion, he clapped Rick on the back.

Rick sagged into the chair, exhausted and elated. He had a fucking goal.

Hector explained the basic physical evaluation they were going to do. Testing range of motion and setting a baseline to measure improvement. Rick stood and let Cruz put him through his limited paces.

"It's time. Based on what I see and what's in your file, you're done healing. It's time to start rebuilding."

Rick nodded. He tried to get excited.

"What are you doing now for PT?"

"I'm, I'm not..."

"And what about diet?"

Rick shrugged. Before, he'd been a foodie. Now, he lived on delivery pizza and ramen noodles when he remembered to eat.

"That's got to change. Real food. Your body requires the protein and vitamins to build muscle. Do you want a referral to a nutritionist?"

"No, I can cook pretty well. I just haven't."

"Hit the grocery store on the way home. That's an order. Meat, eggs, veggies, and whole grains."

An excuse about being tired was on the tip of his tongue. But the look he got from Hector silenced him.

"This last one is important. No judgment. What about the pain pills?"

"I flushed them over a week ago." It felt good to tell someone that.

"Any withdrawal symptoms?"

"Headaches and insomnia. Nothing bad."

"Good. I'll get you started meditating. It will help with the insomnia. And no more naps. Regular sleep schedule. Keep yourself busy during daylight hours. No more couch potato crap."

"Sir, yes, sir." He gave Hector a mocking salute.

Keeping busy during the day. Shit, that was a whole other situation. Maybe he could start on the house. Small stuff while he looked for a contractor. Just dusting Mona's hundreds of knickknacks would take a few days.

"You commit to my plan from now until fall, and I'll have you back running. It might not be ten miles, but if you want to sign up for the Thanksgiving 5k turkey trot benefiting the kid's cancer center here at the hospital, I don't see a problem. We can run, not jog, it together."

Thanksgiving. Shit.

He was skeptical, but Hector's excitement and determination were contagious. The doctors in Miami kept telling him to take it easy. Not to push, not to hope. It had become a habit. But suddenly he had orders and expectations to meet. A glimmer of something like hope dawned.

Seven

"WE HAVE A SITUATION," Maggie blurted out without preamble.

Rick leaned against Mona's front door frame, his expression bland. He wore a black V-neck T-shirt, and an angry looking scar peeked out of the top. It was wider than her finger and started dead center below his collar bones. How far did it extend?

"We do?" he asked through the screen door.

"Yes." If she hadn't been desperate, she wouldn't have come to Rick. For the millionth time, she contemplated passing the responsibility to another neighbor. But no, she was doing this for Mona. Before he came to town, she would have done everything on her own, but now that wasn't an option.

She snatched the stupid screen door open. Talking through it made her feel like an unwanted door-to-door salesperson. "It's Mona's turn to host the front porch party."

"The front what?" He could not look more annoyed with her if he tried.

Rick's workout clothes hugged his chest, and the loose gray shorts showed his long, tan legs and bare feet. Damn, Florida men took good care of their feet. She wiggled her unpolished toes inside her worn-out red Chuck Taylors and committed to giving herself a pedicure tonight.

"All the neighbors take turns hosting an outdoor party every other week in the summer. The dates are assigned a year in advance. Tomorrow is Mona's date on the calendar, and I told everyone I'd handle it. She and Polly started the parties a decade ago after Polly's husband died. And I agreed to host tomorrow in her honor."

"Okay, so you do it." Rick started to turn back into the house.

She caught his arm before he could escape. His skin was warm under her hand, and she felt his muscles tense at the unexpected contact. He looked down at where her hand rested on his bicep, and she gave his arm an affectionate squeeze before letting go. His grumpiness wasn't anywhere near strong enough to put her off. This was for Mona. And him, too. He should meet people besides her.

"I can't have the whole neighborhood on your front porch without you. That's just weird. They would spend the whole night gossiping about how strange you are."

His sigh was loud enough for the whole block to hear. "What do I need to do?"

"Ah, invite me in so we can talk?"

"Maggie, would you like to come in?" He ground the invitation out through a clenched jaw but stepped back and waved her inside.

She smiled at him as she sailed into the house. She almost reached out to pat the center of his chest as she passed, but the scar made her hesitate.

Out of habit, she headed for the kitchen. Along the way, she could see he'd been busy paring down Mona's huge collection of trinkets. The crocheted doilies that littered almost every surface were missing, and she couldn't find a single collectible spoon. It was painful to see Mona's precious treasures packed away, but the freshly polished furniture looked great.

Rick detoured briefly into the living room. He knelt on a yoga mat to pause a meditation video that played on his laptop. She didn't figure him for a Zen kind of guy.

"Coffee, tea?" In the kitchen, she reached for the kettle like she'd done a million times with Mona.

"Here, let me. This is my—er, I live here."

She let him take it. "I still call it Mona's house too."

"That's why I started packing some of her things. It felt like a museum, and she wouldn't have liked me tiptoeing around afraid to move anything." He filled the kettle and put it on the stove.

"Agreed." In the cabinet, she pushed aside a mug with the words 'world's best grandmother' on it to find a pair of plain white ones. She took them out and placed a tea bag in each.

"What do we have to do for the party?" he asked while they waited for the water to boil. His enthusiasm was underwhelming.

"I'll get all the coolers and tables out of the barn. Can you get some non-alcoholic drinks? Then we set everything up."

"I can help get everything out of the barn."

"No, it's fine. I did it for Mona all the time." She waved him off.

"I said I'll help."

There it was: a full macho man moment. Men were so predictable.

"Can you?" She looked pointedly at the scar.

Rick tugged the neck of his shirt up over the ugly mark. "It's been months since it happened."

"That doesn't answer my question."

He clenched his jaw and looked away.

The cautious way he moved combined with the scar left little doubt his injury was horrible. She hadn't meant to offend him. But physical limitations didn't change because of male pride.

The shrill whistle of the tea kettle cut through the silence in the room. Maggie took the pot and poured the hot water over the tea bags. She slid one to him.

He looked up and held her gaze as he rubbed a hand down his jaw and over the back of his neck. "Thank you."

"You're welcome." Look at that—Rick's manners finally arrived from Miami. Took long enough.

"I will try to help you with the stuff in the barn." He sighed and shook his head. "It's been months since I was shot. I have to start pushing myself more." He readjusted his shirt to ensure it hid the scar on his chest.

Hearing him say he'd been shot was sobering. She assumed, but neither Rick nor Jacob Hansen had confirmed it.

"No overdoing it." She held up her pinky finger and waited. She and Evan had a strong belief that the pinky swear was unbreakable.

"Promise." He almost smiled when he hooked his pinky around hers.

Damn, if he managed an actual smile that went all the way, he would go from handsome to swoon-worthy. She could tell he'd have those sexy crinkles at the corners of his eyes. Add in the thick dark hair that made a woman want to run her fingers through it and his smoldering eyes... Oh yeah, he was gorgeous.

"I'll put out some cookies or something, and everyone else will fill in the rest of the food."

"What's potluck fare in Omaha?" He toyed with the teabag in his mug.

"All the regular stuff: mac and cheese, potato salad, funeral ham sandwiches, Jell-O salad." Based on Rick's expression, all the regular stuff was mildly horrifying to him.

"Jell-O salad. That's a real thing? I thought it was an internet joke."

"Food snob."

"Yes. Jell-O should never mix with vegetables."

"Some versions use fruit."

He grimaced. "In the hospital, I had enough Jell-O to last a lifetime. The only way I'm touching that stuff again is if it's laced with vodka."

"I'll put Jell-O shots on the list for the next porch party. Just for you."

The look he shot her way left little question that he wasn't planning on attending the next porch party. Challenge accepted. Not only was he attending tomorrow's party, but she was going to make sure he met all the people Mona cared about in the neighborhood. There was more to Omaha than the inside of this old house.

This grouchy homebody version of Rick didn't mesh with the dashing man-about-town stories that Mona had shared with her over the years. The scar on his chest seemed to be the tip of a big, depressing, life-altering iceberg. And she wanted to help.

Mona would want her to do it.

Mona's legacy was helping people and the community, not a bunch of knickknacks collecting dust. And damn it, she was going to follow in her footsteps, starting with Rick. She would drag him back into life kicking and screaming—or grumbling and huffing, as the case may be.

Ready or not, here comes the neighborhood. And Rick wasn't ready. Expectations, events, people, all the reasons he left Miami. And now Maggie was bringing them literally to his front porch.

"If you can get some bottled water and soda, I'll bring ice from the convention center."

He grunted his agreement and swirled the last of the tea around in his mug.

She had a whole plan, and damn it, he knew he was going to fall in line and do as she asked. It was the sweet girl-next-door thing she had going on. He couldn't fight it. It would be like kicking a puppy.

Every time they saw each other, she made a point of stopping and saying hello or at least giving him an excited wave. At first, he didn't trust it. It's not like her being nice would stop him from selling the house. There had to be an ulterior motive. No one was that nice; she was buttering him up for something.

But it all felt genuine, like her beautiful smile.

Maggie Stewart was dangerous. And he should steer clear. Be cordial and nothing more. Otherwise, evicting her would become a shit show of epic proportions.

"Alright, I'll be here tomorrow as soon as I'm off work. If you want to make my son's day, knock on our door and offer to let him sweep the porch for a few bucks. He'll be home with his babysitter." She stood and moved her empty mug to the sink.

"I'm not an invalid. I can use a broom." The stretches Hector had him doing every morning were already paying off. He was sure he could handle a broom. He'd just stood up without groaning.

"I bet you can."

He might have been imagining it, but he was pretty sure the sweet girl next door had ogled his chest and arms. He reminded himself he was her landlord, nothing else. Fuck. She caught her lower lip between her teeth and raked her eyes over him one last time. He'd been thoroughly eye-fucked.

"It's kind of a tradition. Mona would give him a few dollars, and he would sweep up before every party."

"Did she pay him in dollar coins or two-dollar bills?" Think about Mona, think about cute kids doing chores, think about anything but Maggie's pretty mouth and hungry eyes.

"Yes." There was that gorgeous smile again. His obsession with her mouth was unwise.

"I'm not sure I can compete with $2 bills." He dragged his gaze from her lips and focused on putting the mugs in the ancient dishwasher. "Mona had to have a contact at a bank or something. She's been pulling that trick with all of us kids for decades."

"Show him your FBI badge. I bet he would do it for free."

That would be impossible; his badge was back in Miami. His boss took it the day he'd been put on indefinite medical leave. The painful memory reminded him why he was in Omaha. Pretty or not, Maggie would be losing her apartment.

"Maybe I'll see if I can find Mona's stash of two-dollar bills," he mumbled and closed the dishwasher.

"Umm, alright."

He crossed his arms over his chest and leaned against the counter. Waiting.

She shifted her weight from foot to foot, looking him up and down. After a sigh and a shrug, she leaned in and hugged him. His crossed arms wedged awkwardly between their bodies.

"So that you know I'm a hugger. And I hate talking to you through that screen door." She stepped back, gave him a little wave, and practically skipped out of the kitchen toward the front door.

Yep, she was danger with a capital D.

Eight

RICK PICKED AT THE label on his beer with his fingernail. He leaned against the planter of mint next to the front door, trying to fade into the wall. Maggie and a neighbor were seated in folding chairs nearby. The woman, Ann—or was it Amy?— was in her twenties and had a baby perched on her lap. She and Maggie were discussing baby butt creams. He took a pull off his beer; it was going to be a long night.

Maggie had dragged him around and introduced him to everyone as they first arrived for the front porch party. The people were fine, nice even, but he felt out of place—an outsider. He solidified his position as such when he casually mentioned he planned to sell the house. The older woman he was talking with clutched her pearls in horror at the idea.

After that faux pas, he decided it was better to keep his mouth shut. He used to be good at this kind of event. He'd flirt with the older ladies and buddy up with the men talking sports. But all that was more effort than he could muster up.

"Your grandmother was a great lady."

Rick shifted his attention from the riveting conversation about childcare to the man in front of him. He was younger than Rick by maybe ten years and had a Marine Corps tattoo on his forearm.

"Thank you." He held out his hand to shake. "Rick Cabrera."

"Steven Dawes. That's Amy, my wife, and our baby." Dawes pointed with his beer bottle. "We got married about the time you were on CNN talking about arresting the mayor of Miami. Mona was so proud she had the whole neighborhood watching those press conferences, so be ready. You're a minor celebrity around here."

"So I've gathered."

"Mona touched a lot of lives. Helped me out more than once."

Rick nodded. All evening, people told him stories about how important Mona was to the neighborhood.

"A shame you're going to sell this house. But I can see the appeal of Miami over long, cold Nebraska winters. Pretty women and palm trees." Steven's tone didn't sound like he wanted to trade the cold winter for sunny beaches anytime soon. He was looking at his wife and baby.

"I've got a lot to fix up before the house is ready to sell."

"Good luck with that. I'm a car guy, not a construction guy. I own an auto repair place downtown."

"I might be in the market for a cheap used car. The cost of the rental I have is ridiculous. Any recommendations where to start?" With everything the house needed, he had to save money wherever he could.

"Sure, I can give you a few names." Dawes pulled a business card out of his wallet. "Shoot me an email. I'll give you a few reputable used car lots to check."

"Thanks. I appreciate that."

"I have a couple of service buddies that went into law enforcement when we got home. But FBI, that's next level. Right?"

"Yeah, we're not writing speeding tickets."

Dawes's laughter drew the attention of Amy and Maggie. Maggie's gaze connected with Rick's, and she lifted one eyebrow, giving him a look that said, "See, I told you this was fun." He wasn't sure he agreed. But he was doing it.

"Miami. I bet you've seen it all. Drug dealers, money laundering, human trafficking. Shit, there was that crazy thing a few months ago with the fake painting."

"Yeah." Rick set his beer on the planter and glanced away, wishing Dawes would drop it.

"You know anything about it? Amy followed the story in the news. She was always into art."

"The Vermeer." Saying the name caused sweat to pop out on his skin. Everything about that case still pissed him off.

"Yeah, that one. A hundred million dollars for a painting, huh?" Dawes shrugged at the ludicrous amount.

"Five hundred million."

"You sure?"

Yeah, he was fucking sure. That half-a-billion-dollar painting nearly cost him his life.

"That was the estimated value before the auction."

And suddenly, he was back there—the auction at Vizcaya. The smell of gasoline filled his nostrils, and he could feel the weight of the fire extinguisher in his hands. One moment he'd been spraying down the flames engulfing the fake Vermeer. The next, Klaus Nauman put two bullets into his body.

An echo of pain slashed down his chest. He pushed his hand flat on the clapboard siding of the house. His fingernails dug into the wood. Panic gripped him, making it impossible to breathe. Bile rushed up the back of his throat, and for a moment, he thought he might get sick.

Dawes reached out. "Easy, man. Take a breath." His voice, low and calm, cut through the fog. He held Rick's bicep firmly, not letting go until Rick straightened and pulled away.

"You alright?" Dawes was concerned but not making a scene.

Rick rubbed an unsteady hand over his face, unsure how to answer the question. "I think we're out of ice. I'm going..."

Rick fumbled with the handle on the screen door. He needed a moment to collect what was left of his sanity.

"If you want to talk, find me. We all have our demons," Dawes said. He brushed Rick's hand away and opened the screen door for him.

Rick staggered into the quiet house. The sweat that had surfaced all over his body had left him feeling sticky. Upstairs, he rushed into his bathroom and ripped off his shirt. Careful to avoid looking in the mirror at his scars, he soaked a washcloth in cold water and ran it over his body and face.

He closed his eyes and began one of the breathing exercises from the meditation videos. He counted to three on the inhale. Paused. Counted to four on the exhale. Again. Gradually the adrenaline, fear, pain, or whatever the fuck it was that had flooded his system dissipated. And goosebumps pebbled on his wet skin.

He opened his eyes and met his gaze in the mirror. He looked normal but inside still felt raw. That flashback or whatever it was rattled him.

Fuck.

He pulled a clean shirt from the closet and considered if he wanted to go back out there. He walked to the window and looked outside. A couple of kids chased each other up the sidewalk, playing in the light of a streetlamp. He could hear them laughing. The rest of the voices were an annoying low hum. It would be easy to ignore the party going on right outside if he wanted.

A beat-up older hatchback squealed to a stop in front of the house. A tall, lean man with slightly shaggy hair got out of the car and stalked up the walkway disappearing from view, leaving his car double-parked. Asshole.

Rick worked the buttons on his shirt and kept an eye on the car. Something about it felt off. The way the driver left it to block the street, his lights on, the engine probably running.

Rick was out of the bedroom and thundering down the stairs at the first angry shout, tucking his shirt into his jeans as he went.

The hatchback asshole was going toe to toe with Maggie on the front walkway. She was an average height woman, but the guy was tall. She looked small and vulnerable. Every protective feeling he had for his mother, sisters, and the female victims he dealt with over the years flooded through him. Maggie lived under his roof; she was his responsibility.

"No, Ted, you don't just get to pick him up whenever." She poked the guy in the middle of his chest.

"He's my kid."

"Not that I can tell."

"Leave Mom alone." Evan barreled toward his father, head down to tackle a grown man. He made a beeline for the front stairs to defend his mother.

Before the boy could reach the lawn, Dawes caught him in a bear hug and pulled him to a stop. The ex-marine looked over Evan's shoulder at Rick, expression hard. "You got this?"

"Yeah." Rick didn't break stride, all his focus on the asshole that had grabbed Maggie's wrist and was pulling her toward him. Rick wasn't going to wait to see what happened. His years of experience in the FBI told him it wasn't a good situation.

No man should treat a woman or a child like this. He'd seen it all. Broken restraining orders, kidnapped kids, and too much violence. This wasn't happening on his lawn. And it sure as hell wasn't happing to Maggie.

He didn't have a gun or backup unless the couple dozen concerned neighbors counted. He would brazen his way through. He had done it before in more dangerous situations.

"Let go." Maggie twisted her arm, trying to wiggle free of Ted's grip. He'd been drinking; she could smell it on him. Even if it had been Ted's weekend to have Evan, she wouldn't have let her son in his car. God, she hated the judge that forced her to share custody of her son. It wasn't worth the paltry child support Ted paid.

"She said let go." Rick's voice was sharp, hard. Not to be ignored. And his body language was the same. He didn't look anything like the man that had been moping around Mona's house. This was the charismatic FBI agent from the CNN broadcasts but pissed off. And on her side.

"Who the fuck are you?" Ted's hold on her wrist tightened.

She sucked a sharp breath in through her teeth. She was going to have a bruise.

"Mona's grandson, the FBI agent. And you're on my property. Get off." Rick curved an arm around her. He flicked his eyes down to where Ted held her arm. She was sure she felt a rumble of a growl in Rick's chest the moment before Ted let go.

"Are you sleeping with him to pay your rent, you slut?"

Rick tucked her against his side and ignored Ted's shitty comment. A retort hovered on the tip of her tongue. She wanted to shout, throw things, and cry all at once. Ted was such an asshole. The only reason she didn't give in to the urge to yell at him was Rick's arm around her holding her together. Ted always brought out the worst in her.

"I said get off my property." Rick gently squeezed her against his side. "Now."

"What you going to do? Make me?" Ted wagged his fingers at Rick, taunting him to take a swing.

"No. Not in front of your son. Just go before you embarrass yourself further."

Rick spun and pulled her back toward the house. Amy's husband, Steven, let go of Evan as they came up the stairs but kept his eyes locked on her ex.

Evan threw himself against her legs, wrapping his arms around her waist and burying his face against her. She held on to him. Her heart broke that she couldn't cut Ted out of their life like the cancer he was.

"Has he left?" Rick asked Steven. Rick's arm was still looped around her.

"Yeah, he's slinking back to his car."

"Thanks for having our back."

Steven nodded and returned to his wife's side.

"Let me see your wrist?" Rick held out his hand. She loosened her grip on Evan so he could see it was nothing.

"It's fine."

He smoothed his finger over the red marks. And her chest tightened at his delicate touch on her abused skin.

"Mom, did he hurt you?"

"No, it's nothing." She willed her voice to stay steady and bent down to kiss the top of Evan's head. The whole time Rick's hand rubbed soothing circles over her back.

"If you ever need me to help with him again, please ask. It goes for you too, Evan."

Evan looked up at Rick. His face was red and splotchy, but the tears were already drying. He held up his pinky finger to Rick and waited.

Rick obliged, linking his finger around Evan's much smaller one. "A vow between men, yes?"

"Yes." Solemn, Evan nodded once before he pulled his hand back.

Suddenly she was blinking back tears. Here was the man Mona had talked about for all those years. Solid and good. Despite his injuries, he stood up to Ted and ensured she and Evan were alright. And if life were different... she could easily fall for him. But he was just a handsome diversion that she didn't have time for. He would disappear back to Florida before she knew it.

She sniffed a little and looked around. The party had resumed, and only the nosiest neighbors were still watching her and Rick. She was sure a few heard Ted's accusation. The rumors would be flying fast and furious tomorrow.

"You sure you're good, Mom?" Evan asked.

"Yes. It was nothing."

"Okay." Evan turned to join a couple of other kids his age sneaking cookies from the buffet.

She would give anything to be as resilient as her son. She leaned against Rick, enjoying the support of his arm around her for one last fleeting moment before she stepped away.

"Thank you for handling all that."

He shrugged and put his hands in his pockets. In his world, being a hero was not a big deal.

"The Jell-O salad thing, did someone actually bring one of these mythical creations?" he asked.

"I think so. Why?"

"I'll pay you five bucks to eat a spoonful and not gag."

And holy shit. There it was: the full wattage Rick Cabrera smile. Words failed her. He had a freaking dimple, and the depths of his rich chocolate brown eyes glittered with mischief. It was a good thing she was an overworked, highly responsible single mother, or she'd be aching to do all the irresponsible things with him—to him.

She exhaled and pulled her shit together. "You're on, Cabrera. Your five bucks are paying for my mocha latte tomorrow."

Nine

"I DON'T GET IT. They're stuck in the convention center all day. Then, they hang around at the end of that long ass day and drink cheap wine and eat our generic cheese and crackers. They're doctors, and there are medical device company reps with expense accounts right there. Why stay?"

"Networking," Maggie said. She handed Lena a beer from the nearly empty cooler.

"I think I'd network better over a hundred-dollar bottle of merlot and a steak." Lena used a bottle opener on her keychain to pop the beer.

"They still go to the fancy dinner after the networking at the convention center." As an event manager, Maggie had run enough of those events to know exactly what Lena was talking about. The doctors might preach about good diets, but she was sure they all had Lipitor prescriptions based on how they acted at the conventions.

"Why bother going out with a belly full of bad wine and sad cheese?" Lena shook her head and took a sip of her beer.

"More networking." Rick popped a carrot stick into his mouth.

Lena's eyes strayed to Rick... again. She'd been checking him out since she arrived at the tail end of the front porch party. Lena was many things—a great friend, a talented coworker, and an enthusiastic karaoke singer—but what she wasn't was subtle. Rick had to know she was interested.

But he didn't flash Lena a smile or return the appreciative look.

The remains of the potluck were sparse. The neighbors had eaten like a swarm of locusts, only leaving a few things behind. Like carrot sticks minus dip.

Lena stood and started to fill a plate with some of the leftovers. She surveyed the picked-over offerings and sighed. "I should have stayed and let one of the guys with an expense account pick me up. A nice meal wouldn't suck."

Rick moved closer and elbowed Maggie in the side.

"What?"

He jutted his chin toward Lena, who considered the leftover Jell-O salad. She reached for the serving spoon but stopped short. Only to pick it up upon reconsideration.

"Is she going to eat that? It's got to be a health hazard by now." Rick asked quietly. The lime Jell-O and veggie ring had begun to liquefy.

"Stop. It's not that bad." She fought back a giggle. It wasn't that appetizing either. The bite she had earlier tasted fine. It was Jell-O salad, not ambrosia. And yes, she took Rick's money. A bet was a bet.

Lena hesitated and set the Jell-O spoon down without taking any salad.

Rick raised an eyebrow. "No, I think it is that bad."

Lena moved on to the plate of Maggie's cookies and snagged one before giving up on the buffet.

"So Rick, what do you think of Omaha? Not quite Miami Beach?" Lena batted her eyelashes at Rick and resettled in her folding chair.

"It's about like I remembered." He shrugged and looked out at the dark street.

Lena's gaze snapped to Maggie, a quizzical look on her face.

"Rick would come to visit growing up. We've known each other since I was younger than Evan."

"Yeah, Maggie was the tomboy in ratty sneakers trying to follow all of us older boys." Their eyes met and held for a handful of heartbeats. "Three years older is huge as kids."

She remembered following him and the other boys on adventures all over the neighborhood. He'd always made sure she was included in the fun. When he returned to Florida, the other boys didn't let her tag along. She had a severe case of hero worship back then.

"Guilty as charged. I like tree climbing and bikes a lot more than Barbies. Rick was the cool boy from out of town."

"Not cool, a novelty... I still am." He lifted his beer to his lips. To her ear, it didn't sound like he enjoyed being a novelty.

"Not true. Everyone loved you tonight." After he helped with the Ted situation, she couldn't remember how many people had mentioned to her what a good man he was. And how proud Mona would have been.

He shook his head.

Evan stomped up the front steps and went directly to the buffet table.

"Mom, what happened to the last cookie? Thinking about it was the only reason I survived putting away the chairs in the barn." Evan bounced on his heels, undoubtedly already flying high on the loads of sugar he'd eaten tonight.

"I ate it," Lena managed around the last bite of said cookie.

"Nooooooo." Evan pretended to swoon, leaning on the buffet table for support. "Aunt Lena, I'll starve."

Her son knew how to work a room. Er, a front porch.

"There is a full plate of cookies on the counter in our kitchen. Go grab a few. And if you want to play some video games before getting ready for bed, go for it." It was too late to start preaching moderation tonight. The kid could have another cookie and play some games. He'd had a shitty night, and school was out for summer.

"Yes!" He pumped his fist and took off around the side of the house for the apartment, all three adults watching him go.

"Since it's an Evan-free zone for a moment, fill me in on the latest Ted drama. Your text was too short." She'd texted Lena for moral support after Rick chased off her asshole ex.

"He showed up and demanded to take Evan for the night. I'm pretty sure he was drunk too."

"What the fuck? Didn't he miss his last scheduled weekend with Evan to play in a slots tournament in Michigan?"

"Yep. Degenerate gambler. I bet he shorts me on child support this month." She hated her younger self every time she thought about how she believed she could change Ted. Fix his weaknesses. Yeah, when that didn't work, she'd ended up divorced with a three-year-old.

Rick stood and started cleaning up the buffet table. He took a load of stuff into the house, giving her and Lena some privacy.

Lena pounced the moment the screen door slammed shut. "Forget your asshole ex. Mister FBI is seriously good-looking. He's got a broody Latin lover thing going on. He's a banked fire waiting to flare to life. And sadly, he's not interested in me." She frowned.

"I don't think he's interested in anyone." Maggie shrugged. Poor Lena. She wasn't accustomed to being rebuffed. "He's going back to Miami as soon as the house sells."

"He was barely willing to talk to me. And I've been throwing out *come and get me big boy* glances left and right. You started talking, and he sat up and paid attention. He's interested in you."

"No, he's being polite." Maggie swallowed the last of her beer and tossed the bottle in a full garbage can.

"I think it's more." Lena was seeing something that wasn't there.

Maggie shook her head. "It's not."

But she couldn't help but remember how good it felt when he'd wrapped an arm around her and pulled her away from Ted. Nope, not going there.

"Well, ladies, are we calling it a night?" Rick surveyed the porch. "I'll get the last of it cleaned up in the morning."

"I'll help." If she got up early, she could help before work. There would be plenty of time.

"No, I can handle this. My physical therapist wants me doing more."

"You're sure? You promised not to overdo it."

"I promise." He held up his pinky finger. "Besides, you'll be the first to know if I overdo it. I'll run out of that arnica cream."

"I'll bring you some." She linked her pinky with his to seal their deal.

"Thanks." He lingered at his door, about to head inside.

Maggie paused a moment before leaning in to give him a friendly hug. "You survived, Cabrera. Nice work. Goodnight."

Unlike the last time she'd hugged him, he squeezed her back. "Goodnight, Maggie." His voice was low, and the gravelly undertone sent a ripple of awareness over her skin. He stepped back and gave Lena a nod. "Nice to meet you, Lena."

"Same." Lena stood. "I parked around the side by the apartment. Shall we?"

She and Lena walked down the front steps together.

They had hardly gone ten steps when she spoke. "Maggie, next time, you offer to rub that muscle balm on him personally. You deserve to get some, and I think he wants to give it to you."

"Lena, behave."

They were still laughing when they hugged goodnight next to Lena's car.

Lena's flirting had been both obvious and
harmless. Maggie's hug was the actual danger. The
tangy, herbal scent of her shampoo and her body
pressed into his reminded him of things he hadn't
thought much about since the shooting. The
sensation of a woman beneath him, soft and
yielding. How good she could feel wrapped
around him. Coming apart under his touch.

Lena's parting comment, her advice to Maggie,
had been the tipping point that sent him from
mildly uncomfortable to raging hard-on. It was the
mental image her words conjured that did it.
Maggie, straddling him, her hot, wet center
pressed against his lower back while she massaged
his shoulders.

For the second time tonight, he rushed to his
bedroom before he embarrassed himself. His cock
throbbed hard and insistent against his zipper. He
slammed the door behind him and undid his
jeans.

The idea of her hands on his back, rubbing his
sore shoulder after a long physical therapy session,
pulled a groan from him. Her bare breasts pressed
into his back when she bent forward to whisper in
his ear. He could almost feel her pebbled nipples
abrading his skin.

In a breathy voice, she whispered dirty
promises in his ear. Her teeth nipped his ear lobe.
And she ground her dripping wet pussy against
him.

Fuck. He throbbed painfully. The fantasy played
out in X-rated technicolor in his brain.

He leaned against the bedroom door, his legs
trembling.

He shoved down his underwear and fisted his
length. A shudder ran through his body at the first

stroke. He wouldn't last long. He couldn't remember needing to jerk off this badly since high school. His rough, regular strokes over his shaft were almost painful.

A hundred thoughts of Maggie filled his mind. Each one more erotic than the last.

He bit his lip to keep from crying out. His balls tingled, and the first brutal spasm racked his body. Desperate, he worked over his cock, harder, faster. He saw stars when the first wave of his orgasm almost dropped him to his knees.

He grabbed a towel off the bed and released into the wadded-up fabric.

Inside, he felt hollowed out; it was so intense. His legs shook, and he was lightheaded. He couldn't believe he'd done that. He thumped his head against the door a few times, trying to clear out the remnants of his fantasy.

Fuck. Either Maggie was a witch and had cast a spell on him, or his libido had recovered from the shooting and the pain pills. Because his cock was still hard.

Shit. He was thirty-six years old and was standing in his bedroom with his pants around his ankles and a towel full of cum in his hand. *Fucking pathetic.*

This wasn't anything like rubbing one out in the shower to prove his equipment was still in working order. He'd just fucked his hand while incredibly detailed thoughts of Maggie took over his brain. He'd had sex with a partner that wasn't as good.

He pulled up his pants.

"Keep it together, Cabrera," he mumbled.

A sweet single mom with a fuck ton of responsibilities wasn't his type. He was more of a keep-it-simple guy when it came to lovers. And nothing about Maggie Stewart was simple. No, their lives were tangled together at the moment but destined for different paths.

He should find someone he wasn't about to evict from their home and screw them six ways from Sunday to clear out his brain.

Ten

MAGGIE SET HER COLD beer on the coffee table in her living room and reached behind her back to unclasp her bra. She pulled the lacy torture device out one sleeve. Damn, that felt good after a long day. She should go put on PJs, but that seemed like a lot of work. All she wanted to do was relax.

It was after ten, and she'd just gotten home. Evan's babysitter, Suzie, was a lifesaver, especially on a day like today when she had to go in early and stay late. Summer camp only covered so many hours.

She grabbed her beer and the remote. Choices, choices. Was it a Grey's Anatomy kind of night or Game of Thrones? She needed to power down her brain, so hot doctors for the win.

McDreamy had barely made an appearance on her screen when the singing started. Loud male singing, and wow, was it off-key.

With a groan, she got up from her couch to see who was making all the racket. As soon as she opened the door, she was ninety-nine percent sure it was Rick and a buddy singing in Spanish.

She walked around to the front of the house and found Rick and his friend holding each other up. They swayed, arms clasped as they belted out what had to be a soccer team's fight song or something similar. They staggered back and forth on the sidewalk, seeming incapable of propelling themselves toward the front door.

"Hello, gentlemen." She jogged barefoot toward them while waving.

Rick swung in her direction, pulling his friend along. "Maggie. Hector, this is Maggie. I told you about her."

"Hola, chica." Hector stuck out his hand to shake and almost tipped forward. "He really doesn't want to evict you."

Well, she didn't want to get evicted. But shit happens.

Maggie put a stabilizing hand on Hector's shoulder, holding on until he didn't look ready to face plant. He shot her an adorable drunk thank-you smile. He was a bit shorter than Rick but had more bulk. No question the good-looking man spent quality time in the gym.

"You boys have a fun night?"

"Hell yes!" they shouted in unison.

They were cute drunks. Inebriated Rick had a huge smile and an easy laugh. It was a stark difference from the reserve and restraint she was accustomed to seeing. And judging by the empty street, they were smart drunks too. They must have taken a cab home.

"I have to ta-take you next time we go." Rick squeezed her shoulder and trailed his fingers down her bare arm as he let go. "Best Latin food in Omaha. Almost like being back in Miami."

"Shhh, don't tell my mom, but the mofongo was as good as hers." Hector held a finger over his lips but was anything but quiet.

"I'll be sure to keep your secret. Where were you two?"

"Latin Caribbean food truck."

"Sports bar."

She had begun herding them toward the front porch. It was slow going every few steps she had to steer them back on the center of the path to save her chamomile that lined the front walk from being trampled.

They gave her a play-by-play of the game they had watched. But Hector told her about a baseball game and Rick talked about a soccer match. She'd venture to guess tonight had been more about high-quality male bonding than sports. And it had involved copious quantities of alcohol.

Her two adorable drunks began singing the fight song again without any warning. Louder than before. And two houses down, security floodlights blazed to life. Shit. That was Mrs. Firebaum. The wicked witch of the neighborhood. And she wasn't going to be cool about two drunk men singing in the front yard at almost midnight. She would call the cops. Rick had only been here about a month. She didn't need him getting arrested.

"Come on, guys, keep it down. Please."

"Anything for you, pretty Maggie," Rick slurred, not very quietly.

"Dude, you're loud." Hector wasn't helping.

She all but shoved them the last several feet toward the base of the porch steps. "Up, now." She used her best angry mom voice. No one could ignore it. The tone must have cut through at least some of the booze. The two men managed to make it up the steps with only a few stumbles.

"Keys, Rick." She held out her hand and snapped.

"I'm trying." He fumbled in his front pocket while Hector slumped against the house under the glowing porch light.

Rick moved like he was underwater, slow and exaggerated. He was concentrating so completely, a deep wrinkle furrowed his brow. He swayed on his feet.

"Let me." Maggie pressed him back to lean against the house next to Hector. She then slid her hands into his front pocket—first one, then the other. No keys. This was not how she imagined getting to third base with Rick. She wrapped an arm around him and went for a back pocket.

"Damn, Maggie, you smell good." He nuzzled her neck and pressed his hips forward. His hot breath feathered over her skin. She impetuously tipped her head back, giving him easier access. He shifted and curled one arm around her waist to pull her closer. Her breasts pressed into his chest; heat zinged through her hardening nipples at the contact.

Damn was right. The man had a glorious ass. Hard as stone and begging to be fondled. She was a bad girl. Groping drunk Rick had to cross some serious boundaries.

She snagged a set of keys from the depths of the pocket and extracted herself from the unplanned embrace before things went sideways–er, more sideways. She hoped his memory of tonight would be hazy.

Unfortunately, hers would be crystal clear. It had felt way too good to press against him.

She ripped open the screen door and fumbled with the keys a moment before finding the right one and slipping it in the lock. As she worked, the guys held each other up. Once they were horizontal, she was outta there. Back home to her TV heartthrobs and cold beer.

"Inside, now." She held the screen door and waved her charges past.

They stumbled through the foyer and into the living room. Hector landed facedown on a sofa, and Rick flopped into the old recliner that had been Polly's husband's favorite. The thing had to be thirty years old.

She knelt and tugged off Hector's shoes and did the same for Rick. The men had gone quiet. Finally.

In the kitchen, she checked the fridge and found two bottles of sports drink. And in Mona's junk drawer, there was some aspirin. Perfect.

She left the sports drink and pills on the coffee table and tossed a quilt from the linen closet over Hector. She turned to do the same for Rick. His eyes were open, and he watched her.

"He's good for me." Rick nodded at Hector. "But you're bad."

"I am?" She gently draped the quilt over Rick, drowning in his intense, dark stare.

"Yes. You're Mona's, and I have to toss you and your kid out of this house. Life sucks." He closed his eyes, cutting their connection.

"I'll be fine. I always am." Truer words had never been spoken. She was always fine. On occasion, she could even reach for good. But she couldn't remember the last time she'd been spectacular. She stifled the urge to sigh. Fine was just fine.

"I live in Miami, and you're all sweet Midwest girl next door. And it's killing me." He snagged her hand and turned it over to trace circles on her palm.

Heat rushed up her arm from his gentle touch. She pulled her hand away before the tingles could spread any farther.

"Okay, someone needs to get some sleep." She stepped back out of his reach. The slow, sexy smile that curved his full lips made her belly turn to warm caramel. Fuck, she could make such a bad decision right now.

"I'll dream about you, mi corazón." His voice was heavy with drink, desire, and sleep.

"Good night, Rick." She backed out of the room. She was jogging by the time she hit the front door, her bare feet nearly silent on the old hardwood floors. She didn't want to know what sober Rick would think or remember about tonight.

Hell, she didn't know what to think about tonight.

"I hate you." Rick sat up. The change in position made it feel like his eyes were going to pop out of his head. Once the room stopped spinning, he was going to puke. The cheery chintz drapes and floral wallpaper in the living room were not helping.

"Hydrate." Hector shoved an open bottle of sports drink into his hand. Fucker didn't have the common courtesy to look hungover.

He took the bottle with one hand and raised it to his lips for a tentative sip. Thankfully, his stomach didn't rebel. As he drank, he flipped Hector off.

"Six years and two bullet wounds ago, I would have been like you. Hangovers were a present from Satan that arrived on my thirtieth birthday." Rick rubbed his bloodshot eyes. So much for good eating and sleeping habits. He and Hector had gone off the rails last night.

"Don't hate the player." Hector sucked down his own sports drink.

"Kamikaze shots and beers? What the hell were we thinking?" He couldn't remember the last time he'd seen someone order a kamikaze, let alone drink one. South Beach nightlife revolved around specially crafted bespoke cocktails that cost seventeen dollars a glass. And most tasted like licking a pine tree or snorting flower petals.

"I think we were all hopped up on good food and feeling invincible. That food truck was the shit. It's now my new favorite restaurant in Omaha. I already signed up to follow them on social media." Hector flashed his cell phone at Rick. "That was some of the best Puerto Rican food I've had since I moved here for my Ph.D. program."

"Totally respectable Cuban too." They should have stuck with overeating. The sports bar with buy two shots get a beer free deal had been the scene of the crime against their livers.

"So, this is the house you inherited. It's big. It has a late twentieth-century grandma vibe." Hector straightened a framed needlepoint sampler on the wall that said *home is where the heart is.*

"I've actually started decluttering. When I arrived, my grandma's lace doilies covered every horizontal surface." He'd carefully packed up all the doilies, not sure what else to do with them. So, for now, they were in a box in a spare bedroom along with a growing host of other old lady trinkets: a collection of souvenir spoons, dozens of antique perfume bottles, and every Precious Moments porcelain statue from the last three decades.

"You going to sell it like this?"

"No. Everyone I talk to says I have to renovate to get the best price." He'd barely started on the herculean effort.

"You have a contractor?"

"I wish." He was feeling better physically, but that didn't mean he suddenly knew anything about fixing Mona's house. He could probably handle painting or other basics, but he'd always lived in an apartment. His idea of home repair was to call the super and complain.

"I know a guy. He was a PT client. I'll send you his contact info. Tell him I referred you. I promise he'll give you a fair estimate."

"Hector, have I told you lately I might love you?"

Hector laughed and flopped back on the sofa.

"Seriously. The last few weeks, you've done so much to help me. Thank you."

"I love my job," Hector said with bone-deep conviction.

He'd felt that way about the FBI back in the day when he was young and idealistic. He wasn't sure he could have conjured up that same devotion in the last few years. And after getting shot... Shit, he didn't even want to think about the confusing feelings that sometimes rattled around his brain. He shoved the thought away. His head hurt enough already.

"You're good at your job. I never thought I would be improving this fast. I came here thinking I would sell this house so I'd have a nest egg to live on while I collected disability checks."

"Fuck, no. You're going back to the FBI. Better than before." Hector held up a fist, and Rick obligingly gave it a bump.

Thanks to Hector, he could see the light at the end of the physical therapy tunnel. It was a long way in the distance, but it was attainable.

"I'm starving. Eggs?" he asked Hector.

"Sure thing. I've got some time before my first client."

Rick pulled together a basic eggs, toast, and sliced tomato breakfast, and Hector handled the coffee machine.

"The pretty blond that tucked us in last night, she's the tenant you're evicting?" Hector pointed out the kitchen window where Maggie was tending to her plants.

"Unfortunately, yes. To make me feel worse, she is nothing but nice. Like almost too good to be true nice." Rick stabbed a tomato violently with his fork.

"Like putting her drunk landlord in bed instead of calling the cops nice."

"Exactly." The memories of Maggie from last night were blurry. More a feeling than a clear picture. But he was pretty sure he remembered hugging her. He better not have been an idiot. That was all he needed, another reason for Maggie to hate him. Drunken assault.

"I don't envy you putting her out."

"And it's not only the apartment." He proceeded to tell Hector all about the home-based business Maggie ran from the barn.

"Damn, if I were her, I'd have left your drunk ass on the lawn and turned on the sprinklers. She's a better person than me."

"What else can I do? Give her the house?" Omaha wasn't where he lived. He had no desire to own a house here.

"Maybe you could ask the buyers to keep her as a tenant? She might lose the beauty products stuff, but she'd have her home."

"Hector, again, have I told you I love you? I'll get the real estate agent to make it a condition of the sale. A one-year extension on her lease at the same rent. That's fair, right?"

"Yeah, man, that's fair." Hector looked skeptical.

"What?" He set down his fork; the one-year lease was the perfect plan. What could Hector have against it? Hell, it was his idea.

"You're doing a lot to keep a near-stranger happy."

"My grandmother practically adopted Maggie and her son Evan after Maggie had a falling out with her parents. Mona has been telling me about their lives for years. The guilt was just another thing on my plate. The lease is a brilliant fix."

A one-year lease was the key to him not feeling like a total asshole. He shouldn't be worrying about Maggie when he had his own shit to handle. The welfare of a woman he knew as a kid and her son was a burden he did not want.

Now he had to wipe the hazy drunken memory of nuzzling her neck while she pressed against him from his memory too.

Eleven

MAGGIE PUT DOWN THE garden shears and wiped the soil off her hands on her cutoffs. She tugged her ringing cell phone out of her pocket and almost put it back when she read the screen. Ted. No part of her wanted to talk to her ex-husband. But unfortunately, it was his weekend to have Evan.

She leaned on the planter of mint that she had been harvesting leaves from on Mona's porch. He was going to cancel on Evan, again; she knew it. With a whispered curse, she accepted the call.

"What, Ted?"

"Hey, Maggs. How's it going?"

Her blood pressure climbed into dangerous territory at the whiny sound of his voice.

"Fine."

"That's good. How's Evan?"

"Fine."

He was trying to be friendly. He wanted something.

"I'm gonna take him fishing this weekend."

No, he wasn't. False promises and bullshit were Ted's stock and trade. She learned long ago not to get Evan's hopes up by telling him all the wild things Ted promised to do. But at least he hadn't called to cancel. She had a green market this weekend. And Ted was her court-ordered childcare.

"Great."

A few awkward moments of silence passed. She was about to hang up and get back to work with her plants.

"Maggs, I saw a billboard for that jewelry show at the convention center. It looks big. Are you hiring any extra people?"

"What's wrong with the job you have?" She was sure this was the start of an excuse for why he would be late or short on child support this month. When it came to money, he always had a reason he was broke.

"I'm not going to lie to you. The casino is slow when the weather is nice. So my tips have been for shit." Remorse dripped like molasses off his words.

Ted had fallen about as far as you could and still have a job. From sales manager at a high-end car dealership with a six-figure salary to valet parker at the same casino where he once lost their mortgage payment.

"And you're going to be short this month. Surprise." Not really.

"I'm trying. It's hard to find work. But if you put in a good word for me at the convention center, it would help."

Besides whining, Ted's other major life skills were gambling away all his money and getting fired. Her younger self picked a real winner for a sperm donor.

"What kind of job do you think I can get you? You don't have a college degree."

He dropped out of school while she busted her ass to finish, and it had always been a huge bone of contention between them.

"I don't know, security guard or something, so it pays good."

She snorted into the phone. "Dream on. But with the amount of bullshit you sling, I bet you'd be a natural on the custodial staff."

"Okay, sure. Fine. Whatever. I'll take it. I'm desperate."

Did he just agree to scrub public bathrooms? Fuck. He probably already got fired from the casino job. Liar.

"I will not risk my reputation for you. The jewelry show is huge, and my boss assigned both Lena and me to it. The last thing I need is you finding some way to screw that up for us. Nope. Not doing it. You want a job? There's an application on the website. I'm staying out of it."

"But Maggs. If I have a good steady job where I don't rely on tips, I won't be short on support payments."

"Yeah, you will. You're a gambler. And until you stop, you will always, always be broke." Her throat felt tight, and she hated that her eyes stung with unshed tears. That Ted and his addiction could still make her emotional reminded her she was the same stupid girl who'd married a guy that gambled his college tuition away at an off-track betting place.

"Hey, last month, a big payout on the slots covered my support payment."

"Sure, if you say so." She didn't have the time or energy for this. Ted was an emotional black hole.

The screen door clicked open behind her, and she dashed away any tears that might have managed to escape before turning around.

She smiled at Rick and tuned out Ted's continued whining. Rick somehow looked better every time she saw him. He smiled more now and moved more naturally than when he first arrived. He told her it was all Hector's doing. Six weeks of physical therapy had made a huge difference.

Rick passed her a bottle of water. It wasn't the first time he had come outside to say a quick hello while she tended her plants. He started to turn back toward the front door. She caught his arm, stopping him. Their eyes held, and the connection set a flock of butterflies loose in her belly. She had to stop remembering how good it felt to be in his arms. It wasn't helpful.

"Good luck, Ted. I've got to go." She cut her ex off mid-sentence and hung up the phone.

"Ted the ex?" Rick uncapped his bottle of water. He always made a point to come outside and say hi to Maggie so he didn't feel like a reverse peeping Tom watching her out the window. She wore what he thought of as her gardening short shorts. He had a love-hate relationship with those shorts.

"I was the dumbest college kid ever. What the hell was I thinking with him?" She shook her head, her frustration evident.

"We were all young and dumb once." Hell, he was still dumb. Exhibit A, him lusting after Maggie when he had nothing to offer her.

"Yeah, but you aren't still dragging your mistakes along behind you like an anchor as you approach forty."

"You did get a cool kid out of the deal."

"That I did." She smiled and took a sip of the water he'd given her.

When she licked a stray drop from her lips, he couldn't help staring at her glistening mouth. He ripped his gaze away and focused on the closest planter.

"What's this one?" He fingered a broad green leaf.

"Basil. I use it in my acne wash. It has antimicrobial properties." She took a leaf and rolled it between her fingers before inhaling the fragrance. She held it out to him.

"Really?" He gently held her narrow wrist and took a sniff. "I thought it just tasted good with my mozzarella." He smiled at her, and a flush spread across her cheeks. He liked that reaction way too much.

"Ah, feel free to take a few sprigs if you want it for cooking. Mona would." She stepped back, reached for a pair of shears, and snipped a few leaves from the mint in the next planter.

"I'll have to get some fresh mozzarella."

"Come to the green market this weekend. There is a lady there that sells incredible handmade mozzarella. And you can get tomatoes from a local farm. I'll have a booth too, so you can stop by and say hello."

"I might do that."

"I'll text you the details."

A fancy new SUV rolled to a stop in the drive beside the house.

"Want to watch a man spend his life savings?" he asked Maggie. "That's the contractor Hector recommended. He's going to give me a few thoughts on what it will cost to fix up the house."

"It's just money, right?" She patted his arm.

"Yeah, right." Fuck.

A man about Rick's age stepped out of the SUV. He was tall and well built. His scuffed work boots crunched over the gravel in the drive.

"Hey there! You must be Rick. I'm Kevin Walsh."

Rick met Kevin halfway down the front steps. Maggie followed close behind.

Rick shook the other man's hand. It was rough with calluses. Good to know Kevin wasn't above getting his hands dirty.

"There she is in all her one hundred and thirty years of glory." Rick waved at the house, and he took a minute to notice all the work it needed. Living there, he'd learned to ignore the peeling paint and missing shingles.

"Yes, she's glorious but could use some work. You two have quite a project on your hands." Kevin reached out to shake with Maggie. "I'm sure we can make it your dream house."

"Oh, no, I'm just here for the entertainment. I'm Rick's tenant. It's his money you're spending."

"Well, lovely to meet you anyway." Kevin gave Maggie a closer inspection than he had the house. Rick cursed her gardening short shorts and Kevin's lack of a wedding band.

If a toy company made a Ken doll that was a contractor, it would be this guy. Blonde, blue eyes, easy smile, and perfect hair. He even had a tape measure clipped to his hip on his well-worn jeans. And, no doubt, a permanent address in Omaha.

"Should we start out here?" Rick forced himself not to pull Maggie away from contactor Ken doll.

"Anything you say, boss." Kevin's eyes lingered on Maggie's ass as she started toward the side of the house.

"So, I figure a new roof and a lot of paint outside."

Kevin pulled out a small pad and a pen and began to study the house. "Yes, that would be a good start."

They circled the house, Kevin taking notes on rotted siding, missing shutters, and a cracked window Rick hadn't even noticed. The questions came at him fast. Shingles or metal? Replace the windows? Pave the driveway? New house color? He stumbled through the best he could.

"Whoa, this is a full-scale landscape project back here." Kevin surveyed Maggie's mini-farm. The neatly tended rows and bushes filled every inch of available space behind the house. "This will take a full crew and at least a week of work."

"Rick, I told you I will get you a lawn at the end of summer. No worries." She put her hands on her hips and glared at him.

"Maggie—" He wasn't going to make her keep that promise. He was already going to have to sell a kidney to fix this place. How much could a new backyard add to the tab?

"No, Rick, a deal is a deal." She swung around and pointed at Kevin. "This isn't your problem."

Kevin looked back and forth between them for a moment in confusion. "My momma always said never argue with a beautiful woman."

"Your mother was brilliant." Maggie beamed at Kevin's compliment.

He'd revisit the backyard issue later when Kevin was gone.

"Where would you like to start inside?" Rick asked. "Kitchen? Bathrooms?"

"I like to start at the bottom and work up. Inspecting the foundation of a house this age is critical."

"The basement is Maggie's domain. She can lead the way."

Rick fell into step with Kevin. He hadn't been inside Maggie's part of the house in decades. He was curious to see her space.

The entry area opened into a simple family room with a dining table at the far end. The TV wasn't as old as Mona's, but it wasn't the sixty-eight-inch flat screen Rick left back in Miami either. The comfy looking couch had a video game controller and one of Evan's sweatshirts dumped on it.

Someone had painted the dark 1970's wood paneling a bright white, helping alleviate the gloomy feeling Rick remembered. And Maggie had left the large windows at the far end of the room uncovered, letting as much light as possible into the walk-out basement.

Overall, Maggie's apartment felt tidy and less run-down than the main house. The brighter color scheme and updated light fixtures helped a lot.

"You said you want to look at the foundation. Come on over here." Maggie walked down a small hallway with faded floral wallpaper. At the end, she pulled open a louvered closet door. "Wiggle past the washing machine through that little gap. You'll get the best peek at the original house foundation."

Kevin unstrapped his tape measure and phone from his belt and put them on the dryer. He leaned on the washer and pushed it over as much as it was willing to go. The opening was barely wide enough for him to squeeze through. But Rick knew that it was a full-size room on the other side of the tiny door.

"Hey, Mom." Evan leaned around the corner. "Are any of those cookies left?"

"In the Tupperware on top of the fridge."

"Hey, Rick, you want some?"

"Nah, I'm good."

"Cool." Evan bolted for the kitchen.

"If he keeps eating and growing at this rate, I don't know what I'm going to do."

"Oh, it will get worse. When I was a teenager, I think I spent half the day eating. I was like a bean pole too."

Kevin's reemergence was proceeded by a few muffled curses and a grunt from behind the washing machine.

He stood up and dusted a few imaginary cobwebs from his golden hair. "What is that space?"

"Mona and Polly swore that it was a hiding spot for some crazy great-uncle that ran illegal booze during prohibition." Maggie passed Kevin his tape measure and phone from on top of the dryer.

"The family legend says he set up a speakeasy in the barn and hid the contraband alcohol down here. I have no idea if it's true, but Mona had a couple of old whiskey bottles with Canadian labels. She told me they were from the speakeasy." Rick hadn't thought about that story in years.

"I've only been in there a few times. I kept thinking I would board it up but never did." Maggie turned to walk back toward the living room after closing the closet doors.

Rick hung back with Kevin. "What's the diagnosis? How's the old girl's foundation?"

"She's built like a brick shithouse. So at least you've got that going for you." He clapped Rick on the back.

"I'll take any good news I can get."

Maggie flopped on the sofa with Evan, who was playing video games. "You guys finish up without me. Evan is going to kick my butt in Mario Kart."

Rick and Kevin did a quick tour of the apartment, spending extra time in the kitchen and bathrooms before heading up to the main house. The more things Rick showed Kevin, the faster his pen flew over the pages of his notebook. It was like the guy was writing War and Peace. That could not be a good thing.

Rick leaned against Mona's kitchen counter while Kevin looked through his notes one last time.

"This is a huge project. And now that I know it's a flip, we will focus on the big things that scare buyers and the stuff that makes them pull out their checkbooks."

"That sounds like a good plan." It was good that Kevin had been down this road before because Rick was learning on the job.

"You desperately need a new roof. The exterior dry rot and peeling paint are killing curb appeal. The good news is you have a recently installed furnace. Then it's on to cosmetic upgrades to the kitchen and baths. And new floors and some paint. Done."

Rick gives him a number he had in mind for a budget.

"You'll need all that and more if you want to do it all."

"More?" He was already emptying his retirement savings.

"Here are some very rough estimates." Kevin slid a sheet of paper to him. It had line items like roof, kitchen, first bath, and next to each one, a dollar value that made him want to cry.

He could look into a loan. He had a cousin back in Miami that was rolling in money from his real estate deals; maybe Carlos would act as an investor.

"If we don't touch the basement, it could save a ton. Think about it? An outdated rental apartment isn't going to stop a buyer that falls in love with this house." Kevin stood and started to gather his things.

Rick rubbed a hand over his face. Skipping Maggie's part of the house felt wrong, especially if he got her a one-year lease from the new owner.

"I have to think about the interior. But I agree on the roof and outside paint. When can you start?"

Kevin consulted a calendar on his cell phone. "I can get roofing and paint crews out here in a couple of weeks. You're lucky I had a cancelation."

"Great."

"I don't want to pressure you. But most of my subcontractors are already booking jobs into September and October. If you want to do the inside, get in touch with me ASAP."

"I understand."

Twelve

THE OMAHA GREEN MARKET was hopping this morning. Eleventh Street teemed with shoppers and vendors enjoying the glorious summer weather.

Maggie restocked her lavender bath salts. It was one of her most popular items and was selling better than ever today. She would have to talk with Loess Hills Lavender Farm about augmenting her own harvest. Especially next year when she wouldn't be at Mona's house.

"Maggie, remember me?" The perfectly coiffed television news anchor leaned across the display table and floated an air kiss over Maggie's cheek.

"Cheryl, good to see you. How's your bumper?"

"It's fine." She waved away Maggie's question about her hundred-thousand-dollar SUV like it was nothing. "The tragedy is that we haven't met up for that glass of wine yet. I thought the end of the school year was crazy, but then summer started. My daughter, Chloe, has camp and drama classes and gymnastics. I feel like an Uber driver, not a parent."

"Preaching to the choir."

"Chloe is at rehearsals for her upcoming play at a theater around the corner. I decided to pop in for some fresh veggies, and voilà, you were here. It was meant to be." Cheryl spun around, taking in Lone Tree Botanical's booth. It was very simple:

white collapsible shelves, wicker baskets, and a few vintage apple crates. A hand-carved sign with her logo hung on the tent's back wall.

"It absolutely was."

"I must stock up on your delicious products." Cheryl turned to a shelf to inspect the handmade soaps, lifting a few to her nose. Maggie passed her a shopping basket when she began to collect one of every variety.

"Any word on that new teacher?" she asked Cheryl.

"The gossip I heard from a PTA mom is that the school is still interviewing. Fingers crossed they get our kids someone fabulous."

"Otherwise, you know we will hear about it." Evan took school very seriously and wouldn't tolerate a teacher he didn't think was up to his standards.

"Daily." Cheryl rolled her eyes, and they both busted out laughing. She and this woman must hit happy hour. She might have a free night sometime in the next decade, maybe after Evan got a driver's license.

"Maggie."

She turned to see Rick inside her little tent.

"Rick, you came." She was shocked. She'd texted him the info, but that he actually appeared was unexpected. She rushed to give him a quick hug; one of his arms briefly wrapped around her back.

"You got me thinking about fresh mozzarella," he said when she stepped back.

"The cheese lady is on the next aisle." Maggie pointed in the general direction of the best fresh mozzarella in Omaha.

"I've shopped there before. She has great stuff." Cheryl inserted herself into the conversation. Her eyes ran up and down Rick and then back to Maggie, curiosity written all over her face.

"Where are my manners. Rick, this is Cheryl. Her daughter goes to school with Evan. Cheryl, this is Rick, my landlord."

"Lovely to meet you." She held out her hand for a friendly shake. Then, turning, she hid her face from Rick with her hair and mouthed *he's hot* to Maggie.

Maggie agreed. Rick was looking as tasty as that gourmet cheese. Dark jeans and a simple black T-shirt that clung to his upper body. Broken-in flip-flops and mirrored sunglasses hooked in the neck of his shirt gave him a bit of Miami flavor.

"You look familiar..." Rick cocked his head.

"I'm a news anchor on channel seven." Cheryl put her hand on Rick's bicep and squeezed like she was checking for a ripe melon at one of the produce stands.

"That must be it." His doubtful tone made Maggie think he didn't watch the local news.

"Oh, there's that billboard on I-80 too. I get recognized everywhere since that went up. It's kind of ridiculous." She laughed self-consciously and dropped her hand from Rick's arm. He stepped back well beyond her reach.

"It must be strange to see your face like that." Maggie couldn't imagine looking at her face twenty feet tall.

"To be honest, it's not my favorite part of my job."

A few giggling teens bopped into Maggie's booth. They laughed and looked at their phones as much as they shopped. Rick edged away from the incoming group.

"Well, I'm going to go find that cheese. Maggie, see you at the house." He scooted around Cheryl and ducked out of the booth. Maggie got the distinct impression that high estrogen levels had sent him running.

"Girl, that is a wow. Your landlord is gorgeous." Cheryl fanned her face with one hand and pressed the other over her heart.

Maggie laughed. "Thanks, I guess." What else could she say to that?

"As one sex-starved, lonely, overworked, single mom to another, please tell me you are planning to cut that pony from the herd, tie him down, and ride him hard."

Maggie's cheeks burned at Cheryl's comment. She might be worse than Lena.

"Cheryl!" Maggie pointed at the teen girls, mildly horrified they might have overheard.

"Please. Teens today hear much worse on social media."

"I'm going to see if they need any help. I'll be right back." She tried to ignore the little voice in her head that was yelling *giddy up, cowgirl, let's go rope us a man!* while she went to check on the teens. Other than one wanting an artistic picture of Maggie with her products for Instagram, they were just browsing. As she talked with them, Cheryl added more products to her shopping basket.

"Okay, it's just us now. Spill. Hot Rick, what's the deal?" Cheryl dropped her overflowing basket on the display table and propped her hip next to it. Maggie started tallying up her order.

"Hot Rick is not for me. One, he's my landlord." She put down a bottle of bath salts and counted off the depressing facts on her fingers. "Two, he's leaving Omaha as soon as he sells the house I live in. And three, I don't think he's interested."

"He's interested. Otherwise, he wouldn't be at the green market. It's in the bro-code handbook. Green markets, art fairs, and foreign films are strictly prohibited activities unless there is a chance of getting laid. He was here because of you. Thus...he's interested." Cheryl seemed to think she had it all figured out.

"That doesn't change the other impediments."

"He's the perfect fling. Yes!" Cheryl squealed louder than the teens that had just left the booth.

Maggie shook her head. "I don't think that's a good idea."

Maggie wasn't that kind of woman. One-night stands, vacation romances, hit 'em and quit 'em games had never been of interest to her. If the man in her bed wasn't there because they were trying to be with each other long term, she didn't want him.

"Don't knock it until you try it. We're getting older. Our boobs are starting to need that push-up bra more every year, our asses aren't as perky as they were, and don't even get me started on the chin hairs. Those fuckers. I had to buy a magnifying mirror and special precision tweezers. The closer I get to forty, and I'm closer to it than you, the more I realize that now is the time to squeeze every drop of enjoyment out of life before it's too late. I say grab that man, a bottle of good wine, and some sexy lingerie. And enjoy the ride."

"You are nuts. Awesome but nuts. And a fling isn't me."

"You never know until you try. And that's one fine man to broaden your horizons with." She put her credit card down on the table and reached for a few more lip balms to add to her haul. She practically bought one of everything Maggie stocked in her booth.

"I'll keep that in mind."

"You do that. This was great, girl talk and most of my Christmas shopping in one stop." Cheryl leaned over and kissed Maggie's cheek. "See you soon." She waved and disappeared into the ever-growing crowd of shoppers on Eleventh Street.

A new surge of customers kept Maggie busy. Her items sold better every year. A few of her most loyal customers even stocked up in case she ran out of their favorites before the summer green market season ended.

She should prioritize looking for a new living situation that would allow her to start her mini-farm over. Or, like the extra lavender, she would have to buy her raw ingredients from others. That would cut into her profits and make paying for

Evan's school harder. She and Mona should have planned for the inevitable better.

She smiled robotically at the customer she was ringing up—the tremulous thoughts taking up way too much brain space. The next year was going to be a hell of a challenge.

When the crowd started to thin around noon, Rick reappeared.

"So, how were sales?" He lingered just inside her booth, not getting close enough for a hug.

"Great, better than last weekend." She stacked and straightened stock as she talked. A few last-minute customers might appear in the next thirty minutes before the market officially closed.

"That's good, right?" He met her eyes and sent her one of those rare, smoldering, five-alarm-fire Rick Cabrera smiles. Her insides melted and knees weakened. He should have been a TV heartthrob. That look would have made him famous.

"Yeah." She turned back to the tray of lip balm she just straightened and did it again. "How was shopping?"

"Pretty cool. Actually, very cool. We don't have farmers' markets like this in Florida. I got incredible stuff. I met this rancher. He sold me all this awesome beef. We talked for like half an hour about cuts and cooking techniques. Grass raised beef versus grass-finished beef." Rick held up a bulging bag with a local ranch's logo. It had to have half a cow in it.

"Wow, you're going to eat well."

"You should join me tonight. I imagine you've been on your feet all day, and you need a glass of wine and someone else to cook?" He made the offer so offhand, with no anxiety or concern. It seemed natural and uncalculated.

Maggie had the word no on the tip of her tongue. It was the smart answer. But damn, wine and a steak sounded like nirvana. She deserved to enjoy something, even if only a good meal. She firmly reminded herself that Rick was not on

tonight's menu no matter what bad ideas Cheryl
had put in her head.

"I'll see you about five o'clock?"

"Five o'clock it is."

Thirteen

RICK SAT IN HIS new-to-him crappy used SUV and rubbed a hand down his face. What the hell was he thinking inviting Maggie for dinner?

He hadn't planned it, but she looked exhausted, and he had all this food. It was the nice thing to do. And lately, when he thought about Maggie, he tried to think of nice things to do for her. It was his way to make up for all the upheaval he was causing. He brought her garbage can in from the curb. He gave her the better parking spot in the driveway and got her water when she gardened in the heat. He was being nice. Dinner was just one more nice thing.

It was a good thing he brought an old cooler with him for his green market purchases. He had a stop to make on the way home. You didn't cook gorgeous steaks on the sad rusted out thing that passed for a grill at Mona's. He turned the key in the ignition and aimed for the nearest strip mall.

He pulled into the parking lot of a big box home improvement store. The line of gleaming grills out front drew him in. Grilling was one of his favorite ways to cook. It kept the kitchen clean and didn't heat up the house. It was sensible to buy a grill for him to use while he was in Omaha.

He was not spending five hundred dollars on a grill to impress Maggie. But he planned to leave it for her when he went back to Miami. It was the nice thing to do.

How could the word nice mean so many different things?

He selected a top-of-the-line but smaller sized grill with all the bells and whistles, including a special high heat area that promised to sear meat at near a thousand degrees. He could almost taste the ribeyes as he and a sales associate loaded Maggie's new grill and some propane tanks into his SUV.

Across the parking lot was a massive wine and liquor shop. Can't serve red meat without a nice bottle of wine. He pocketed his car keys and headed for the shop.

"Hello, sir. Can I help you find something?" A gray-haired man with a wine specialist tag intercepted him at the entrance to the store.

"Ah, I'm looking for a red wine to go with grilled steaks."

"Sounds like date night. I have a Bordeaux that will work perfectly."

Yeah, it did sound like a date. The only things missing were candles and a bouquet of flowers.

"Not a date, just doing something nice for a friend," he corrected the wine specialist as they strolled to the French wine section of the mega store.

"Friends are important in this life. Don't ever take them for granted. Ah, here you go. A small vineyard with a fairly unknown name but a wonderful robust wine. Tastes better than most of the stuff twice its price. A personal favorite."

The label had a drawing of an ancient stone chateau among fields of lavender on it. "I'll take two bottles."

"Perfect. Anything else."

"No, I'm all set." Time to go home before he found himself at a florist.

Back at the house, he got busy setting up the new grill on a small patio off the side of the barn.

Once dusted off, the old wrought iron patio set was plenty serviceable. He hauled the rusted grill out to the curb and finished sweeping off the patio with enough time for him to prep dinner and grab a shower.

He wandered outside a little before five to find Maggie finishing what he'd started. She had a red and white checkered tablecloth spread on the old table and cushions tied onto two chairs. In the center of the table, an oversized mason jar filled with a mix of wildflowers sat next to a few votive candles.

"Aren't they pretty?" Maggie pointed to the flowers.

"Yes." He wasn't looking at the flowers. She had captured all his attention. She wore a cotton sundress, nothing fancy or overtly sexy about it. But the last golden rays of the sun burnished her hair and gave the simple dress an ethereal glow.

"Another vendor gave them to me while I was taking down my booth." She leaned across the table and lit the candles.

He pulled his eyes from her and went to work opening the bottle of wine he'd brought outside. Planned or not, their friendly dinner looked very romantic—flowers, candlelight, and fancy French wine.

And part of him liked that more than was prudent.

He poured the wine and passed her the first glass, careful not to touch her fingers. One touch of her skin would lead him to crave another.

"A toast?" He held his glass up.

"To?" Her smile was light, friendly, and not at all coy or seductive.

"A successful day at the green market." He may have a bunch of nebulous desires swirling around inside him, but Maggie appeared to be taking this night at face value. A relaxed dinner with a friend.

They clinked their glasses, and he consciously smothered all his weird thoughts. He'd shared plenty of meals with a woman that weren't designed to end in sex before. Hell, he and Ava King, his friend in the US Attorney's office, did it often. That was all this was. He needed to chill the fuck out with the romantic thoughts. Too much daytime television was warping his brain—stupid Hallmark channel.

The wine was like liquid red velvet, thick and soft. It would be killer with the steaks.

"Like it?" he asked.

Maggie nodded and pulled the bottle over to examine it.

"It's the French version of this house on the label. Once the guy showed me, I had to buy it."

"I bet renovating the chateau might cost more." She tapped the bottle with one finger.

He laughed with her. It was that or cry. He was still chuckling when he headed into the house to retrieve everything for dinner. On the way back, he turned on the small coach light on the side of the barn so they would be able to see when the sun set.

The farm-fresh tomatoes and mozzarella were perfect topped with Maggie's basil. Better than he'd had in any restaurant. They chatted about her customers and the other vendors at the market while enjoying the salad and some fresh bread.

"Obviously, you liked our green market. What about the rest of Omaha?"

"It's growing on me. After so long in Miami, this place is a total change, but it's not bad." He hadn't missed much about Miami other than his family.

"Like?" She rested her chin on her hand, waiting for his answer. In the low light, her eyes sparkled with interest.

"SoBe wasn't my scene anymore. You know?" He shrugged.

"Nope. What's SoBe?"

"South Beach. When you see a movie showing beautiful people club hopping and partying all night in Miami, that's South Beach. And for years,

I was into it. I knew all the bouncers, the valet parkers, and the bartenders at the hottest clubs. I never waited in line and was treated almost as well as the guys throwing around wads of hundred-dollar bills."

"But?"

"But I was starting to feel like I was the old guy in the club. When the girls I'd meet were more than a decade younger than me, it got... a little strange. Suddenly, I wasn't a hot young guy with connections anymore." The realization had taken time, but it slowly dawned on him that going out felt like work and not play.

"Ouch. You were a cliché." She was totally making fun of him.

"Yeah, my ego was shredded." He chuckled.

Youth was currency in the trendy bars. As he aged, his worth fell. And worse, the older a man, the bigger the bank account he was expected to have. Not like a good job and a 401K but like owning a yacht or private jet. FBI agent did not meet that expectation.

"Damaged ego aside. What about your job at the FBI?"

"I miss the people I worked with. Great team." He trusted his fellow agents with his life. That kind of bond was rare in this world.

"I sense a but coming here too." She listened intently; her eyes held his, and she didn't fidget or reach for her phone. She focused solely on him.

"No job is perfect. But it's my life. I'm an agent."

"Sure, I understand."

He loved being an agent. But there were a thousand things he didn't miss. And the longer he was away, the less he wanted to deal with the mountains of useless paperwork, uncooperative judges impeding investigations, and most of all, his boss. The man's questionable decisions were a big part of why Rick got shot. The bureau had taken his loyalty and rewarded him with two bullets.

"When I got here, I wasn't sure I'd have the option of returning to the field. Hell, that's why I came. I thought I could sell the house, and I'd have a windfall to go with my disability checks."

"You weren't that bad, were you?" Maggie thought back to the first days Rick was in Omaha. His stiff movements and constantly grim expression. The scar she'd glimpsed on his chest. Maybe he had been that bad but also good at hiding it.

"Yeah, I was a mess—in pain and weak. But Hector is a miracle. He says it's all timing. I came to him exactly when I had healed enough to start regaining strength and mobility. But the doctors back in Miami kept telling me I was lucky to be alive." He rubbed the heel of his hand over his sternum as he spoke.

Lucky to be alive. It was difficult to swallow her wine past the lump that had formed in her throat at the thought.

She coughed and sputtered, forcing the wine down.

"You okay?" He rubbed a hand down her back.

She nodded.

His hand lingered on her back, sliding slowly up to her nape. His thumb grazed the base of her skull, and goosebumps rose in response to the delicate caress. She wanted to melt.

She could drown in the depts of his dark eyes aglow with banked desire. Her breath caught. He was on the edge of his seat. If she leaned forward, she could kiss him. She licked her lips; temptation was within reach. Want versus need. Smart versus rash. The debate paralyzed her. She gripped the arms of her chair as indecision seethed inside her.

"Mom, I'm home!" She jolted back, her son's voice like a bucket of icy water.

The door into the backyard from the walkout basement slammed in Evan's wake. He raced across the yard toward them.

Rick drew back from her, eyes closed, and cleared his throat. The gruff sound was somehow both sexy and uncomfortable.

That was the hottest near kiss in the history of Nebraska. Fuck, her panties were wet, and her heart raced from one touch. Rick should come with a warning label: bad decisions ahead.

She blew out a breath and tried to get her brain into mom mode. She stood, her arms out to hug Evan, who crashed into her. She kissed the top of his sandy blond head before letting go.

"I thought Dad was dropping you at camp in the morning?"

"He had a thing. Whatever." Evan shrugged like he couldn't have cared less. "Hey, Rick."

"Good to see you, Evan." Rick gave Evan a fist bump.

"Did he at least feed you?" It wasn't the first time her ex dropped Evan off without warning and un-fed. More than once, Mona had taken Evan in when Maggie had been stuck at work.

"Drive-through junk food, yum! And he bought me a new video game. Can I go play it?"

She picked up her phone to check the time. "Go rot your brain for a few hours before bed. I'll be out here with Rick."

"Yes!" He ran back to the house faster than he came out to hug her.

"Does that happen often?" Rick asked.

"Ted flaking out on parenting responsibilities?" She snorted. "You met him. What do you think?"

"I think he's an ass."

She lifted her wine glass. "I'll drink to that."

Rick clinked his glass with hers.

"What about a steak?"

"Best offer I've had all day." Other than an almost kiss with a gorgeous man from Miami. She took another sip of wine. Good thing Rick had brought out a second bottle.

"She's ready for her inaugural run." He leaned over and checked the temperature gauge.

He looked as excited as a kid on Christmas to use his new toy. He turned knobs, readied his BBQ tools, and set out a pair of clean platters. It was the most excitement she had seen from him since he'd arrived. She was glad to get a glimpse of him enjoying life. Even if it was just one night, she was sure the relaxed, happy guy with the spatula in one hand and a wine glass in the other was the real Rick.

He deftly placed the spectacular looking steaks on the grill. The sizzle and aroma of cooking beef started her taste buds watering. He added an array of fresh squash and mushrooms next to the meat.

She joined him at the grill. It was fun to watch him expertly turn and position the food. "Not your first time operating a pair of tongs?"

"Definitely not. Wait until you see the perfect set of cross-hatched grill marks I'm putting on these babies." He gave the two steaks a quarter turn and rolled the mushrooms.

"I don't remember the last time I did this." She topped off both their glasses.

"Based on that old grill I tossed out, a long time."

"More I meant kicking back with a friend to have a nice meal. Lena and I try to get together for dinners or happy hour. But between Lone Tree and Evan, I don't have much free time. If I'm outside, normally I'm doing something with the plants." If she was inside, she was cooking, or cleaning, or working, or doing laundry. Her list never seemed to end.

"It does seem like you are constantly in motion." The look he gave her was a blend of pity and amazement.

"Most days, I'm running on caffeine and pure determination. Sleep is for the weak."

"I better not let Hector get a hold of you. He's big on balance and letting the body recharge when needed."

"Single moms don't get that often." She was running from morning until night.

"I don't know many single moms, but from where I'm standing, you have the hardest job out there. And you do it well. Evan is a cool kid." He pointed at the house with a pair of tongs.

"Thank you for that." Inside she felt stretched too thin most days. But if the rest of the world thought she was doing a good job and Evan loved her, maybe she did have it figured out. At least until the next crisis.

Rick plated up their meal with the same grace he'd cooked it. The food was insanely good. After her last bite, she kicked her sandals off and propped her feet on an empty chair. She tilted her head back and looked at the stars.

One deep breath in, one out.

She relished the warm summer night and the soft breeze that teased her hair. She had a full belly and the littlest buzz from the wine. If only she could return to this memory the next time she was tired, stressed, and hungry.

Still looking at the stars, she said, "We should do this every Sunday. It's so nice."

"Yeah, nice," he echoed.

Fourteen

WITH THE WINDOWS ROLLED down and some old-school Nirvana playing in his shitty car, Rick enjoyed the endorphins from an awesome workout with Hector. After two months, that's what his sessions with Hector were now—workouts, not PT. He wasn't back to normal yet, but he could see that the FBI physical fitness test would be doable by the fall.

He parked in the drive next to the house and got out just as Kevin, the contractor, pulled up. They had a meeting to go over the final color selections for the exterior paint.

Kevin got out of his SUV with an overstuffed file folder and a grim expression. Odd, because last Rick checked, he was the one paying the enormous invoices to fix up this house, and Kevin kept the profits.

They met on the front path and shook hands.

"Good news or bad news first?" Kevin asked after pleasantries were exchanged.

"Fuck." So much for the endorphins. "Hit me with the bad news."

"I got the results back from the lead paint tests we did inside the house. And the basement apartment and the original sections of the house that weren't renovated back in the seventies need remediation."

"Lead paint."

"It's pretty common in a house this age." Kevin nodded and passed Rick a stack of lab reports from the folder.

"Is it safe to live here?" His first thought was of Evan. He was sure he remembered that lead paint was terrible for kids.

"As long as no one is eating the paint, it's fine. But the removal is going to cost extra. And you'll have to vacate the house for a few days. Your tenant too." Kevin looked almost apologetic.

"How much more?"

Kevin ruffled through the folder again for an estimate. "About ten grand."

Rick groaned. Why did everything seem to cost about ten grand?

"And I have to get a special crew in here. So that's another delay. We're looking at October."

"Of course." Nothing about home remodeling was easy, cheap, or fast. Those shows on the home and garden channel were absolute bullshit.

"Great. I'll get the remediation crew scheduled." Kevin unclipped his cell from his belt and fired off a text.

Poof, there went some more of his retirement savings.

His siblings had been jealous that he'd inherited Mona's house. Lucky bastards. He was about ready to call home and give this money pit to any family member that wanted it. How Mona had let things get this rundown, he didn't understand. The deferred maintenance was bad enough, but lead paint... Ugh. There were laws against selling houses with lead paint.

"Good news. My carpenters and roofers will be here in the morning to start on the roof and dry rot."

"Sounds good." This house was going to eat him, his retirement savings, and his rainy-day cash in one big bite.

"Ready to make final paint choices?"

"Sure." Let's spend more money.

"I'll get the samples."

Rick waited for Kevin to get a box from his SUV. Then he followed him up the front porch so they could paint swatches on the house.

He'd narrowed down the choices to four options. He took a small can and brush from Kevin and got to work while the contractor did the same. They chatted about ideas for the inside remodel while they worked.

"Hey, you two know you're both painting with a different color?" Maggie teased as she strolled up the path.

Rick turned, a retort on the tip of his tongue. Whatever witty thing he'd been about to say vanished. Maggie must have come from an important meeting. She was dressed to kill in a dark navy skirt suit, her hair pinned up, red heels, total hot CEO look. Ideas he had no business entertaining filled his mind. He imagined bending her over a big, polished desk and sliding that skirt up her thighs. He'd bury his fingers in her hair, pulling it loose so he could wrap it around his fist.

Since the near kiss in the backyard, nice had taken on a whole new meaning...nice and dirty.

"Samples. It's final decision time." Kevin smacked him on the back. "Want to help old Rick here pick?"

Rick wanted to both punch Kevin for talking with Maggie and buy him a beer for covering for Rick's lapse. He had been staring at her like he'd never seen a woman before. He focused on redirecting his blood flow from his dick to his brain.

"I'd love a woman's opinion." Rick focused on closing his sample paint can.

"Alright. Tell me the color names."

"Coventry Gray, Saybrook Sage, Aegean Teal, Newport Blue." Kevin pointed to each swatch in turn.

Maggie stopped halfway up the steps and cocked her head, considering her options. "What color for the barn?"

Kevin dug into his box again and painted a fifth swatch on the wall. Caliente. The name and deep red color were perfect. Rick was sure about that pick. It was his way of leaving a dash of Cuban spice on the Omaha house. Sure, the new owners would never know, but it was his inside joke.

"Easy. Coventry Gray."

"You think?" He joined her on the steps and looked back at the house. He liked the gray but thought it might be boring.

"No green. It'll look like Christmas with the barn that color. And the blue will look like a Fourth of July theme. The teal is ugly. That's simple— Coventry Gray."

"Are you always this logical and decisive?' He was astonished. His mother had taken a month to pick a color for her living room. And all the choices had been whites.

"Dude. I'm an event manager and single mother. My wheelhouse is efficiency and organization. I can't afford to fiddlefuck around when it's important. And I know the crew starts tomorrow." She put up her hand for a high five, and he obliged. She was the boss.

"You heard the woman. Coventry Gray it is."

"I'll get it ordered. And sorry about the bad news." Kevin packed up his paint samples, gave Maggie another lingering look, and headed for his SUV. It was her red shoes and killer legs. No man was safe.

"Bad news? Wonder if yours is worse than mine." She leaned against the porch railing and toed off her heels, sighing in relief when she stood flat-footed.

"The house has lead paint." He moved next to her, but not too close. He wasn't a masochist.

"Ouch, sounds expensive."

"Oh yeah. It is. But not dangerous for now."

"I think I win. My asshole ex got a job at the convention center."

"Shit. Want a beer to drown our misery in?"

"Hell yes."

He headed inside to grab a couple of cold ones. At least he could fix his lead paint problem with money. Poor Maggie was stuck with her ex until the guy did something stupid to get fired.

"You should join Evan and me for dinner. I have a crock pot full of spaghetti sauce cooking. I'm just going to boil some pasta and toss a salad." Maggie wasn't going to lie. Commiserating with Rick while sharing a couple of beers on the front porch reminded her of doing the same with Mona and Polly. Except the two widows had been more likely to sip chardonnay. And the octogenarians didn't inspire hot, tingly sensations in her belly.

The women had been smart, savvy, and an essential part of her support network, especially right after she left Ted. More than a surrogate grandmother or landlord, they had done so much for Maggie and Lone Tree. And she missed their companionship in the evenings.

"I don't think I should impose." He made no move to bolt from the porch either.

"You fed me the other night. It's fair to let me return the favor."

Rick peeled the label on his bottle, considering her offer. "That was a nice meal."

They both looked up, their gazes locked, and all the hot needy feelings that their almost kiss on Sunday created flared to life...only fifty times stronger. Six feet of front porch separated them, and she started to cross the distance. But before she took a step, sanity returned. What she was experiencing was pure animal attraction. Blind lust. Unreasonable and pointless.

She sighed and closed her eyes, severing the sizzling connection between them. She didn't do flings. Rick had to stay in the friend zone.

"If you help set the table, I'll let Evan kick your ass in video games after."

He took a pull of his beer, straightened, and nodded. "Friendly dinner it is."

Rick and Evan made a production of setting the table while she chopped up a simple salad and boiled pasta. The two of them were hilarious to watch elbowing for position and trying to fold the napkins into swans.

Having Evan around seemed to ratchet down her and Rick's attraction to a reasonable level. At no point during dinner did she want to climb over the table and straddle Rick.

"Mom, I'm done." Evan took his dirty dishes and bolted for the kitchen. "Can Rick and I play Xbox now?"

"Let me help your mom clean up, and I'll be right out." Rick scooped up her plate and a few serving dishes.

"Thank you. I always love cleanup help. Evan and I take turns, but a nine-year old only can do so much." She followed him with the remainders.

He took a spot at the sink, rinsing plates and loading the dishwasher while she packaged leftovers and tidied up.

"There's another front porch party coming up at Jacob Hansen's place." She'd been meaning to invite him for a few days.

"He was the lawyer for Mona's estate." Rick scrubbed the crockpot as he talked.

"Yes, he handled all Mona's business. You should come to meet him."

"Okay." His reply sounded more like a question than an agreement.

"Rick, it's a party. It's fun. Not a chore." She had her hand on her hips, and her mom voice activated.

"Sure. If you say so." He sighed and flipped off the sink, done with the dishes.

She tossed a damp, wadded-up towel at his head. "When you got here, you had an excuse for being anti-social. You were in pain. But now, nope. You're rejoining the living one porch party at a time. Oh, and I expect you to bring something for the potluck."

"Jeez, I'll go. And I'll cook something." He plucked the towel off his head and held up his hands in surrender.

"I thought so."

She turned her back to put a few spice jars away. A muted crack was the only warning before a quick flash of mild pain shot across her butt. She whirled around with a squeak—one hand rubbing her ass cheek.

Her plaid dish towel hung from his right hand. He'd made it into a rat tail whip. That son of a bitch.

She reached for the kitchen sink sprayer, flipped on the faucet, and took her best shot, right at his chest.

He froze for a moment, eyes wide while a jet of water soaked his shirt before he had the presence of mind to pull open the refrigerator door and hide behind it.

"You can't hold out forever, Cabrera." She was between him and the exit from her galley kitchen. Her evil laugh echoed around the small space. Her index finger hovered over the trigger for the sprayer.

"You've got killer aim with that thing." He ducked his head around the side of the fridge door.

"Put down the towel and come out with your hands up." She imitated all the cop shows on TV.

"I surrender." He laughed as he made a show of dropping the towel whip and slowly closing the door.

"Smart call." She let go of the sprayer, and it slithered back into the sink.

Rick's shirt was plastered to his chest and abs, every ripple and valley outlined by the wet cotton. He looked like some kind of advertisement for men's cologne. Her fingers wanted to explore every contour. He bent down, rescued the towel off the floor, and tried to dry off his shirt.

"What are you guys doing?" Evan stood in the doorway, hands on his hips. Disapproval radiated from every wrinkle in his almost ten-year-old forehead.

She looked at Rick and he sputtered. She had no good answer. He started laughing and tried to explain.

Fuck it. She owned a mop. She reached for the sprayer and took them both out, laughing harder than she had in ages.

Fifteen

"I'M COMING." RICK SHOVED his feet into a pair of flip-flops and headed for the door. The roofers must want him for something. He pulled open the house door and stopped. Evan and a pretty young woman stood on the other side.

"Hi, I'm Suzie." She waved through the screen door.

Evan, like his mom, apparently didn't like to talk through a screen door. He yanked it open and set a bag with a tangle of television cables hanging out the top at Rick's feet.

"Hi, Suzie. I'm Rick. Can I help you?"

"I have to go. It's an emergency. My mom was taken to the hospital." The girl gripped her phone with white knuckles and kept looking at the screen like she wished it would ring.

"And that brings you to my door?"

"Duh, Rick. She's my babysitter." Evan looked at him like he would be riding the short bus to school if he didn't keep up.

"I called Maggie. She didn't answer. But Evan says you're cool, and Maggie would be okay with you watching him in an emergency. Otherwise, I have to take him across town with me to the hospital."

"Suzie, Mom will not care. I'll be safe with Rick. He's FBI!" Evan wormed his way between Rick's hip and the door frame. "Bring the Xbox, Rick.

You owe me a game. We never got to play after spaghetti."

He could hear Evan's sneakers slapping on the wood floors as he bolted for the family room. It was a good thing Rick had upgraded Mona's TV last week. He wasn't sure an Xbox could have been connected to the dinosaur he'd donated to goodwill.

"I guess I got this." He shrugged. "Go find out about your mom."

"Thank you so much. Maggie might be late. She's managing an event tonight." She leaned up and kissed Rick's cheek before jogging down the front porch steps.

Rick had grown up with plenty of nephews and cousins. He could handle a cool kid like Evan. Heck, might be fun to blow up some zombies and wreck some video game cars. Better than looking at more tile and paint samples.

He scooped up the video game console and followed Evan.

After an excruciating twenty minutes, Evan proved he was smarter than Rick by almost single-handedly hooking up the game console. Rick took a controller. Game on.

Rick hadn't had a beat down like this in years. Evan was crazy good at these stupid games. If he was going to keep hanging with this kid, he'd need an Xbox of his own so he could practice. Maybe Hector would want to help him train for this competition too.

The only pause in the slaughter was so Rick could call in an order for pizza. Extra cheese only for the champion and veggie with sausage for him. His fingers would start cramping soon. He couldn't wait for the food to arrive.

The doorbell's bong-bong saved him from getting lapped again in the racing game they were playing. It was humiliating that a kid who wasn't tall enough to see over a steering wheel beat him in a car game. He trained in precision driving at the bureau.

"Pizza, Champ. Hit pause and go wash up."

Rick paid and brought the pizza into the kitchen. He looked at Mona's plates and shrugged. He grabbed the roll of paper towels from the counter and ripped a few off for him and Evan. He popped open both boxes as Evan found his way to the kitchen and plopped in a seat.

Evan recounted several of Rick's epic gaming fails around bites of pizza.

"Alright, you win. Evan, you are the best. The undefeated champion." Rick bowed dramatically, kowtowing to the master.

Evan held up both hands, one with half a slice of pizza in it, and jogged around the kitchen like a prize fighter after winning a world title fight. Rick laughed and ruffled Evan's hair as he passed by.

Evan sat and put down his slice. "Are you really an FBI agent?"

Evan crossed his arms and looked hard at Rick. This was important.

"Yes." Rick put down his pizza, wiped his hands, and held the boy's stare.

"You're sure? I don't see a gun or a badge. Or anything." Evan searched the room like one of the prerequisite items might suddenly appear and appease his concerns.

"I'm on vacation because I got hurt." Rick tugged down his shirt collar a few inches to expose the top edge of his scar. Evan's eyes widened. "My badge and gun are in Miami. I get them back when I'm all healed up."

Evan considered his answer. "Can you still arrest someone?"

"Why would I do that?"

Evan sighed. "I don't really want to arrest him unless you have to. I want you to stop him from doing something that will stress Mom out even more."

"He who?" In the pit of his stomach, he already knew the answer.

"My dad."

Yep. He knew that guy was trouble.

"When I was there last weekend, Dad had friends stop by. The one guy paid me twenty bucks to go outside and play so they could talk. I took the money but hid in the kitchen, so I could listen. I think... I think they're going to do something bad at Mom's work." Evan started ripping little chunks out of the paper towel under his half-eaten pizza.

"Tell me what you heard." Rick waited while Evan thought for a moment before speaking.

"They were pointing at a map of the convention center. And talking about doors and security guards. Something about a loading dock."

Rick rubbed a hand over his face. Maggie said Ted was working on the janitorial staff at the convention center. Security was above his paygrade.

"Did you see the map?"

"I found it later. Dad stuffed it in the pantry."

"Was it like a brochure or like building plans?" Any details he could get might help him decide if Evan's theory was nothing more than a misunderstanding by a smart kid with a fanciful imagination.

"Plans, the big sheets like that contractor guy you have working on the house carries around."

Blueprints. Not good. Blueprints made Rick think heist. That meant a plan of some kind, not just janitors with a pipe dream about making a big score.

"Why did you decide to listen in?"

Evan looked away, uncomfortable with the question.

Rick patted his hand. "Evan, I'm FBI. It's my job to ask questions, remember?"

"Yeah, okay. My dad has problems, and Mom says I'm smarter than him. And if I need to misbehave to do what's right, I have permission.

Like the time he tried to get me to help him cheat at cards."

"You can cheat at cards?" This Ted guy was more than an asshole to put his kid in that situation. Images of gritty backroom card games and the kind of scumbags that played at those tables filled Rick's mind.

"I have a really good memory, and I see math everywhere. So card games are easy."

"Tell me what you mean, you see math." Rick remembered Maggie calling Evan a genius, but seeing math was like Goodwill Hunting shit.

"Numbers just make sense, you know?" Evan shrugged and took a bite of his pizza.

"Remind me never to play poker with you, kid." He snagged a new slice from the box and took a bite. The grease and carbs were a weak distraction from all the information Evan had dumped in his lap.

A degenerate gambler, a friend that paid a kid twenty bucks to go away, and a map of the convention center. It sounded like a recipe for twenty-five years in the state penitentiary.

Evan was right. This was another thing to stress out Maggie.

"Hello, Maggie." It was after eleven o'clock. Rick sat on the top step of the porch waiting for her. He got up as she approached and slipped his cell into his pocket.

"I'm so sorry. Let me get Evan, and we'll get out of your hair." She started toward the front door.

"Wait up. We need to talk." He caught her shoulder and squeezed it.

Nothing good in this world had ever followed those words. Her first irrational fear was he'd somehow sold the house. It only had three-quarters of a new roof, but that didn't stop her from freaking out. On its heels was the worry he was about to tell her that it wasn't his job to watch her kid.

"Sure. The workshop?" It had been a hellishly long day, and she struggled to find her voice past the tight feeling in her throat caused by all her disconcerting thoughts.

"Yeah, Evan shouldn't overhear this." Rick led the way around the side of the house.

Fuck. Rick must be pissed he'd been saddled with Evan all afternoon and evening.

It had been one of those days. It started when she forgot to charge her cell phone and snowballed. Her event this evening had been a near train wreck. It was a technology presentation, and the convention center Wi-Fi melted down ten minutes before the start. The caterers were late, and the bartender dropped a case of high-end scotch. Great day. Plus, Suzie's mom.

She kicked a small rock with the toe of her black flats.

Rick turned at the sound, then froze, looking at the backyard. "Look, fireflies. Rare to see those in Miami."

Her mini-farm was aglow with the fireflies buzzing from plant to plant, enjoying the warm summer evening. It was magical. She'd miss this place when she had to leave.

"One more good thing about Omaha." She gave him a weak smile and waited for him to look his fill.

He watched, head tilted, for a few moments before moving to open the barn door.

Inside, she flipped on a few small lights. The rich smells of rosemary, mint, and lavender seemed to wrap around her. The heavy herbal scent was a balm to her frayed nerves. Lone Tree was more than a revenue stream. She was passionate about her products and the plants she grew to make them.

She sat on her stool at the workbench. Across from her, Rick braced his hands on the tabletop and dropped his head.

He looked up, his eyes searching her face before he spoke. "How bad of a guy is your ex?"

"What?" He could have knocked her off the stool with a feather. That was about the last topic she expected him to bring up.

"Evan has some concerns. He shared what he heard and saw when he was with Ted last weekend. It sounded like your ex is planning a robbery at the convention center."

She couldn't even find the words. The gibberish she sputtered out was a mix of curse words and threats to Ted's life. A stress headache bloomed to life, pounding behind her eyes. This was the cherry on top of the shit sundae that had been her day.

"Thank you for telling me. It's not that Ted is that bad, but he is that dumb. I should have known something was up when he got a job at the convention center. He's not the type to take a job cleaning—too humiliating."

He nodded.

"And I was worried you were upset about watching Evan."

"No, I like him. Cool kid. I told you it was fine in my text." He waved off her concerns.

"I know, but...thank you for the help today. I'm grateful. Knowing he was safe with you was pretty much the only good part of my day."

"You're welcome. I'm happy to help."

"In the morning, I'll call Ted and tell him not to do anything stupid." She rubbed a weary hand over her face, probably smearing what little makeup she had left after a twelve-hour day.

"I don't know if that's the best way to handle this. From what Evan told me, Ted isn't in this alone. If his partners are in charge, you could become a target. An impediment that needs to be handled."

"Needs to be handled. Great." She dropped her head to the tabletop, resting her forehead on her folded arms. She had enough to worry about already.

She turned her head to the side to see Rick. "Like I don't have enough to do this summer. I have a green market every weekend for the next four weeks. I barely started looking for a new place, and now I have to figure out how to keep my ex out of jail." She buried her face back in her arms like the ostrich with its head in the sand.

Rick's hand settled gently on her back. "Let me handle your ex."

"You have the house and PT. It's not your problem," she mumbled, head still hidden. He started tracing comforting circles on her back.

"Hector's flexible. And Kevin has brought me estimates, plans, budgets, ideas, and samples. But he hasn't been able to commit a crew to do the work. Once the roof and exterior paint are done, it will be weeks before he has time to get back here. You weren't kidding about construction in Omaha. It's ridiculous. It makes me wish I'd watched home improvement shows instead of the food network while bedridden."

She turned her head to look at him. He stopped caressing her back. His warm brown eyes looked so trustworthy and earnest. "You're sure?"

"It's nothing. I'll make a few calls." He let his hand slip away, and she instantly missed the connection. "Get me Ted's full name, birth date, and social security number."

"Okay, thank you." She struggled to sit back up, the weight of the day pressing down from all directions.

She laid her hand in the center of his chest for a beat before slipping off the stool and giving him a hug. She pressed against him. He was tall, strong, and so easy to lean on. She smelled her arnica balm on his skin, and it only added to his appeal.

Rick Cabrera was a good man. He had stepped up to watch her son and promised to look into her ex's stupidity. Those two things were better than chocolate and flower bouquets.

"Come, let's get Evan and pour the two of you into bed. You look exhausted." He kept one arm around her as they turned to leave the barn.

She flicked off the lights as they passed the switches, and Rick pulled the doors closed with one hand. "I could barely open these doors when I first arrived."

She remembered.

He draped his arm back over her shoulders as they walked up the drive to the house. He squeezed her close to his side, matching his stride to hers. "I couldn't do this either. This shoulder was practically frozen."

"You're getting better." So you can go home to Miami.

"Finally."

They paused at the foot of the front porch steps. The light from the house outlined Rick's profile perfectly, highlighting his strong jaw. She laid her head against his chest and relished the restful pause, letting her worries and responsibilities go— living in the moment.

He cupped her jaw in one hand and tilted her head. His eyes focused on her lips; she instinctively slid her tongue over them. His other hand found her hip, his thumb resting on her waist. She closed her eyes and tried to burn the moment into her memory. His smell, his warm, steady hands. She relaxed further into his embrace. It felt so natural to be close to him.

"Maggie." He sighed her name over her mouth before he dipped his head for a kiss.

Tentative and fleeting, he teased her lips with a delicate caress. Her pulse pounded in her ears, and her skin prickled alive with sensation wherever their bodies touched. She gripped his forearm, her nails digging into his shirt sleeve. He didn't plunge in and ravage her. No. He savored small tastes that left her starving for more. She whimpered into his mouth, her knees weak.

He placed a final chaste kiss at the corner of her mouth. He pulled her flush against him and pressed their cheeks together.

"Mi corazón," he whispered in her ear.

They stayed locked in each other's arms, the sounds of the quiet neighborhood surrounding them.

Unfortunately, life's responsibilities and realities awaited her as soon as she stepped out of his embrace. But she indulged in the senseless fantasy that was Rick Cabrera for a few moments longer.

Sixteen

RICK FLIPPED THROUGH A home design magazine sitting at the big table in Mona's kitchen. A white porcelain farmhouse sink caught his eye. It would be perfect. He looked for the price in the fine print. Shit. His first car cost less than that. But he stuck a sticky note on the top of the page anyway. Maybe he could find a cheaper one that looked like it.

He closed the magazine and pushed it under a folder from Kevin with the most recent estimates in it. He was so over penny-pinching and paint swatches.

Time to do something more in his wheelhouse. He reached for his cell, fired off an email to Ava King, and dialed her office number.

"Ava King," she answered on the second ring.

"How's my favorite US Attorney and dog mom?"

"Rick Cabrera, is that you? Nah, it can't be. You sound almost happy."

"Gee, thanks."

Ava had been one of the few friends that kept trying to jolt him out of his depression after the shooting. It hadn't worked, but the woman never gave up. Hell, she made him go to a drag queen brunch in an attempt to lighten his mood.

"I can't take all the credit. The physical therapist I have out here is amazing. He's like a personal trainer, a shrink, and a spiritual guru all in one.

He's got me in the gym, meditating, and even eating healthy. All real food, nothing processed."

Except for half a pizza he ate yesterday with Evan. And he might have scarfed down another cold slice for breakfast with his green smoothie this morning. What Hector didn't know would never hurt him.

"I love Hector. Get me his address. I'm sending him a fruit basket or something."

"I'm sure Hector would love some fresh-from-Florida oranges, but it's not necessary."

"Rick, don't make me stalk him to get his address." She would do it too. Tenacious was the perfect word for Ava.

"Fine. I'll email it over." He scrawled a reminder note on the sticky pad so he didn't forget.

"How's Omaha?"

"It's growing on me like a fungus."

"That bad?"

"Joking. It's a surprisingly cool city. And no hurricanes."

"I couldn't do it. I'd miss the ocean." Ava's husband, Jackson, was a true boat guy, and the two of them and their dog spent a lot of time sport fishing.

"More like Jackson would never leave the ocean, and you'd miss him."

She laughed. "Don't knock boat ownership until you try it."

"I have no desire to own a hole in the water that sucks up money. I've already got a house like that."

"Ugh, sounds awful."

"The renovations will cost, but the profit potential is there to make it worth it." He hoped he didn't run out of cash before realizing that profit.

"I'm glad it's going so well up there, but since you called me at work, I'm guessing there's more to your call than a proof of life?"

"I already sent you an email. I have a childhood friend here, and her ex is giving her and her son problems. I want to help. Can you run her ex in the system see what you find? Pull known associates as well."

"You're helping a woman with a kid who is a friend, as in you're not sleeping with her?"

"I'm not sleeping with her..." The memory of last night derailed his train of thought. The way she felt cradled in his arms. She was so sad and exhausted, and he'd wanted to make her feel better. He went one gigantic, unforgettable step too far. Because that kiss...holy fuck.

"But you'd like to. I can hear it in your voice." Ava cackled in his ear; her laugh overflowed with devious delight. "Old Rick is back. The ladies of Omaha aren't going to know what hit them."

"It's not like that, Ava." He wasn't his old self, not yet, but he was getting closer.

"You ask her to go dancing yet? I mean, if this Hector guy is as badass as you say, you should be almost back in dancing form by now."

"I could probably handle a little salsa dancing. My shimmy might not be in full effect. But, no, I'm not taking her dancing, just helping with the ex."

"Come on, Rick, you need to get back in the saddle."

He had zero interest in getting back in the saddle, as Ava called it. Even before the kiss that violated his vow to stay away from Maggie seventeen different ways. He hadn't been on the prowl at all. Cheryl, that TV reporter, Maggie's friend Lena from work, some hot co-ed at the university gym. Not one had turned his head or tickled his fancy. What the fuck happened to his mojo? And why hadn't he noticed it was missing until now?

He even forgot to flirt with Ava at the start of this call. Shit.

As soon as he got off the phone, he was going out and going to score a number off some random woman. Get back in the game to prove he still had it. It was mid-morning; he could try the grocery store. He'd gotten a date more than once in the produce section. It would get his mind off last night's kiss better than anything else.

He sighed into the phone. "Maggie was my grandmother's tenant. And once the house sells, I'm leaving. It would be a dick move to get involved with her only to turn around and evict her before leaving town. I'm only helping with the ex."

"Alright, I'll let it go."

"Thank you, Ava. Maggie was like family to my grandmother. And her son's a good kid. They don't deserve the shit this guy puts them through."

"I understand. You'll have the info in an hour or less." Ava hated these kinds of cases as much as he did.

Domestic issues were difficult for everyone involved—law enforcement, the justice department, and the families. His least favorite case at the FBI were parental kidnapping cases. From the outside, you couldn't know what was best for the kid, but this time he was on the inside, and he knew.

"Thanks for the rush service. Talk soon, mi amorcito."

"No problem, Rick. Keep doing what you're doing. You sound great. Goodbye."

So much for trying out his mojo in the produce department. Ava always kept her word. It would be better to stay at home and wait so he could get to work digging through Ted's life as soon as the file hit his inbox.

And, if he was honest, his enthusiasm for hitting on a stranger in the grocery store ranked just above his urge to learn to play the accordion or look at more tile samples with Kevin.

"Come on in," Maggie called. A wave of lust or nerves or some other inconvenient emotion zipped through her. Only Rick would be knocking on the door to her workshop at this time in the evening. He stopped by most nights when she worked, keeping her company and even helping. Last week, he'd stuck labels on soaps and tied bows on gift baskets. It had been nice to have company while she worked. But that was before the kiss.

"Hey, Maggie, how was your day?" He stepped inside but lingered in the doorway. He shoved his hands deep in his pockets.

"Good. Busy. You know." She looked up. Damn, he was handsome. His dark hair was tousled, and there was a shadow of stubble on his face. She tore her gaze away, her cheeks heating as she remembered how his scruff felt pressed against her.

He cleared his throat.

She smiled uncertainly.

Last night's kiss rendered their typical easy banter awkward and stilted. And she hated it.

She wiped her hands on a towel and capped the bottle of sage and lavender lotion she had filled. She walked around the worktable and stopped a few feet from him. Rick was still Rick. There was no reason to feel weird.

"It was just a kiss." She put her hands on her hips and jutted her chin out.

"Yeah?" He met her gaze straight on, matching her defiant energy.

"It happened. We're both adults." She shrugged, faking a nonchalance she didn't feel. "Water under the bridge."

"Can't un-ring the bell."

"Can't put the toothpaste back in the tube."

"Time to move forward." He smiled, seeming to get on board with her plan to face this issue head-on.

"Exactly, forget it happened." Yeah, she wasn't going to succeed in forgetting anytime soon, but she would try.

"Sure. We'll forget...it happened." His words trailed off like the idea of forgetting wasn't sitting well. But from her perspective, it was the safe option.

"Exactly." Her reply came out a bit tortured instead of bold, but it would have to do.

"Exactly." He squeezed her shoulder and gifted her one of his handsome movie-star grins.

"So, Rick, how was your day?" She moved back to her spot at the worktable and pushed a case of bottles and a roll of labels toward him. He plopped down in the stool he'd used the other night and began carefully sticking them on.

Back to normal, thank God. Or the new version of normal, where she longed to shove her bottles of lotion aside, climb on top of the table. and attack him—but didn't.

"Good. I spoke to my friend, Ava, in the US Attorney's office."

"About Ted?" Worry about her ex had gnawed at the back of her mind all day. Part of her wanted to take her concerns to her boss, but she decided to wait and see what Rick learned. With her luck, if she got Ted fired somehow, it would blow back on her. And she would end up fired right along with him.

"Ava pulled his criminal history. All pretty low-level unexciting stuff. But his most recent arrest was for running an illegal lottery."

"You're kidding me. What an idiot." An illegal lottery sounded beyond shady.

"He got hit with a fine and a slap on the wrist."

"They should have given him a smack in the head. It might have knocked some sense into him." She would bring Ted's little lottery indiscretion up with a family court judge at her next opportunity.

"What worries me is the others arrested with him on the lottery scam. Three guys that all work together in a pawnshop across the river in Council Bluffs, Iowa."

"Great. Scum from the casinos, I'll bet." Ted practically lived at the casinos across the river.

"It looks that way. One has a pretty serious rap sheet. He's listed as a part-time employee at the pawnshop, but Ava looked at some tax records for me, and we think he's the de-facto owner. The other two are fronting for him because he would never qualify for a firearms dealer's license with his record. And guns are the bread and butter of most pawnshops."

"So what now?"

"I'm going to buy a gun."

"Jesus, Rick. Isn't that a bit drastic? Can't we call the cops?" She knocked over the lotion bottle she was filling, spilling it all over her worktable. There were days she wanted to kill her ex, but only metaphorically.

"And tell the cops what? A brilliant nine-year-old thinks his dad is planning a thing? This is better."

"Shooting someone is better?" She wiped up the spilled lotion with short angry swipes.

"No. I'm not going to shoot anyone. Relax." He reached out and caught her wrist. He took the towel and finished cleaning up the mess. "I want to check out the pawnshop. See how shady these guys are in real life."

"Then I'm coming with." She crossed her arms over her chest. Her ex was her problem.

"Nope." Rick tossed the greasy towel into a hamper on the other side of the room. "Pretty woman like you the pawnshop guys would remember and talk about. It could tip off your ex. Me, I'm some random Latino from Florida looking to buy a gun. Nothing exciting about me."

There was plenty exciting about Rick. His smoldering good looks. The way his eyes ran over her body when he called her pretty a moment ago. And how being pressed to his broad chest made her feel—all very exciting.

"I don't like your plan, but I understand your reasons."

"Smart and pretty." He bent his head and concentrated on sticking on another label.

Seventeen

RICK SPED ALONG THE highway past the convention center where Maggie worked on his way to Iowa. He zipped over the state line without hardly noticing. It was a novelty compared to the all-day drive it took to get out of Florida. His cell phone's GPS program directed him to one of the first exits inside Iowa—East Broadway. A small blue sign on the side of the road welcomed him to Council Bluffs: population 62,000. Shit, in college, the stadium at Florida State could seat 80,000 people for a football game.

Potholes were plentiful on East Broadway, and the businesses lining the street had seen better days. He passed a second hotel that offered rooms by the hour, confirming this wasn't the fancy side of Council Bluffs. At a stoplight, he looked down the cross street. A clinic with a sign offering quick cash for blood plasma was the nicest building he could see. How desperate did you need to be to open a vein for money?

His GPS notified him his destination was ahead on the left. Jokers Wild Pawn and Loan was in a small whitish-gray clapboard building. It shared its parking lot with a deserted do-it-yourself coin-operated car wash. Rick pulled his shitty used SUV into the front parking spot. It fit perfectly in the sketchy neighborhood. He missed his Charger.

The only window on the front of the pawnshop had thick black bars and a flickering open sign blocking his view of the interior. He was going in blind.

He pressed a bell next to the front door and was quickly buzzed inside. As low-end pawnshops went, this one wasn't the best or the worst he'd ever been inside. Hung from the water-stained drop ceiling, flimsy cardboard signs pointed customers to the different departments: televisions, computers, tools, guns. Very typical.

The back of the shop had a long faux-wood-grain counter displaying jewelry under glass, and behind the counter, a floor-to-ceiling gun case held an impressive array of handguns, shotguns, and rifles. Two employees sat on tall wooden stools behind the counter.

The older guy with a soggy, half-chewed toothpick clenched in his teeth looked up from the CCTV security monitors in front of him and gave Rick a nod. It was Earl Whitestone, the part-time employee that he and Ava thought owned the shop. Old Earl had put on some weight since his last mug shot.

Jameson Green, the other man behind the counter, was obviously in charge of customer service. He'd also been arrested with Ted for the lottery scheme. Jameson waived Rick over with a big smile showing a gold tooth. "What can we help you with today?"

"I'm in the market for a nine-millimeter. Glock or M&P if you've got one. Something reliable, not flashy. I'm keeping it in the bedside table. You know what I mean?" Rick let a little accent flavor his English. He'd been born and raised in Miami and spoke English as perfectly as any news broadcaster, but that didn't mean that occasionally he didn't borrow a Cuban accent to give a certain impression.

"The world's heading down the shitter. Got to protect your own, I always say." Jameson turned and unlocked a section of the gun case filled with handguns.

"Amen."

Jameson laid a cloth out on the glass and placed a few handguns on top for Rick to inspect. He reached for the black semi-automatic closest to him, and something inside him rebelled. A weird sensation that started in the pit of his stomach coursed through him. He clenched his fist and shook it off.

He forced his fingers around the rough grip of the Glock. Sweat on his palm made his hold clammy and tenuous. It was the first time he'd held a gun since getting shot. He needed to man the fuck up. A gun didn't shoot him. A criminal did. A gun was just a tool—a tool of his job as an FBI agent.

He set the Glock down and took up the M&P by sheer force of determination. The smaller M&P felt less uncomfortable in his hand. The other options Jameson laid out were chromed-up flashy things Rick wanted no part of owning. The M&P would have to do.

"Nice weapon." Rick pulled the clip, checked the barrel to confirm it was empty, and clicked the trigger. The click of the trigger sent a creepy feeling crawling up the back of his neck. "I'll take some ammo too, if you've got it."

"Good choice." Jameson set the M&P aside and turned to lock up the case. Rick took a quick inventory. These guys were sitting on a veritable arsenal. If they were planning a robbery, firepower wouldn't be a problem. "Can I see your ID?"

Rick passed over both his Florida license and his gun permit.

"Miami. You're a long way from home. How's the weather down there?" Jameson cocked his head and waited, completely invested in Rick's answer. Was he preparing for a tropical vacation after whatever they had planned?

"Hot, humid, and it's the middle of hurricane season right now, so I'm pretty happy here in the Midwest."

"I feel ya." Jameson went back to the paperwork for the gun.

Rick glanced at Earl, who hadn't said a word the whole time. Earl casually flipped his toothpick to the other side of his mouth.

Nothing else exciting to see at the counter. Rick strolled the shop. He still hadn't found conspirator number three, Nelson Myers. Maybe there was a back office he could peek in.

Shit, he should have bought the TV for Mona's here. He double-checked the tag. It was bigger than what he got and half the price. Next to the flatscreen was a new Xbox system. Rick scooped it up and took it back to the counter.

"Video games? You don't look like the type."

"My, uh, girlfriend's kid likes to play." Referring to Maggie as his girlfriend didn't feel as strange as it should. Down that path lay a million landmines.

Jameson set out a few boxes of ammo for Rick to pick from.

He took a twenty-count box of hollow points and two large boxes of generic ammo to shoot at the range. He needed to practice and get comfortable with his new purchase.

"Smart man. Get the kid on your side. You'll get laid all the damn time."

The buzz of the front doorbell cut off whatever answer he might have said to Jameson. Nelson Myer swaggered into the shop, swinging a plastic grocery bag in one hand. Happier than a pig in shit.

"Earl, I got um." Myer dumped the bag out on the jewelry counter. Rick turned to see what all the excitement was about.

"Nice work." Earl's toothpick barely moved as he talked. He reached for one of the bright blue shirts and held it up. The back had event staff in block letters, and when Earl flipped it around, the logo for the Omaha Convention Center was embroidered on the chest.

The shirts weren't a smoking gun, but they were damn close. The shirts and the conversation Evan heard were almost enough to take to the Omaha police. Almost.

Earl caught Rick staring and dropped the shirt on the counter. "Nelson, put these in the back." Earl's dead eyes stayed on Rick as he spoke. The look was one Rick knew well. The cool stare of a hardened criminal.

"Yeah, boss man, no problem." Nelson scooped up the shirts and disappeared into an office behind the counter. Earl spit his toothpick in the garbage can next to him and pulled a new one from his shirt pocket.

Rick wrapped up his transaction with Jameson quickly. He'd seen more than enough to convince him to keep a close eye on Ted. He never wanted Maggie or Evan dealing with a man like Earl.

He texted Maggie from his car, asking her to get him Ted's work schedule. He had all the bits of the puzzle, but he needed them to fit together before he involved the authorities.

No problem. I'll get the schedule. See you at the Front Porch Party.

He groaned when he read her reminder about the party before he turned his car back toward Omaha.

Eighteen

RICK JUGGLED MONA'S 1970S avocado green crockpot and knocked on Maggie's door. Evan ripped the door open like he'd been standing on the other side, waiting to pounce. Evan's babysitter, Suzie, rushed up behind him with a backpack slung over her shoulder.

"Rick!" Evan held up his fist.

"My man!" Rick bumped his knuckles and ruffled his hair.

"Smells good." Suzie nodded at the crockpot.

"It's ropa vieja." The rich beef, tomato, and oregano scent had filled the house all day, reminding him of home. The nostalgia had convinced him to call his mother. The forty-minute call had ranged from laughter to tears—on her part, not his. It wasn't awful. He enjoyed talking with her, hearing about his family. A long way from when he dodged calls and family dinners.

"You cook. That's hot." Suzie looked him up and down slowly. She was a striking woman. Pale ivory skin and mahogany red hair, a strand of which she was curling around her fingers. She'd been so upset last time they spoke he hardly noticed how attractive she was.

"Ah, thanks. It's my mom's recipe. Speaking of, how is yours?"

She giggled and patted his arm. "Thank you for asking. It turned out to be nothing. Indigestion, believe it or not."

He waited for the zing of triumph he normally felt when a pretty woman flirted with him. It was a rush and a challenge wrapped up in a tempting feminine package. He loved it. The game. The hunt. Getting a phone number was often the best part of a relationship. Everything was possible—new and exciting.

Nothing. No zing.

No expert pickup line sprang to the tip of his tongue.

Confused, he looked down, breaking eye contact with Suzie. "Evan, buddy, tie your shoe so we can head out."

What the fuck was going on?

He was Ricardo *Effing* Cabrera; he charmed the ladies. He made panties wet and got phone numbers stuffed in his pockets. It was what he did. He was fun and charming. The guy every woman wanted to take her out on the town. Men across Miami dreamed of having his charisma and smooth moves.

If he lost his mojo, what did he have left? Dance moves?

"Good to see you, Suzie. Can you lock up? Evan and I should get moving." He stepped back as he spoke, getting some distance—time to consider what had happened.

"Sure, I can handle it." A momentary pout of her lips was the only sign she gave that he missed his opportunity to make a play.

"Come on, Rick, let's go. Mr. Hansen has the coolest dog."

"Lead the way." Rick fell into step on the sidewalk behind Evan, still unable to think of the perfect pickup line for Suzie.

Hansen lived on the next block. As soon as they turned the corner, they could see a small group gathered on the front porch of a fully restored home about the same age as Mona's. It was gorgeous. The house was painted a rich sage green with black shutters and white trim. The front porch had a bench swing and pots of geraniums. He made a mental note to ask Hansen if he did the renovation.

Evan called out to one of his friends and bolted past the last couple of houses to meet up with a boy about his age on the lawn. Rick shook his head and kept walking. As much as he complained, he wasn't totally annoyed about going to the party. Just because he got tired of clubbing didn't mean he wanted to become a hermit...well, not anymore.

"I'm Jacob Hansen, and you must be Rick Cabrera. I recognize Mona's crockpot. Here, let me take that." Hansen took the ropa vieja and set it on the potluck table on the wide front porch. He plugged the crockpot into an already overloaded power strip. "Smells like Mona's. Nicely done." He patted Rick on the shoulder.

"Maggie is bringing rice."

"Those commercial rice cookers at the convention center are a dream. Maggie would do the same when Mona made Cuban food. See, you're fitting right in. Stepping into your grandmother's shoes." Hansen smoothed his white hair and added a serving spoon to the crockpot.

"No, no, I'm here to renovate and sell. Just like you advised me."

"It's a hot market. But until then, you're a great addition to the neighborhood." Hansen was the grandfatherly type, but Maggie swore he was a cutthroat and brilliant attorney.

"I wanted to ask about your home. Did you do the remodel?"

"It's not a remodel. Over the years, I did a lot of updating, unlike Mona."

"I was wondering about that. Why did she let everything go?"

"She and Polly had other priorities."

"Like what?"

"That's a long conversation. Make an appointment with my office. Come in; we'll talk. Maybe the end of August, I'll be done with my current case then." Hansen bent down, fished a beer out of a cooler, and passed it to Rick.

That sounded like a lawyer's answer—evasive.

"Ah, there she is now." Hansen gave Maggie a one-armed hug while taking a huge foil pan of rice from her as soon as she stepped onto the porch.

"That's enough rice for an army. We should plan a sushi-making class for the whole neighborhood with the leftovers." She leaned in and hugged Rick. Her whole body pressed into him. He wrapped his arm around her lower back, enjoying the feeling of her hair sliding over his cheek before he reluctantly let go. The smell of her herb-scented shampoo lingered.

"Nah. You know this crowd. They're like locusts. There won't be anything left." Hansen removed the foil from the pan of rice.

Maggie laughed with Hansen and unbuttoned her black suit jacket. Rick zeroed in on the flash of bright pink lacy camisole stretched over her breasts. She shrugged out of her blazer, and the feeling he'd been missing when Suzie smiled at him hit like a ton of bricks. His mojo wasn't missing. It was tied to the one woman he shouldn't have anything to do with.

He wanted to pull her back against him and peel the skinny straps of her top off her shoulders with his teeth. And that was only the beginning. Vivid fantasies of them tangled together played in his head. Tousled sheets. Sweaty skin.

"Right, Rick?" she asked him.

"Ah, what?" He'd lost the thread of the conversation, distracted by thoughts of getting naked with Maggie.

"I said you were happy to make the Cuban food. A taste of home and all that." She wrinkled her forehead and gave him a healthy dose of side-eye for his odd behavior. If she only knew...

"Yeah, it reminded me of my mom."

"Aww, that's sweet. I'm going to go find Evan." She waved and skipped down the steps toward a herd of kids playing tag in the yard. The sway of her ass in her pencil skirt was utterly engrossing.

Hansen clapped Rick on the back and chuckled. "I think Omaha is growing on you."

"Yeah, like a fungus."

Hansen picked up a half-empty beer from the potluck table and clinked it against Rick's. "A rather lovely fungus."

The older man turned to welcome the newest arrivals, leaving Rick with his thoughts of Maggie. He needed to get his head on straight. Single moms scared him. Commitment gave him hives. And a complication like a criminal ex-husband should send him running. Everything about his beautiful, sweet, sexy, soon-to-be evicted tenant said do not touch. But damn, his fingers itched to feel her skin.

What kind of lowlife started anything with a woman under these circumstances? If he didn't keep his wits about him, he would be that kind of lowlife. A satisfied lowlife.

Focus on being nice. Only nice.

He drained his beer and tossed the empty in a garbage can. Steven Dawes and his wife were talking with Maggie across the way. He should thank Dawes for the recommendation on where to buy a used car. The Ford SUV he got wasn't pretty, but it ran great and was cheap.

The front porch party was starting to wind down. Amy and Steven had left fifteen minutes ago when the baby decided to get fussy. Rick had spent much of the night hanging out with the gang of guys Maggie thought of as the cool husbands.

They were a group of guys that were still young enough to look good in their jeans but old enough to have successful jobs or businesses. But not so successful that they were resting on their laurels. Rick seemed to fit into the group without trying, laughing and talking sports like one of them.

Maggie shrugged her black blazer on and picked one of the last rice crispy treats off a platter. Jacob Hansen wasn't a cook, never had been, but he could run a microwave, so his contribution to most every porch party was a ridiculously massive pyramid of marshmallow cereal treats. She bit into the gooey square and almost wept. These things were so good—the mix of salt and sweet with the perfect hint of childhood nostalgia.

Rick was at the other end of the buffet table, wrapping the cord from Mona's crockpot around the handles. She snagged another rice crispy treat for him and walked over.

"I guess the ropa vieja was a hit." The inside of the slow cooker looked like it had been licked clean.

"I think so, and I see half a ring of Jell-O salad left over there. It restores my faith in the Nebraskan's palate, picking good Cuban food over gelatinous ooze." He raised an eyebrow in the direction of the lime Jell-O before turning back to her.

They were chest to chest, so close she could see the sexy little wrinkles bracketing his eyes.

"Dessert?" She held out the rice crispy treat.

"What is it about those things? I think everyone ate like five apiece, myself included." He caught her wrist and pulled her hand closer. "So damn delicious," he murmured, his voice husky and his eyes fixed on her lips.

He bent his head, and her heart fluttered in anticipation of a kiss, but instead, he took a bite of the treat right from her fingers. He closed his eyes and moaned as he chewed, his hand still wrapped around her wrist. Her pulse ratcheted up, and she wondered if he could feel it racing.

She couldn't tear her eyes off his mouth and had to squelch the urge to moan along with him. Fuck, she hoped she remembered to charge her vibrator. Her attraction to her landlord was providing plenty of fodder for her self-pleasuring fantasies.

He swallowed and opened his mouth to pluck the other half of the treat from her fingers. Heat flashed across her skin when his lips grazed her fingertips. He winked and let go of her hand while he savored the last bite.

She cradled her hand against her chest and firmly reminded herself Rick was permanently relegated to the friend zone. But part of her was begging for a conjugal visit. Friend zone be damned. She shook her head to clear out the unwise thoughts.

"Ready to walk back?" she asked.

"Sure. Where's Evan?" He glanced around the last few stragglers at the party.

"He went home with his friend Samuel to spend the night. Those two boys were hopped up on sodas and desserts. Sam's mom is a brave woman agreeing to that shit show."

"I don't know. I bet they crash quick. The one I feel bad for is Hansen's dog. Those two boys played fetch with him all night."

"Nah, Shadow loves it. It keeps him in shape for when Jacob's grandkids visit."

They said their goodbyes to Jacob, thanking him for hosting.

Rick put his free hand at the small of her back as she navigated the front steps. Her heels weren't that tall, but the chivalrous gesture made her melt.

They turned up the street, strolling back toward the house. "Admit it, you had fun tonight. You were all smiles and laughs hanging with the guys."

"It was a good night. Nice weather, friendly people, and no cameo appearance from Ted.

Speaking of... Did you manage to get me his schedule?"

She printed Ted's schedule as soon as Rick had texted asking for it. She hated that he had to help her handle this kind of situation. She was accustomed to doing things by herself. Accepting his help with Ted's idiocy was smart but made her feel like she was shirking a responsibility.

"I have it. It kills me he would be dumb enough to get involved with this kind of thing. He's a long way from being a perfect dad, but at least Evan has someone. He goes to jail, and then what? What does that leave for Evan? I don't understand why he would risk it."

"Maggie." He stopped walking under a streetlight and caught her upper arm, turning her to face him. The soft overhead light illuminated his earnest expression. "I've seen so many men and women make stunningly bad choices. As an FBI agent, I would see the absolute worst people had to offer to their fellow man. Mostly over money. Sometimes power. And on rare occasions, a distorted version of love drove them. You can't try to understand their motivation. They don't think like the rest of us. Something inside them is damaged."

Her breath caught on the knot in her throat. She hovered between wanting to scream and cry. The years of frustration with Ted seemed to culminate in this situation. Even though she'd left him, he was managing to mess up her life again. She'd never get out from under his cloud of shit.

She dug Ted's schedule out of her handbag and passed it to Rick. He opened the paper, scanned it, and checked his watch.

"Come on, let's get you home." He resumed walking a bit quicker than before.

"Easy, tiger. What's the rush?"

They were almost home.

He rechecked his watch. "Can you take the crockpot? I'll get it from you later."

"Rick? What's going on?" She cradled the crockpot in one arm and grabbed him before he could bolt.

"If I leave now, I can tail your ex when he gets off work. It's Thursday night, and he has Evan all weekend. If he's meeting up with the pawnshop guys, it will be tonight." He shifted his weight back and forth, ready to sprint the moment she let go of his arm.

"I'm coming with you. Get the car. I'll deal with the crockpot."

"Maggie, there's no need."

"All this is not your responsibility. It's mine. I'm coming with."

Rick sighed but nodded.

She ran down the sidewalk and up the front steps. She ditched the crockpot under one of her planters and jogged to Rick's SUV idling in the street.

Nineteen

RICK HAD TAILED ENOUGH suspects in his years as an FBI agent to know what he was doing. The goal was to keep a few cars between his car and the subject's. Not make rash moves like unexpected lane changes that might draw attention. And it was helpful if the driver or co-pilot knew the city.

Maggie's local knowledge made tailing Ted much easier. She predicted many of his moves before he made them, allowing Rick to follow with almost no chance of suspicion.

He leaned forward and turned down the radio. "What's out this direction?"

The area they were in wasn't one Rick had visited during his stay in Omaha. He was sure they had crossed into Iowa a few turns back. The street was dark with a few industrial-type buildings lit up along either side of the road.

"Okay, let me think. Um, the airport. A small casino. The jail?" She tapped her index finger against her lips as she rattled off the options.

"I have five bucks on the casino." He flipped the music back up. They'd been enjoying a 1990s greatest hits marathon while following Ted. So far, Ted had made a very brief stop at a gas station, hit a drive-through for food, and then made a quick stop at his apartment where he changed clothes in record time. While they tailed Ted, they recounted memories the old songs prompted. He grudgingly admitted having her company made the night better in many ways.

A few miles up the dark four-lane road, Ted's car slowed and coasted into the left turn lane, his signal blinking.

"Oh, yeah, and there's that." She pointed and tried to stifle a giggle that slipped out anyway.

Rick slid the SUV into the turn lane two cars behind Ted and glanced at the business he was headed for. At first, it looked like a five-star restaurant complete with a fancy circle driveway and porte cochere. It took a moment to find the discreet but well-lit sign among the extravagant landscaping—the   Peppermint   Pony: A Gentleman's Club.

This was not going to end well.

Rick pulled into the large parking lot and parked in one of the few open spots with a view of the club's entrance. They watched Ted drop his keys in the valet's hand and take a ticket. He clapped the bouncer on the back in a familiar gesture that made Rick suspect this was one of his regular haunts.

"I'm going in. You stay in the car. I want to see if he's meeting anyone." He would be in and out so fast she wouldn't even notice he'd gone.

"Stay here. You're kidding, right? That idiot is my problem, not yours." She was pissed.

"What if Ted sees you?"

"So we keep to the shadows. He knows your face, too." She looked beyond determined.

"I'm not taking you in a place like that." Absolutely no fucking way.

"That's ridiculous. I've been in a hundred dive bars that weren't as nice as this place. And they're just boobs. I have my own." She cupped and lifted her tits to emphasize her point. The movement drew his eyes like a tractor beam to her prominently displayed cleavage. He gritted his teeth so hard to contain a groan his jaw hurt.

"It's not appropriate." Mona would kill him, er haunt him, if he took Maggie into a place like this.

"Prude. You're from South Beach. Isn't every nightclub there a seething mass of scantily clad people rubbing on each other to techno music? This is almost the same thing. Hell, I bet the Peppermint Pony has better music." She unbuckled her seat belt.

"A strip club isn't a dance club. And this one is near the airport and the jail. We're not talking about a high-end Las Vegas burlesque show." And he didn't need the memory of Maggie inside a place like this to drive him even more insane.

She snorted at him and started digging in her purse. "The Peppermint Pony is the classiest strip joint in Iowa."

Jesus, the *classiest strip joint in Iowa*. There was a claim to fame...or infamy.

"Why do you know that?" He should have kept his mouth shut. He was so going to lose this argument. Hopefully, Mona's ghost would forgive him when he caved.

"Please. I wasn't always a workaholic mom. I was a fun college girl. I did things and went places. I've been in a strip club before." She flipped down the visor and popped open the mirror to slick on a coat of dark lipstick.

He didn't want to know she'd been in a strip club. He had a hard enough time sticking to his self-imposed boundaries. What boundaries? He blew past those when he chose to literally eat out of her hand at the party earlier tonight. But flirting with her was as natural as breathing.

She tugged off her suit jacket and again plumped up her breasts. She dragged her lace cami lower, letting the top of her black bra poke out.

"Maggie," he half whined, half groaned. He should back the car out of this spot and head for Omaha. Tailing a suspect often took an unexpected turn, but this was off the charts.

"Man up, Cabrera. Let's do this shit." She pointed to the front of the club, her other hand on the door handle. "I want to see some boobs and spy on Ted." She popped open the car door and got out.

"Mona, I tried." He killed the engine and rushed to catch up with Maggie who was boldly striding toward the entrance while fluffing her hair.

He caught up with her as they reached the porte cochere. Before he could take her arm, she turned and looked in a blacked-out window at her reflection.

"I think my skirt is too long. What do you think?"

"Shorter is always better," answered the valet parker with a wink.

"He's right." A few quick rolls of the waistband and her work-appropriate skirt became a mini.

Rick was speechless, taking in the whole picture. His brain was robbed of blood as it flowed south to other areas. His sweet girl next door looked entirely too fuckable—from her red lips to the patent leather heels. She was hot.

The wolf whistle from the parker pretty much summed up the way he was feeling better than words.

"Come on, baby," she purred. Her arm snaked around his waist. "Let's go see what kind of trouble my asshole ex is into." Her breath whispered over the skin of his throat as she spoke, the intimate tone totally at odds with her angry words.

The mention of Ted helped pull his brain back into his head and out of the gutter. He had work to do. Then he could go home and jerk off to the image of sexy Maggie that was indelibly printed in his memory.

He draped an arm over her shoulders and pulled her close. The distinctive scent of her shampoo tickled his nose. "Alright, beautiful, here we go."

Bass throbbed in the dark club. The focus of the room was the long, low stage and catwalk in the center. At the apex of the stage, a spotlight highlighted a pole and lone dancer.

He maneuvered Maggie toward a quiet area next to a woman in an almost nonexistent bikini selling beer from an ice-filled trough. The shadows were deep in the secluded corner, a perfect place to scan the room without either of them getting recognized by Ted.

"She's good." Maggie leaned up to speak in his ear without taking her eyes off the woman performing on the main stage. The stripper whipped around the pole and dangled upside down. Topless or not, she was a serious athlete and sexy as hell as she gyrated in time to a popular Rihanna song. Maggie shifted back against him, her ass pressing dangerously close to his cock while she swayed to the music.

He put a hand on her hip to hold her in place and eased back a few inches to regain his focus. He searched the room methodically. The shifting shadows and flashing lights made it difficult to see faces. A large party at a table next to the stage caught his attention. A man with his back to them at the table could be Ted.

"Let's get closer." He pulled Maggie deeper into the club. Maggie drew a few curious glances as they weaved past other customers, and he wrapped an arm around her, staking his claim. The smokey air was thick with a mix of sweet perfumes from the girls that wandered through the club looking for clients to pay for lap dances.

He found Maggie a seat at a bar close to the stage and kept a possessive arm around her. "I think that's Ted?"

"Oh, shit." She turned and buried her face in his chest. "Yeah, that's him. And I know almost every guy at that table. They all work in food service at the convention center. The third guy from the end is Gary, and it's his thirtieth birthday."

Maggie's hand rested on his right pec muscle. The heat burned through his shirt. She felt good pressed against him.

"This is a bust. He's just making friends at his new job." She sighed and patted his chest, about to hop off the stool.

He caught her wrist like he had at the party earlier and pressed her hand back on his chest. "I'd agree, but take a quick look at the older guy in the corner by the stage with two ladies in his lap."

She turned for a moment and then swiveled back, managing to somehow press even tighter into his body.

"That's Earl Whitestone from the pawnshop. And it looks like he's footing the bill for tonight's party." He nuzzled her neck as he spoke in her ear and watched Ted's table. He savored the feel of her hair sliding over his jawline. He wasn't worried they'd notice him or Maggie. They were too focused on the stage.

Earl had a roll of cash in his hand, peeling off bills for the girls entertaining his guests. A wave from Earl, and Ted hopped up and scurried over to speak to him. When Ted moved back from Earl, he had a handful of cash and looked like a man on a mission.

"Fuck. We've got to move." Ted was zeroing in on the bar where they sat. Earl must have him playing waiter or something. Heading for the entrance wouldn't work. They would practically run into Ted.

Maggie took one look over her shoulder and hopped off the stool. "This way."

She pulled him toward a dark doorway guarded by a huge bouncer with crossed arms—the champagne room.

The bouncer looked at Rick, and a slow, knowing grin spread across the man's face. "I'll need your credit card, and if you don't have a preference, I'll get Misty in to take care of you two. She loves couple's dances."

He was going to go to hell for this but fuck it. What a way to sin. He passed the bouncer his credit card without delay.

The bouncer directed them to a low black leather love seat in a secluded corner of the VIP room. Maggie sat, and Rick joined her. His hand landed on the bare skin of her thigh.

She hadn't been lying earlier. She'd been to a strip club before. Twice, if the Magic Mike male burlesque show counted. Her only trip to a gentlemen's club was during college. Her friend, who was low on cash and desperate, decided to try and win a wet T-shirt contest. They didn't call that girl Terri Tits for nothing. She'd won five hundred bucks that night at a run-down cowboy strip joint on the wrong side of town.

The Peppermint Pony was next level compared to that place. It felt like an upscale dance club. Except for the beautiful topless women. And the grinding. And the cash. Okay, it was nothing like a regular club other than the music and the furniture.

The night with Terri had been a seedy adventure, not sexy at all. But tonight...was different.

"Misty is on her way. Here's your champagne." The bouncer served her and Rick, then left the bottle in a free-standing ice bucket next to their couch.

"You okay?" Rick turned to face her; his eyes bored into hers.

She wasn't sure what he saw because she wasn't sure what she felt. She felt all the things. Nervous, uncomfortable, curious, sexy, and about a million other things that were too nebulous to name. And pissed off at Ted. But Rick's hand on her leg felt right, and when he caressed the skin, heat flared in her belly.

She drank half her glass of champagne in two long swallows. "Yeah."

"We don't have to do anything. We can hang out for a few minutes while Ted is at the bar."

"Ah, sure." Her teeth sank into her lip, holding back the words she wanted to say. She wanted to see what would happen. With the dancer, with Rick. All of it. She couldn't remember the last time she had been this keyed up. Her nerves tingled at the thought of what if... She shifted her legs, crossing them to trap Rick's hand.

"Maggie," he growled in her ear. "What are you doing?"

"I want the dance. You paid for it. We should get it." She couldn't believe she had said that. But she was committed. It had been too long since she had done anything that scared her in a good way. Harmless, sexy, fun, and scary. A moment to pretend she was more than a mom. More than Ted's ex.

He sat back and held up his pinky finger. "You're sure?"

"I swear." She linked her finger around his and sealed the deal. She needed this tiny rebellion like her plants needed water.

Rick downed the remainder of his champagne and put the glass on a table next to him. He took her mostly empty glass as well. "I think you'll need both hands for this."

He glanced meaningfully toward a woman slinking in their direction. She was tall and lean; long black hair fell well below her shoulders. She wore a glittery black dress cut down to her navel with long slits exposing both her legs and killer platform heels.

What the hell had she agreed to? The dancer was a goddess.

"I'm Misty." The dancer knelt in front of her and Rick, a sweet smile on her full red lips. She put one hand on each of their thighs.

"Misty, I'm Rick and this is Maggie. She's in charge tonight."

"Nothing as sexy as a man letting the woman lead once in a while. Right, Maggie?"

Maggie nodded. Her heart was pounding like she'd run a mile. She couldn't have spoken if she'd had something to say.

"I'm going to start by teaching you a few moves you can practice at home. Okay?" Misty nodded to the bouncer, and the room darkened, turning from reds and pinks to cool blues.

Misty slid over, so she was now kneeling between Maggie's feet. The Eurythmics' "Sweet Dreams are Made of This" filled the room, drowning out the muffled music from the main stage.

Misty's hands wrapped around Maggie's ankles. She squeezed before her hands slipped up and over Maggie's thighs. Her hands were soft, smooth, delicate. So unlike a man's. Misty pressed Rick's hand higher under Maggie's skirt, his fingers a hairbreadth from the edge of her panties. Maggie's breath stalled. Rick shifted closer and pulled her so she leaned half her back against his chest. His breath ruffled her hair, and he caressed her thigh.

Maggie was trapped between Rick and Misty. She wanted a leap out of her comfort zone? Well, here she was. She exhaled out the doubts and questions threatening to rob her of the moment.

She tilted her head back on Rick's shoulder and looked through her lashes at Misty. The dancer slithered up from the ground, every twitch and sway in rhythm to the music. The velvet of her dress slid over Maggie's bare legs, sending goosebumps over her flesh. Rick's solid chest rose and fell behind her. His breath was irregular and harsh in her ear.

Misty's cheek brushed over Maggie's throat. She threaded her long nails into Maggie's hair and straddled her left leg, her knees sinking into the couch on either side.

"Move with me." Misty brushed her lips over Maggie's ear.

"Yes." That she could do. Wanted to do. Needed to. Her hips lifted, rubbing against Misty's thigh. Rick's hand, still on her other leg, gripped hard. She could only imagine what he was seeing. The thought sent a spike of arousal through her.

Maggie reached out tentatively for Misty's hip, seeking the connection so they could move together—really give Rick a show. Something inside her unfurled at that idea. It was empowering and sexy to think about reducing Rick to a puddle of desire at her feet.

She lost herself in the sensations—the music. The movement. With her whole body, she pressed up into Misty's soft, yielding curves and then back into Rick's hard chest. Every touch layered sensations one on top of the other. She let her eyes slip half-closed and relished the sensations. Rick's labored breaths encouraged her bold actions.

Misty's bare skin was everywhere, hot and petal-soft. The dancer guided Maggie's hands over her exposed body. Rick moaned in her ear, the sound rough and sexy. Maggie lifted his hand from her thigh and brought it up to skim over Misty's body with hers.

"Fuck, Maggie." His words were a feral growl that she felt all the way to her aching pussy.

"Poor man. You should give him some attention." Misty shifted off Maggie's lap and guided Maggie to straddle him.

She and Rick froze for a moment.

His eyes glittered like onyx, and his chest rose and fell with each shuddering breath under her hand. They were balanced on the edge of a precipice. One touch and they would fall over.

Misty didn't wait for them to decide; she pushed them off the cliff. She tipped Maggie forward into

Rick. It was like falling into an inferno. His hands were everywhere. One buried in her hair, the other under her skirt, grabbing her ass and grinding her wet center against his hard cock.

The weeks of dancing around each other had led them to this moment. Their mouths crashed together in an explosion of pent-up desire. The ferocity stole the breath from her lungs. She grabbed a handful of his shirt and rocked against him. She was so turned on it hurt. She whimpered into his mouth and dug her nails into the back of his neck.

They broke apart, their breathing jagged and eyes locked. God, she wanted him.

"Take him home and fuck him until he can't walk." Misty cupped a hand around Maggie's jaw, tilted her head toward her, and sealed their lips together in a brief but smoldering kiss. "You can thank me next time."

Twenty

I'M NOT THE KIND of man that has sex with a woman like Maggie in a car. He repeated the mantra leaving the club, in the parking lot, and all the way home. His cock pulsed in rhythm with the chant in his head.

It didn't help. He could still feel the imprint of her lips on his. The kiss in the club had only been the beginning. He'd kissed her up against the door of the car and at the last three stoplights. She was addictive, and this had bad idea written all over it.

He barely got the SUV in park in the driveway, and Maggie was climbing over the armrest into his lap. She shifted, grinding her hips against him. His cock pressed painfully against his fly. He took her mouth for a deep, hard kiss, his hand under her skirt, palming her bare ass.

Imagining her thong was killing him.

She arched up, one hand on the roof. Her ass lifted and bumped the horn. She shrieked, and he couldn't help but laugh as he buried his face in the crook of her neck.

"Please, Rick." She moaned.

"Mi corazón. You're killing me." He reached between them and undid his seat belt. "Not in a car." He kissed her again. Then once more before he shoved open the door.

Somehow, they tumbled out of his SUV without either of them falling on their ass. He pinned her against the car with a hand on her shoulder, holding her at arm's length. Despite the desire urging him to bury himself inside her, he knew he should try to convince her this was a lousy idea... himself too.

"I'm your landlord. I shouldn't sleep with you." But fuck...he wanted to.

She bit her lip and smiled like a siren in a movie. "My hot landlord."

"I'm leaving soon." The complications and consequences would be worth it, or at least his cock thought so.

"I know. And I don't care. I want you." She was breathless.

He caged her against the car. He was grasping at straws, looking for roadblocks to the inevitable. "You have a kid."

"Who is on a sleepover. I'm a full-grown woman. I know what I want." She arched up and pressed her lips to his throat. The sharp sting of her teeth sent a bolt of pleasure straight to his cock.

She was seduction incarnate. Watching her at the club had been the single hottest thing he'd ever seen. Having her naked under him would be incomparable. Fuck it.

She was a witch, and he was at the mercy of her spell. Tonight would either bind him to her more closely or set him free.

He took her hand and started toward his front door. She didn't follow.

"I have condoms. Do you?"

"Your place it is."

He trailed behind her and pressed kisses to her neck as she fumbled with the key in the door. Inside the dark apartment, he shoved her against the first empty wall and sealed their bodies together.

He hooked a finger in the center of her camisole and pushed it down. The lacy shirt and the tiny peeks of her black bra had been killing him all night. He reached behind her and undid her bra.

He filled his hands with her breasts, teasing her nipples to hard points.

Her hands were under his shirt, nails scratching over his abs. She snaked a hand up his chest, lifting his shirt as she explored his body. She grazed the edge of one of his scars, brushing over one of the dead spots where his skin no longer had functional nerves. The odd lack of sensation sent a wash of ice water through him. He pulled back; something ugly and painful lodged in his stomach. He couldn't do this. He pushed her hand away, and his shirt fell back into place.

"Hey, what just happened?" She cradled his face in her palm. Her eyes saw too much.

He shook his head. He didn't have the right words to answer her question. He grabbed her hands and pinned them above her head. He took her mouth, letting his uncertainty fuel the kiss. She moaned into his mouth, and he ravaged her lips, taking all she had to offer. More. He needed her passion distracting him from his insecurities.

"Bedroom," he mumbled when they broke apart.

He pulled her into the dark bedroom and caught her wrist when she tried to flip a light switch.

There was no way he'd show her his scars right now. She'd either run screaming from the ugly sight or worry about hurting him. The only thing hurting him was the hard-on he had been sporting all night. Now wasn't the time.

He practically tripped over her bed, falling on the mattress with her wrapped in his arms. He lifted up and ripped off his shirt and flung it away. Anticipation made him clumsy as he pulled at her clothes in the dark. He needed to touch every naked inch of her.

He toed off his shoes, and they thumped on the hard floor. The noise was deafening in the otherwise quiet house. Her legs wrapped around him, and he reached for her ankle, lifting her leg to remove her sexy shoes.

From there, he skated his lips up her long, perfect leg. He used his fingers to savor every curve he couldn't see. Listening for every gasp of pleasure and moan, learning what she liked. He tasted the soft skin behind her knee, and she squirmed away. Hands around her thighs, he pressed her legs apart, making room for his shoulders. Her hips lifted from the bed. Damn, he was dying to taste her.

"Please." Her plea was more whisper than words.

He pressed his mouth to her center. Fuck, her thong was still on. Unceremoniously he tugged it aside to bare her pussy to his ravenous mouth.

His name spilled from her lips, and she raked her nails over his scalp. He would happily stay here working this beautiful, sexy woman toward release forever. She thrust up to meet his mouth in a desperate rhythm that fueled his appetite.

"So close, so close," she mumbled into the dark. She didn't need to worry. He'd get her there.

He sucked her clit between his teeth, and her hips shot off the bed. He cradled her ass in his palms, angling her so he could feast. Every one of her sweet moans and gasps shot directly to his cock, making him ache. He redoubled his efforts. He wanted her more than close. He wanted her coming on his tongue.

She imploded. Her trembling thighs closed around him, holding him to her center. He sucked and savored every drop of her release, not stopping until she was limp.

He yanked her thong down her legs and shucked his pants off, then crawled up her body, mapping his progress with his lips and hands. He stopped to nip at her belly button and suck her hard nipples. She tangled her fingers in his hair and held his mouth in place over her breast.

In his mind, he created a rendering of her body by touch—exploring the dips and valleys of her shape. Her soft skin was like hot silk beneath him.

She was exquisite, arching and writhing into every caress.

She tugged him up the last few inches to seal her mouth to his. She wrapped her leg around his back, and her wet core sizzled against his cock. Electricity shot through him; he was on the verge of losing it. He gritted his teeth to regain a modicum of control.

"Condom." He choked out the word on a gasp as she rotated her hips again.

She wiggled out from under him and shuffled through a drawer. Then pressed the foil packet into his hand.

He barely remembered putting the latex over his dick. As soon as he was ready, he caught her leg, pressed it over his shoulder, and slid home. She was tight and hot, so fucking spectacular. He thumbed her clit; he wanted her ready to explode. He wasn't going to last. It had been too long since he'd been inside a woman. And not one in his memory had ever felt this amazing.

Her short nails dug into his arms. Sweat slicked over his body, and he fell forward over her. Any control he'd tried to salvage slipped away into the dark.

He gathered her in his arms and thrust into her. Her name tumbled from his lips, along with a string of nearly incoherent curses—in a mix of English and Spanish. He pressed short, hurried kisses over her face and neck. He couldn't get enough of her. She locked her legs around him, clutching his hips. Her screams filled the room just as he felt her spasm around his cock, and it pushed him toward his own spectacular end.

Slowly, he returned to reality. Holding her next to him, their labored breathing filled the quiet room. Her hand strayed across his chest, and he caught her wrist before she encountered one of his scars. He pinned her hand low on his waist far from his injuries. There was a time and a place for that discussion and it wasn't now. Maybe it was never.

Maggie was hot. She kicked her legs out from under the blankets and curled on her side. Her top leg slipped up and over the source of all the heat. A man. Not just any man—Rick.

His arm wrapped around her, and she snuggled into his bare chest. If she stayed right here, her eyes closed, she didn't have to try to understand last night. Cocooned in her bed, there was no real world and no consequences. The one thing she was sure of was she didn't regret any of it.

She sighed. She sucked at sleeping in. She was hard wired to leap up before her alarm clock buzzed. She scrunched her eyes closed, trying to convince her brain to shut off and fall back asleep. She counted to fifty before she gave up.

Rick was asleep on his back, holding her with his left arm. His face looked good relaxed in sleep, his lips soft and hair a wild mess from her hands. She let her eyes slide down his chest.

The weak sunlight that managed to seep into her bedroom was enough to reveal what the darkness had disguised last night. She knew to expect a scar over his sternum, but this wasn't like any other surgical incision she'd seen. It was nothing like the small precise line her C-section had left on her belly.

The scar was a thick, bright white line. A stark contrast to his rich tan skin. It started at the top of his sternum and went down his chest, branching off to curve under his right pectoral muscle. The flesh looked like the doctors had torn into him without finesse.

He'd been gutted, sliced, ripped open.

She winced, remembering how he froze last night when she tried to pull his shirt off by the front door. An injury like that left scars on more than just skin.

He shifted under her; his breathing changed. He was awake.

"I died for a few minutes right when the medics got me to the hospital." His voice was rough, scratchy from sleep and emotion.

He moved her hand to the center of his chest, atop the ugliest part of his damaged flesh. She curled closer into him, keeping her hand exactly where he placed it.

"The ER doctor cracked open my chest. It was filling with blood. Bullet fragments had sliced into my aorta. Others had lodged in my lumbar spine. He performed cardiac massage on the chance I might come back." He let go of her wrist to trace the white line under his right pec.

"Rick, you don't have to tell me—" She felt awful getting caught examining him like he was a freak at the sideshow.

"I know." He turned and kissed her temple. He was tense in the bed next to her, staring at the ceiling.

She ached to make this easier on him, but there was no way. If he wanted or needed to talk, the best thing she could do was lie still and listen, offer her silent acceptance.

"They had to shock my heart back into rhythm. It took three tries. I met the doctor who held my heart in his hands. At the time, he thought it was hopeless, but he said he was trained to try and save every life he could. His belief in that kept him working on me. If a different doctor had been in the ER, they might not have gone to the extreme of a resuscitative thoracotomy." Rick stumbled over the medical term like the words were trapped in his throat.

It was sobering. A different doctor, and he would never have come back into her life. She squeezed her eyes closed against the sudden sting of tears and turned her head up to press a kiss under his clenched jaw. Her touch appeared to trigger a moment of release for him, and he exhaled loudly.

"I was lucky." He rolled toward her, pulling her beneath him and burying his face in the crook of her neck. His ragged breath scorched her skin.

She couldn't imagine facing her mortality the way Rick had. Knowing you died, and the only reason you survived was another person's stubbornness. Their willingness to fight for you when you couldn't.

She wrapped her arms around his back, and they lay pressed together for a few precious minutes.

A shudder wracked his body, and he pressed a bruising open-mouthed kiss to her neck. He moved above her; his frantic touch burned her skin. And she willingly sank into his fevered caresses. If this was the exorcism he needed to escape his ghosts, she would give it to him.

Twenty-One

"MAGGIE, KEEP IT SIMPLE. Eggs are fine." Rick sipped coffee in Maggie's small kitchen. He wiped a few more bits of glitter off his shirt. Apparently, Misty had left her mark, and not just on his psyche. When he noticed the sparkles, he almost didn't put it on but decided that he'd rather glitter than subject Maggie to the sight of his scars over breakfast.

She leaned into her refrigerator. Her skintight leggings were almost as bad as her gardening short shorts. The woman had no idea what a great ass she had.

"I know. What about Mona's spinach quiche?"

"I said no fuss. You're crazy."

"No, I have the crust already made. I'll dump everything in and bake. No problem."

"It sounds great."

She started pulling out all the ingredients and mixing up another dish guaranteed to remind him of vacations here in Omaha when he was a kid.

A few minutes later, she popped the finished quiche in the oven. "The secret is the mustard."

"If you say so."

"I do. Actually, Mona did." She poured more coffee and sat at the breakfast bar with him.

"We should talk about last night." He didn't want to ruin the mood, but the issue had to be addressed.

She sputtered and forced down her sip of coffee. "Agreed."

"It was a lucky break." He could have put off following her ex until next week and never caught him with Earl.

"It was?" She cocked her head. "I kind of saw it coming."

"It was just what we needed."

"I guess."

"No, trust me, we've got something tangible." No way Omaha PD would ignore this kind of link.

"Okay?" She drew out the word and wrinkled her forehead.

"I think local PD should be our first stop." He rolled his right shoulder. It got an intense workout last night, but it felt good other than a few twinges.

"What the hell are you talking about?" She held up her hands in confusion.

"Last night. Ted. What else would we need to talk about?" He stopped manipulating his shoulder and focused on her.

She sighed and rubbed her forehead. "Never mind."

"No, this is me minding all of it. Spill." He hated that it looked like he managed to give her a migraine.

She muttered something unintelligible under her breath, then with a huff sat up in the chair. "The sleeping together part of last night."

"And once this morning." He stole a grape from the bowl in the center of the counter and popped it in his mouth.

"Rick. Come on—"

"And I think what you want to talk about isn't the sleeping parts either." He took another grape and flashed her a ridiculous grin while he chewed.

"You're hopeless." She plucked a grape from the bunch and pelted him in the chest with it.

"Back to Ted and the pawnshop guys."

He was winning the award for best avoidance of an uncomfortable conversation. Talking about the status of their relationship, or lack thereof, was a minefield he would rather avoid. Historically, he bailed on sleepover dates long before breakfast and meaningful conversation. But he literally lived here, or almost here. And he had no idea what to say about last night.

It was spectacular.

And he wanted more. More of last night. More of this morning. More of them talking while she made her beauty stuff in the barn. More was a foreign concept to him. He had always been the fun guy, the just-one-night guy.

Wanting more didn't change that he had a life and a job waiting back in Miami.

Yeah, wanting what he couldn't have would only lead to regrets.

"Ted was the worst decision I ever made."

He stood to rub her shoulder. The last thing he wanted for Maggie was more regrets. He would not do that to her. She snuggled close and sagged into him. Her trust felt too good.

After a moment, she sat up straight. "Thanks for letting me indulge in a minute of self-pity. So, what's the plan, Agent Cabrera?"

The words he was going to say lodged uncomfortably in his throat. No one had called him Agent Cabrera since he arrived in Omaha. The title felt like it belonged to someone else. He'd been a patient with an injury for too long. FBI Agent Rick Cabrera was a stranger.

He cleared his throat and tried to recapture his thoughts. "I think we should call and set up an appointment, try and get at least a Sergeant or Lieutenant to sit down with us."

Maggie nodded.

"You don't happen to be friends with anyone on the force, do you?" It was amazing to Rick how she knew the whole neighborhood. Why not a few city cops, too?

"No. I could ask around at work?"

"It's not important. It might have made things simpler, but it might not. I'll play the FBI card." The injured, on leave from the bureau in a strange city FBI card. He might get more respect with a novelty badge from a toy store.

"Thank you." She smiled, and he knew he would make it work.

"When we go, bring a list of all the upcoming events for the next six months at the convention center. And the names of who the police can talk to that are in charge over there."

"That's easy enough. Anything else?"

"I have the info Ava in the US Attorney's office dug up to give them. And then we sit back and wait."

Maggie took her first bite of the spinach quiche as the front door banged open. Evan was home. He dropped his backpack by the door and rushed over to join her and Rick at breakfast.

She pulled him in for a hug. "How was the sleepover?"

"Awesome. Sam got a new set of bunk beds."

And her son came home without a broken arm, so yay for a small victory. Rick and Evan did their standard fist bump. Evan either didn't care or didn't notice that Rick had on the exact same clothes he wore to the porch party last night. And he was rocking epic sex hair. That was entirely her fault, but his hair was like thick silk. She loved it.

"Get a plate. I'll cut you some quiche."

"Nice!" Evan got a plate and took a seat next to Rick.

Rick told Evan he bought a game system yesterday to practice for their next epic battle. The trash talk flew fast and furious between the two. She could barely keep up. Watching them joke around had a part of her remembering why getting involved with Rick wasn't a good idea. She didn't bring men into Evan's life so that they would leave.

Then again, sex or not, Rick was in Evan's life and had always planned on leaving.

"Mom, I'm done." Evan took his dishes and put them in the dishwasher; as he turned, he pointed at Rick. "Dude, where are your shoes?"

"Ah, I..." Rick shoved a huge bite of quiche into his mouth and looked at her with desperation.

"He was so excited for Mona's quiche he left them at home." She took a sip of coffee to hide her smile.

"Cool. You know it's good quiche when you can't even taste the spinach." Evan headed for his room, snagging his backpack as he ran past.

"Nice save," Rick said after a gulp of coffee.

"I briefly thought about letting you flop around looking for an excuse, but it's better this way. Now you owe me." She laughed like an evil queen in a Disney movie.

"I've never been with a woman that had kids. Or had kids I knew about. I didn't know what to say." He rubbed the back of his neck and avoided her gaze.

"Shocking. Single moms aren't a hot commodity in South Beach nightclubs?"

"It's not that. It's me. I'm not what those kinds of women are looking for." He rose to put his dishes in the dishwasher.

"Those women?" She couldn't stop herself from asking. The phrase always made her cringe.

He made a slow and noisy production of loading the dishwasher.

"Rick!" She snapped his name, and he thumped the dishwasher closed before turning to face her.

"The kind of women looking for a new dad for their kid. I'm an FBI agent. I looked good without my shirt on, but my bankroll was insufficient to keep a woman like that around."

"An FBI agent is a good job. Or am I missing something?"

He leaned against the counter and ran a hand over his face, his exasperation telegraphed by each motion. "Miami isn't like Omaha. Money rules the world down there. I was a fun guy with a pretty face."

She didn't have a good reply for him. Their situation guaranteed that their relationship had no future. From his perspective, she wasn't different from those women, using him for a fun night with a hot guy. But that wasn't why she had slept with him. Was it?

"You're also a good man." She stepped into him and laid her head on his chest.

He wrapped his arm around her and kissed the top of her head.

"If you say so." His cynical tone made her want to smack some sense into him.

After a moment holding her close, he put his hand on her forearms and moved her aside.

"Looks like dishes are done. I should go. I'll text when I get an appointment set with Omaha PD." As he spoke, he edged toward the door, hands shoved in his pockets.

"Sure, I don't go in to work until three P.M. If you need to talk—"

"Okay then, I'll be in touch." He waved and bolted for the apartment door, still barefoot.

"—I'll be in the barn," she finished to an empty room. Well, that was a weird and awkward end to their first night together.

Twenty-Two

"YOU ARE SERIOUSLY DRAGGING ass today, my friend," Hector said of Rick's lackluster performance on the rowing machine.

"I'm here. That's about all I have for you today." He almost canceled his physical therapy appointment. He had the cell phone in his hand and his finger on Hector's name. But instead, he dragged his ass into his shitty car and drove to the university gym. The crap Hector would give him if he skipped a workout wasn't worth it.

"Getting here is the most important part." Hector patted him on the back.

"No. No life-improving yoga meditation empowerment crap today. I just can't." Rick shoved back with more energy than he'd expended thus far in his workout. The zing of the rowing machine's flywheel brought a smile to Hector's face.

"Reality it is. It's time we started you running. I reviewed the FBI physical fitness test. Two of the four exercises required it: the sprint and the 1.5-mile run."

"I'm more worried about the pull-ups." And though he wasn't going to tell Hector, he had a new worry: requalifying on his weapon.

He went to the shooting range yesterday. He did fine. His aim was good. The little M&P he bought was a nice gun. But mentally, the visit took it out of him. He'd had to force himself to pull the trigger every single time. He left the range with a migraine and sweat dripping off him. When he got home, he grabbed a beer and zoned out in front of the TV while a mind-numbing cooking show played. And that sure as shit wasn't progress.

"Yeah, not going to lie to you, the pull-ups are going to suck. Your shoulder was practically frozen when you came to me. What you're doing on the rowing machine was impossible, so you are making progress toward those pull-ups."

"Yippie, progress." He let go of the rowing machine handle, and it snapped home. The loud thwack drew a couple of glances from the happy-go-lucky college kids. They were so young. He kind of hated them for it right now.

"Alright, asshole, we're hitting the track." Hector grabbed a towel and disinfectant spray for the rowing machine.

Rick heaved off the machine and took the cleaning stuff from Hector. When he finished the wipe down, Hector was MIA. So he walked toward the indoor track. He didn't need Hector for this. He had his old-lady-approved walking workout memorized.

"What are you doing, Cabrera? We run the outside track today. Get you some vitamin D. It's a natural mood enhancer. Get a move on." Hector shoved Rick's sunglasses and a bottle of water at him and turned for the exit.

He trailed Hector across the parking lot to the university track. As they walked, Hector fidgeted with his smartwatch. Rick scuffed his shoe against the pavement. This was either going to be empowering as hell or in ten minutes he'd be sprawled on the track clutching his chest.

"Here's the drill. Two minutes jogging. Five minutes walking." Hector took off almost before he finished his sentence.

Rick surged after him with a grunt. In a few strides, he found his rhythm, feet striking the track, his arms pumping lightly. The cadence he knew better than his heartbeat, the six-minute mile. The incidental tug at the scar tissue across his chest was nothing but an inconvenience he could ignore.

He was running.

He caught up to Hector, and together they jogged in silence until the watch beeped.

"Nice work."

Rick tried to answer, but his lungs were burning. He gasped a few deep breaths in and out. His endurance was pathetic. But at least he was getting somewhere. But it was so fucking slow.

"What's up with you today?" Hector wasn't even breathing fast. Jerk.

"Nothing," he managed between gasps.

Hector walked silently next to him for half a lap around the track. Rick's breathing settled, and his stride lengthened.

"Care to elaborate on the nothing that's making you such a dick today?"

There were about fifty things pissing him off.

The estimate for the house renovations kept increasing. He'd already talked to his cousin Carlos about coming on as an investor. It was a little humbling to get schooled on the pitfalls of real estate investing by the kid he taught to hit a baseball.

"That fucking house is bleeding me dry."

"And...that is not new."

Rick shook his head. Hector didn't get it. He was on a path—about to get a Ph.D.

Rick struggled to fire a gun without going catatonic yesterday. The doubts about his future with the FBI were weighing down everything. The only reason he'd worked so hard to repair his body was to get his badge back. But now, he wasn't entirely sure he wanted it. The physical demands didn't scare him anymore, but risking his life was another thing. Was it worth it?

He almost died serving his boss's over-inflated ego and trying to save a stupid painting.

He tried to put his thoughts about his future into words, but nothing would come out. Hector's watch beeped, and Rick felt like he'd been granted a lifeline. He set off at the same blistering pace he'd run the first interval. It was harder this time around. His legs were rubbery and the perfect rhythm elusive.

"Hey, you can dial it back, you know. Take it slow. I'd rather not have to hold your hair while you're puking. We have two or three more sets to do."

Speech wasn't an option, so he flipped Hector the bird and lowered his speed to something more like a jog.

As his feet pounded on the track, he thought about Thursday night with Maggie. He spent a lot of time remembering the way she felt, how she tasted, and the perfect way they fit together. It was verging on obsession.

He'd strategically avoided her all weekend. No calls, no texts, no accidental hellos. That situation was a ticking time bomb waiting to blow, and he had no good idea what to do about it. This kind of frustration wasn't something he'd felt over a woman before.

Hector's watch beeped. They shuffled back to a walk. Rick was gasping, Hector serene.

"So the house and..." Hector was like a dog with a bone—relentless. At least he waited until Rick's breathing normalized.

"My mother called this morning." Her call was the most recent annoyance on his list.

"Guilt trip?" There was a hint of laughter in Hector's voice.

"Oh, and it's not just her, my sisters too. They all want me to come back to Miami." He loved them, but he needed time and space. He wasn't done here...yet.

"Family is hard. The more you loved them, the more difficult they can make your life."

"I spent a lot of time with my family. Dinners, holidays, you know."

"Sure."

"But..." Rick threw up his hands. He had no way to make them happy—more frustration.

"But being close allows them to be a huge pain in the ass."

"Exactly. I get it. They want me home. But in Miami, everything was one step forward, two steps back. And they were right there, breathing down my neck. The sympathy made me want to scream at them to go away and mind their own business."

"The support was stifling."

"They need to wait and let me do what I need to do. When the house sells, I'll go home." Their concern was added stress. He didn't understand why they couldn't see that.

"And here you're improving. Thriving."

"Yes. But I don't live in Omaha. This is like a vacation. Temporary. Pretend." The last word caused a painful tightening in his chest as he said it.

Hector considered his words. The beep of the watch interrupted the moment. Before Rick could take off, Hector grabbed his upper arm.

"Or could your new life in Omaha actually be more real than your past?" Hector let go and sprinted up the track, leaving Rick in his dust.

After a second to consider the disturbing and insightful question, Rick took off after Hector. Maybe if he pushed harder, he could drown all these feelings in a haze of physical exhaustion.

She heard Rick's car door slam, and her heart stuttered. They'd been avoiding each other since

Thursday night. The hot, sexy, wonderful night. And it had gone on long enough that she was feeling awkward.

There was no avoiding Rick today; she was tending the mint in the planter right next to his door. She had a stranglehold on a weed that poked up through her plants, and yanked it out with a bit more force than necessary.

Time to do this.

They were adults. She could manage to be cool. Yes, that was her. *Ms. Cool.*

She glanced over her shoulder to watch Rick make his way toward the house. His dark gray shirt clung to his sweaty chest, and his workout shorts showed off his long, tan legs. She'd never had a thing for a man's legs before, but damn, Rick's were gorgeous. Lean with defined muscles.

Exhale. Mind out of the gutter. There was no way she'd keep her cool if she focused on his body. She plucked out another offensive weed.

The fact was post-workout Rick looked a hell of a lot like post-sex Rick. The memories flooded through her: him pressing her into the mattress, scoring his back with her nails, and the whispered Spanish in her ear. Her panties were going to melt if she kept up this trip down memory lane.

She rolled her neck like a prizefighter getting ready to go in the ring. Focus. Be cool.

"Hi, Maggie." He stood right behind her—his proximity sent tingles racing up her spine.

She spun. The way her heart was racing was anything but cool. She leaned her ass against the planter and dropped her handful of weeds on the ground.

"Hi, Rick." She wiped her dirty hands on her jean shorts. And his gaze followed her every move. He swallowed hard when she shoved her hands in her pockets, dragging her shorts low, baring a slice of stomach below the hem of her faded T-shirt.

He took a step back and sighed. "I heard back from the police department. A Lieutenant Morris can meet with us tomorrow at nine. Will that work for you?"

"I have another nighttime event at the convention center Tuesday and go in late, so yes, that will work."

"Okay, that's what I was hoping."

Their conversation was stilted and formal. She forced her lips into a normal smile—at least, she hoped it was normal—and wracked her brain for something to say.

"Thank you, for helping with Ted..."

"Maggie, you don't need to thank me." He shook his head.

"But I want to." She pulled her hands from her pockets, grabbed his upper arms, and gave him a quick hug. Nothing passionate or sexy, just a friendly reminder to him she was a hugger. Breaking the touch barrier was necessary if they were ever going to get over this weirdness.

His hands brushed over her waist as she pulled back, his fingers inches from that sliver of skin between her low-slung shorts and her shirt. It took all her willpower not to lean into him, to rub her suddenly hard nipples over his chest.

Nope, not going to happen...again. Or so she was telling herself.

"So, whose shitty car do we want to take tomorrow?" He smirked.

"Hey, speak for your car but not mine. Bertha is lovely." She punched him lightly in the arm.

Their eyes met, and they started laughing. The tension dissolved like it had never been.

"Lovely, really? It's missing a bumper. And since when was that decade-old hunk of junk called Bertha?"

"Since right now. And I got the A/C fixed, that's why she's lovely." It might be Nebraska and not Miami, but August heat was oppressive when you were in traffic and had no air conditioning.

"You should see my Charger. She's lovely. Black, fast, and the purr on her engine." He rolled his eyes and moaned. "That's a car."

"Does your beauty have a name?"

"Gisele."

"Like the supermodel?"

"Exactly."

"That is so incredibly you." She shook her head. Even his car's name reminded her that he wasn't from Omaha. Miami might as well be another planet—the land where supermodels and fashionistas play.

He shrugged. "You'd love her."

"I'm sure."

"Alright, I'll see you in the morning. I've got to get cleaned up." He plucked at his sweaty shirt where it stuck to him but didn't make a move toward the front door. He studied her with his head cocked to one side.

"Did you have a good workout with Hector?"

"Yeah, it was challenging." He drew out the last word until it sounded like a question.

"Is that good?"

"I'm not sure yet." He shook his head and slowly moved to go inside.

"See you in the morning," she called as he opened the door.

Yeah, she was still totally, irrevocably attracted to Rick. And their chance at a future was about the same as snow on Christmas in Miami. It was unfair.

And the big question was what, if anything, could or would she do about it.

Twenty-Three

MAGGIE GLANCED UP AT the billboard on the highway. It was Cheryl. Thirty feet tall, perfect TV smile, and not a single hair out of place. Cheryl, whose prescription for happiness included Maggie riding Rick hard and often.

The stallion in question was driving. They chose his shitty car for the trip downtown to Omaha PD over hers since it had a full gas tank.

Maggie turned the radio down. Her mother always, always held uncomfortable conversations in a moving vehicle. No need for intense eye contact, and neither party could walk away. It worked a charm. She'd used it on Evan more than once.

She sighed, licked her lips, and plunged headfirst into shark-infested waters. "So about the other night—"

"Right now?" He pulled his eyes off the highway for a brief moment to give her a look of absolute disbelief.

Rick wanted to bolt; she could see it in his eyes. Damn, her mother was a brilliant woman.

But his only escape would be to hurl himself out of the moving SUV, so he would be having this conversation with her. Right Now.

"Are we pretending it didn't happen? Or what?"

"I don't know." He ran a hand through his hair. "What do you want?"

"An end to the weirdness. And I don't want anyone to get hurt." Not her, not him, and not Evan.

"Sure, I get that." He drummed a finger on the steering wheel.

"So…"

"So…"

"Jeez, Rick. Help a girl out. I'm trying to be an adult about this when all I want to do is stomp my feet and pout. The guy I had this amazing night with is leaving town never to return." She huffed and slammed her back against the car seat, arms crossed just like Evan when she told him no.

Rick put his hand on her thigh. His touch burned through her navy work slacks. Every nerve ending in her body stood at attention waiting for his next move.

"Nothing in life is fair. Or easy."

Something in his tone made her think he was talking about a lot more than them.

"How long are you staying?" She hadn't pinned him down on a date. The less she knew, the easier she could pretend that she didn't need a new place to live: God, another item on her long-ignored to-do list.

"I guess at least until Thanksgiving. Hector signed me up for the turkey trot 5K. If I can finish in less than twenty-five minutes, I should be ready for the FBI fitness test. And Kevin should be done with the house by then if I don't run out of money."

"That's close to four months." That was an eternity in the dating world. She'd been in more than one relationship in her life that started hot and heavy and petered out in six weeks or less. There was no guarantee they'd last that long. But if they did, saying goodbye would fucking hurt. But how good could he make her feel until then—

"Yeah, about that long."

What would be worse, wishing she'd seized the moment and had a fling with a gorgeous man or letting him go at the end?

She could almost hear Cheryl and Lena egging her on. Reminding her there weren't men like Rick handing out spectacular orgasms on every street corner. Especially not to a thirty-something single mom.

"What do you want?"

"Ah, mi corazón, I want a lot of things." He squeezed her leg and muttered something in Spanish under his breath. *Why the hell did she take French in high school?*

He pointed the SUV down a highway off-ramp, and the navigation program on his phone directed him toward the police station.

She studied him as he drove. The pinched tightness that had been around his eyes and lips when he first arrived was almost entirely gone. The flat scowl he sported had gradually disappeared over the weeks. A relaxed smile was now his usual expression.

She patted his hand that was still on her leg before lifting it off and setting it on the gear shift. She wasn't sure what the hell they were, but now wasn't the time to figure it out. He turned when she moved his hand and gave her a sad smile that seemed to echo her thoughts.

Rick parked in the lot in front of the Omaha Police Department. The building's 1970s architecture traded elegance for function. It looked like a squat concrete castle fortified for battle.

"Time to talk to the police. You ready?"

"As I'll ever be. Thank you again for the help."

"Let's see how this goes before you thank me." He turned off the ignition.

Rick had been in a million government buildings. They tended toward neutral colors, but OPD headquarters was a sea of unrelenting beige. Every surface was a tone ranging from dull almost-white to weak not-exactly-brown. It made his eyes cross.

The only interesting things in the building were the many depictions of the department's unique buffalo shaped badge. It was on almost everything but the bathroom doors.

A desk sergeant led them to Lieutenant Morris, chatting with Maggie about the weather as they traversed the maze of hallways and offices. Rick had forgotten about the sameness of civic buildings, the hum of fluorescent lights, and the buzz of too many people in too little space talking on desk phones.

He tugged at his suddenly too tight tie. A vision of him chained to a desk in the FBI's Miami office for the next twenty years filled his mind. The unrelenting boredom, mountains of paperwork, endless hours of database searches. It could be his future if he weren't a field agent.

"Here you go." The desk sergeant knocked on a door with Morris's name stenciled on it before opening it for them. "This is Maggie Stewart and Rick Cabrera for you."

The lieutenant stood to shake hands and make introductions. He was maybe five or so years younger than Rick. He was in good shape, clean cut, and neatly dressed. Morris must have climbed the ranks quickly to have this level of seniority at his age. Rick hoped he was still ambitious. That would be good for them.

"Would you like me to call you Agent Cabrera? I understand your situation with the FBI is in flux." Morris sat back behind his desk now that the initial pleasantries were over.

"I'm on medical leave after an incident in Miami. What we're talking about today has zero to do with the FBI, so please call me Rick." He'd spoken with a department administrative assistant to schedule the meeting and mentioned his FBI credentials and his status because he didn't want any misunderstandings or bruised egos.

"Alright then, Rick and Maggie, the message I received said something about a robbery. What do you have for me?" Morris's hands hovered over a computer keyboard, ready to take notes.

"Maggie's son came to me concerned by a conversation he overheard while with his father. His father and a few friends had a set of plans for the convention center and were discussing exits and security." Rick jumped right in. No reason to draw this out.

"I work at the convention center, and my ex-husband, Ted Kurtz, recently took a job there as well. He's not a guy that likes manual labor, so a position on the janitorial staff was... uncharacteristic." Maggie chose her words carefully, and he silently applauded her effort not to sound like a bitter ex-wife.

"That's pretty vague information. How old is the boy?"

"Ten next week," Maggie said.

"Evan is a very smart kid, so I take his concerns seriously. I called in a favor with a friend at the US Attorney's office, and she pulled some records for me." Rick slid a USB drive over to Morris. "After reading up on Ted's life and known associates, I thought I would look closer."

Rick gave Morris a rundown on his trip to the pawnshop in Council Bluffs. He hit all the highlights from the event staff uniform shirts to the paper trail pointing to Earl Whitestone as the shop owner. He also filled Morris in on the evening at the Peppermint Pony without mentioning that Maggie had joined him on that adventure.

Morris's fingers flew over the keys as Rick spoke. The notes he was taking led Rick to believe he was interested in what they had to say.

"Maggie, can you tell me about your ex-husband?"

"Ted is a gambler. It's a sickness that is slowly ruining his life." Her weary tone said more than her words ever could. "If he owed enough money to the wrong people, I could see him involved in almost anything to get free of the debt."

"And Ted is working at the convention center now?"

"Yes."

"Did you help him get the job?"

She laughed cynically. "No, the opposite. I'd love to see him fired, but I have zero control of the janitorial staffing. I work in sales and event management. The divisions between our departments are part of why we came to you and not my boss."

"And the other part?"

"If Ted is involved in something like this, I want records I can take to a family court judge so I can keep my son safe. One of these men paid Evan twenty dollars to go outside and play. Instead, Evan chose to eavesdrop on them. What if he'd been caught? The thought of what might have happened makes me sick."

Morris nodded and stopped typing for a moment to reread his notes.

"Do you have any specific information pointing to what event they are targeting?"

Rick shook his head.

"If you would like it, here is a list of the upcoming events and an org chart with all of upper management's names and phone numbers." Maggie pushed a file folder across the desk.

Morris took the folder and thanked her.

"It's probably nothing, but when Ted originally called asking me to help him get a job at the convention center, he mentioned a position as security for the upcoming US Diamond and Fine Jewelry Show."

Maggie hadn't told him that before. It could be important or be a distraction.

Morris grumbled under his breath. "We've heard some chatter on the street that the show is a target."

Morris slipped the phone list out of the folder and read the names. "I'll get on the phone with your head of security again today and repeat my concerns. I'll also reach out to Council Bluffs police and see what I can learn about the Jokers Wild pawnshop. Thank you both for your information."

Morris punched a button on his phone, calling an admin to lead them out of the maze of beige that was the OPD headquarters.

As soon as they stepped outside, Maggie stopped and grabbed his arm. "That's it? A thank you."

"Yeah. I don't have a way to keep us looped into the investigation. Being on leave from the FBI, I have less pull than a private citizen. I don't even pay taxes in this city."

She put her hands on her hips and sighed. "This sucks."

"How about I buy you a beer?

"Ummm, it's nine forty-two A.M."

"Bloody Mary it is!" He caught her hand and started down the sidewalk toward some restaurants and bars they'd passed driving in.

Twenty-Four

"Winner, winner, chicken dinner!" Rick pointed at a sandwich board in the middle of the sidewalk. It advertised brunch and buy one get one free Bloody Marys until one o'clock. Not a bad way to repair a dismal Tuesday.

Maggie glanced at the building's brick façade. "Looks decent."

Rick pulled open the glass door for Maggie. The trendy brewpub was a few blocks from the police station lot where they left his car. He pressed a hand to the small of Maggie's back and pulled the door open for her. The exposed brick and dark wood paneling was a welcome escape from the bright sun outside.

"Table for two?" the hostess asked as she picked up a couple of menus. Behind her station, tall windows offered a view of the gleaming beer brewing equipment.

"Yes, please. And bring on the Bloody Marys." Maybe after a couple of drinks, he could handle the questions Maggie brought up in the car without looking or sounding like an ass.

"Right this way. I will put in that drink order as soon as you are seated. You want the Cadillac or the bare bones Marys?"

"I can't believe I'm day drinking on a weekday." Maggie glanced at him; her smile was almost a grimace.

"It's not a crime." He wrapped an arm around her shoulders and bumped her hip with his.

"You are a bad influence."

"Exactly." He pulled her close to his side. The smell of her shampoo stirred up memories of their night together. And he squeezed her close before relaxing his hold and reminding himself to keep it platonic.

"Fuck it. If we're doing this, we should do this right." She patted him on the chest, her hand lingering over his heart. "I vote Cadillac," she told the hostess as she scooted out from under his arm and into their booth.

"Cadillac all the way," he agreed. It was fun contributing to the delinquency of an upstanding, working, single mother. Was this a good idea? Hell no. Was he doing it anyway? Hell yes.

"I'll get your drinks sent right over." The hostess left them with their menus.

"This place is cute." Maggie looked around, studying the restaurant and the other customers.

"You don't get out much between Evan and two jobs, do you?"

She rolled her eyes so hard he thought she might sprain something. "My summers are the busiest. I have the plants to care for and all the green markets. As soon as it gets cold, things calm down a lot for Lone Tree. I only do the one holiday market if I have stuff leftover."

"Why the side hustle?" At the green market, her booth had been popular. He had seen plenty of people carrying bags filled with her products. But it was a crazy time commitment when she had a good job at the convention center.

"Lone Tree's profits pay for Evan's tuition at private school. He's not just smart. He's brilliant."

"He said something to me about seeing math. Is he like Good Will Hunting?"

"Pretty much. I don't understand it completely, but the teachers at his school do. You should see his math homework. It looks like he stole it from

NASA. I want the best for him. And the best thing I can do is nurture that brain of his. I can't give him a better father. Ted is who he is. But that school is incredible. So I make it happen."

He understood mothers that would do anything for their kids. He had a whole family full of those kinds of brave, fearless, passionate women back home in Miami. That was half the reason why his temporary relocation to Omaha was driving his mother crazy.

"You're a great mom."

"Thanks, I guess." She shook her head like she didn't deserve the compliment. "Most days, I don't feel like it. I'm stressed out or overtired. I wish I had more time to give Evan. And myself."

"It's not about a lot of hours. It's what you do with those hours. He has a great personality and a big brain. He'll go far in this world. And that's all you."

"Are you trying to make me feel less guilty?" She shrugged and opened her bundle of silverware.

"What are you feeling guilty about?"

Maggie was superwoman; she managed a million responsibilities flawlessly.

"My son is at summer camp. I just reported his dad to the cops. And now, I'm day drinking." She reached out and intercepted her giant Bloody Mary from the waitress.

Rick could smell the horseradish before his glass hit the table. Sticking out of the top of the pint glass was a skewer with a veritable charcuterie board on it. He plucked a slice of salami and a cocktail onion off the end and popped them in his mouth before removing the obstacle from his glass.

He took a sip. Tangy tomato, some heat, and a nice hit of vodka at the end. Perfect.

"It's all me. I'm a bad influence. You said so yourself. But seriously, when was the last time you went out day drinking, or dancing, or to happy hour? Even great moms have to have fun." His mother was proof of that. She and her gal pals were long-standing regulars at some of the hottest restaurants in Miami. She and her buddies had been keeping each other sane for years. Her group had weathered raising kids, divorces, and even the death of a husband together.

Maggie sipped her drink and thought about her answer. "Lena drags me out sometimes. She uses best friend guilt to overpower mom guilt."

"I knew I liked Lena."

Maggie picked up her menu and made a show of checking out the options.

She was so different than the women he usually dated. They were party girls flitting from bar to bar and man to man. Everything about Maggie said warning, stay away, serious relationship ahead. She oozed commitment from her pores. She was nothing but complications. Delicious complications.

They placed their orders for the house special breakfast skillets that sounded like they might soak up all the booze in the Cadillac Bloody Marys that kept showing up at their table.

"Grease and carbs. Hector's going to kick your ass," she teased around a fork full of potatoes and eggs.

"What happens at the brewpub stays at the brewpub."

"Strip clubs have that rule, too, apparently. You didn't tell Morris I was with you at the Peppermint Pony."

"No, that memory is all mine. I'm not sharing it with anyone." His voice was gruff, deeper than normal. He hadn't meant to sound so possessive.

"So, you're not good at sharing? I don't think Misty would agree." A flush crept up over her cheeks, and she licked the salt off the rim of her glass very, very slowly while holding his gaze.

And fuck, his cock jerked in response. Erotic wasn't a bold enough word to explain watching Maggie and Misty.

"Maggie. This... We shouldn't." He ran a hand through his hair, clutching the roots to try and distract himself.

"Shouldn't what? We already did." Her eyes glittered with temptation.

"You're a woman that deserves it all. Romance, dates, and a future. I'm in no position to give you that. The best I can do is offer something casual until I go back to Miami." He hated every word, but it was all true. His future was behind a desk at the FBI in Miami.

"I can do casual. I want casual. I'm crazy busy. I can't devote time to a relationship. It would be another thing to feel guilty about neglecting. What I deserve is some hot sex and orgasms. Multiple orgasms." She purred the last word with her eyes closed and head tossed back.

"What happens when I leave?" He had to ask, had to play devil's advocate so he would have a clean conscience. Even as he tried to talk her out of this, he wanted her naked beneath him, trembling at his touch.

"Rick, whether or not we have sex again, I'll miss you when you're gone. No strings. No promises. No guilt. Nice and casual."

He slammed back the last of his drink. They needed their check and an Uber. No way after four – or was it five? – Cadillac Bloody Marys was he driving.

She was tipsy before noon. And it felt lovely. Maggie snuggled against Rick's shoulder. She turned and pressed her lips to his throat. She sucked and nipped until he dropped his head and gave her a full, deep, intoxicating kiss. He cradled her jaw and then shoved his fingers up into her hair, sending sparks rushing down her spine.

He released her mouth and nipped her earlobe. "Behave. I already told you I don't share, and that includes putting on a show for a nosey Uber driver barely old enough to shave."

She giggled into his chest. Lena and Cheryl were right. She deserved to feel sexy and wanted. She deserved a few dozen, or hundred, no-strings-attached orgasms. And God as her witness, she was going to enjoy every last shudder, gasp, and touch until Rick left for Florida.

They stumbled from the car at the house. She immediately turned toward the entrance to the apartment. He stopped her and pulled her toward the front door.

"My bed this time." His hot breath tickled over her skin, and he pressed his already hard cock against her. "I want my sheets to smell like you."

Fuck, that was hot. Her pussy clenched. "Condoms."

"Handled." He fished his keys out of his pocket, and she sagged against the clapboard siding next to the front door waiting to follow him inside.

He leaned his hands on either side of her and pressed his body against her. She instantly grabbed his ridiculously spectacular ass and offered her lips.

"This feels a little familiar, especially your hands on my ass."

"That night you were the one leaning on the wall to stay upright. And I'm nowhere near as hammered as you and Hector were." She laughed, the kind of silly drunk laughter that had her eyes watering and her gasping for breath.

"Good because I want your full participation in this." He threaded their fingers together and ripped open the screen door and then unlocked the front door. He all but ran up the steps, pulling her along, and she loved it. This kind of excitement and anticipation had been lacking in her busy life for too long.

Once they were inside the front bedroom that Rick used, he slowed down, way down. Drugging her with deep, open-mouthed kisses that stole her reason and left only want behind. When he lifted his head, and she opened her eyes, his intense stare reflected her own need.

The lacy curtains at the window let in the midday sun. She slowly undid his tie, working the knot loose and unthreading the long strip of silk from his collar. He didn't flinch when her hands went to the buttons on his shirt.

Before she opened the two halves of the unbuttoned shirt, she paused. He was holding his breath and still as a statue.

"Can you ignore them?" He caught her wrists in his hands; the tension in his shoulders wasn't desire.

"Of course." His scars were his hang-up, not hers. The marks spoke of what he'd survived. And despite whatever he thought, his body was spectacular. Lean hips, a gorgeous ass, and a hard slab of muscle for a chest.

He closed his eyes, but the tension didn't wane. Instead, it grew, filling the room with an unwelcome weight. She twisted free from his grasp and reached for his tie on the dresser. She pressed it into his hands.

"Go on." She spun, putting her back to him, and pulled her hair into a low ponytail at the nape of her neck. She sank her teeth into her lip as she waited for him to act. Indecision and desire battled. Had she done the right thing? Hell, was there a right thing in this moment?

"Maggie." Her name tore from him, and he settled the strip of silk over her eyes. When he pulled the knot tight, her belly clenched with anticipation.

The blindfold amplified everything. The sound of his shirt falling to the ground was as loud as a gunshot. And every part of her quivered, waiting for him to touch her.

He enveloped her from behind, undressing her slowly, with infinite care. Kissing and exploring every bit of skin he revealed. The tug of his callused fingers over her skin sent fire rippling through her. She squeezed her thighs together, trapping his devious fingers against her aching center.

"You're a fantasy. Naked. Blindfolded. Trembling." He turned her to face him. He trailed one finger down over her breast, around her hard nipple. Goosebumps rose in the wake of his caress.

She spread her hands, searching for him. The hot skin of his chest and stomach scalded her fingers. She undid his belt and pants by touch, fumbling to free him from his underwear. She closed her hand around his length, stroking from base to tip. It was his turn to tremble. He pressed his forehead to hers and murmured her name.

With each stroke, he seemed to lengthen and harden in her grasp. His hips pressed forward, his hands dug into her upper arms, pinning her in place. He didn't need to worry—she wasn't going anywhere. She lavished attention on him, twisting and tugging until his breathing was nothing but guttural moans and harsh gasps.

His need for her, so raw and desperate, made her hurt.

He tore her hands off him and attacked her mouth. His cock pressed between them. The evidence of his desire was slick on her stomach. She tried to hook her leg on his hip, desperate for friction, for relief. He pulled her back a few steps. Then he was gone. She reached out, and her hand landed on his shoulder. He was sitting on the bed.

The rustle of a condom wrapper and the squeak of the mattress. Then his hands dug into her waist, and he pulled her to straddle him. Her knees pressed into the bed on either side of his hips. Slowly, he filled her inch by exquisite inch. She clutched his chest, her anchor to reality. A shudder ran through her. His cock stretched her perfectly, filling her.

"Ride me. Let me watch you." He fell back on the bed. The cool air of the room was a stark contrast to the heat rolling off her body.

The blindfold was freedom. Cocooned in darkness, inhibitions that might have stifled her wanton display never materialized. She tossed her head back and ground down on him, taking her fill —reveling in the sensations.

She tilted forward to find the perfect angle to rub her clit with each thrust. Churning deep within, her orgasm was building. He wrapped his fingers around her thighs, digging into her flesh, demanding she ride him.

The whimpers that tore from her throat morphed into shouts.

"Tell me." He insisted on more from her.

His name, prayers, curses, everything. She'd never been so vocal during sex.

She worked herself against him until her pussy clenched. Wave after wave of pleasure washed over her. She fell forward onto his chest, and he wrapped his arms around her. She rode out the longest orgasm she could remember, trembling and twitching in his arms for what felt like ten minutes while he throbbed deep inside her.

He rolled them over, pulling her under him. He cradled her head for a moment before snatching off the blindfold. She blinked, and his face came into focus above her as he thrust into her. His expression was feral.

His mouth crashed against hers, his kiss all consuming.

Sensitive didn't begin to explain what she was feeling. She convulsed under him, digging her nails into his back as her spine bowed. He thrust again. Holy fuck. His teeth sank into her shoulder. The nip of pain meshed perfectly with the intense pleasure.

He was a man possessed as he fucked her. His hands seemed to be everywhere. Gripping. Holding. Stroking. His hard thrusts were punctuated with groans of her name. His rhythm increased to a brutal pace as he pounded out his release. His head thrown back and arms shaking with the effort he held himself above her, his gaze locked with hers.

He collapsed against her, spent. She coasted her fingers over his back and down to grab his ass. He rolled off and grumbled something about needing to toss the fucking condom as he left the bed.

She glanced at the bedside clock. She had time to nap before work, but this was supposed to be recreational sex. Not a relationship. She forced herself up despite her weak legs and gathered her clothes. If she stayed, it would muddle up their deal.

She was tucking in her shirt when Rick emerged from the bathroom. He froze and took in the scene, a look of confusion on his face as he reached for his shirt and tugged it on.

"Work?" he asked from the far side of the room.

"Yeah."

She shoved her feet into her shoes without looking at him. On the ground, his blue tie lay next to the condom wrapper. Something about the items made her want to kiss him goodbye and invite him over for dinner tomorrow. Or at least climb back in his bed. But that wasn't their deal. This was fucking. Stress relief. Casual.

She turned. He leaned next to the bathroom door, shirt and underwear on. His hair was still tousled from her fingers.

"I'll find my way out." She hurried for the door.

"You're sure?" He shifted away from the wall to follow her from the room.

"Yeah, no problem." She hoped she looked casual as she scooped up her purse and headed out. She wasn't sure about protocol in this situation.

"Talk soon," he said, his arms crossed over his chest.

She gave him a wave and dashed out. Halfway down the stairs, she regretted the awkward wave. She should have grabbed a handful of his shirt and kissed the hell out of him. Too late now.

Twenty-Five

"GIVE!" MAGGIE LUNGED ACROSS her desk at Lena, only half kidding around. Lena held a mocha from the café up the block. Chocolate and caffeine: the most perfect combination in life. She knew that delicious aroma anywhere.

Lena danced back. "Nope, not yet. Spill."

"I have no idea what you're talking about. Give me the coffee, and no one gets hurt." Maggie held up her stapler like a gun.

"You've been smiling way too much for the last two weeks, yawning in staff meetings, and I'm pretty sure that's a hickey."

Maggie fluffed the silk scarf tied around her neck. The annoying thing had one job. One job: hide her hickey while she was at work. Lena wouldn't let something that salacious go without a full interrogation. Her hickey was the end of keeping her arrangement with Rick quiet.

The casual plan was working. Pretty well. They both got plenty of orgasms. But keeping it casual also seemed to involve them spending a great deal of time together.

"Rick and I are keeping it casual." Even she heard the question at the end of her statement.

"Rick, who was helping you in the workshop all last week." Lena cocked her hip and waited.

"It wasn't a big thing. He was keeping me company while I worked."

"Okay. Weren't you having a beer with him on the porch last night when I called?"

"Evan and some other neighborhood kids were in the park playing. We were keeping an eye on them. It wasn't like we planned it." She shrugged.

"And didn't he help you take down your booth at the green market Sunday?"

"He stopped by to get some cheese, and it worked out that way." She'd been grateful for the help. Summer was almost over, and her enthusiasm for setting up and taking down her booth at the market was waning.

"Really?" Lena's disbelief was tangible.

"Yes." Maggie tried to grab the coffee and missed.

"You are in your mid-thirties rocking a hickey. That man put his mark on you. There's nothing casual about that in my book." Lena pointed at her neck. Little did her friend know, there were actually two hickeys. But the one on the inside of her thigh didn't need a scarf to hide it.

"No, Lena, it is. He's leaving in a few months. Remember, he lives in Miami." She held out her hand, making grabbing motions with her fingers, desperate for the mocha. It was the only thing that could make this conversation tolerable.

"So, we have phones and airplanes. And these things called moving vans. There are options."

"No, don't fill my head with ideas." She was doing enough of that on her own. The other evening, she watched Rick teaching Evan to play soccer in the yard. Yeah, that was the stuff fantasies were made of. And she found herself coming up with a million ways to turn a fling into long term. It wasn't a good idea.

"But you are sleeping together?"

"No, that's the only thing we aren't doing. No sleepovers. Just sex." She laid down that unspoken ground rule the day they went to the police station, and they had both stuck to it.

"Let's recap, shall we. Then you can have your precious mocha. He helps in the workshop. You have drinks together on the porch some nights. And you live in the same house. What about meals?"

"Not all the time." Dinners together started because Evan challenged Rick to another video game marathon. She cooked a big pot of chili. He'd been so appreciative she kept inviting him to eat dinner with her and Evan.

"Occasional meals. Anything else that the casual non-couple does together?"

"He washed my car for me. And he's going to help at the green market when he can." And he no longer hid the scars on his chest from her.

"Are you kidding me?" Lena shoved the mocha at her. "Rick is a fucking unicorn."

"It's not like that. We don't plan any of this stuff. We're friends helping each other out." She took the long-awaited first sip of the sweet, dark, chocolatey coffee. So good. Worth every moment of her interrogation.

"I'm not buying it. You two missed the turn-off to casual so far back you can't see it in the rear-view mirror. Casual is a two A.M. text that says: *Yo, girl, you busy?* What you have, my dear Maggie, is a supportive boyfriend and the start of a meaningful relationship. I know women at this stage in our lives don't expect that, but holy shit, girl, you have it." Lena put her hand up for a high five, and Maggie left her hanging.

"It's casual." She shook her head, reminding herself as much as Lena what the reality was.

Lena snorted at her. "I've got twenty bucks that says it's the best sex of your life. Am I right?"

Maggie cursed Lena's far too smug grin.

"I'm not paying up on that." Maggie took another drink of the mocha and checked the time. The big boss, Morgan Drews - CEO, had sent a company-wide memo that morning about the emergency meeting. They had better get moving if they didn't want to be late.

"Come on. We have a meeting." She shooed Lena toward the door.

"I left my coffee on my desk. We have to stop on the way." Lena headed out, muttering about good sex and great men.

After a quick stop at Lena's office for her coffee, they made their way toward the grand ballroom on the upper level. Maggie couldn't remember the last time there had been a full staff meeting and never on such short notice.

"What do you think this is about?" Lena asked as they rode the elevator.

"Maybe Drews is quitting?" Maggie had no idea what else would warrant a last-minute meeting of the entire staff.

She and Lena found seats as five men filed onto the stage at the front of the ballroom. Morgan Drews was joined by two US Diamond and Fine Jewelry Show representatives, the convention center's head of security, and Lieutenant Morris of the Omaha Police. Maggie instantly knew what the meeting was about. The mocha she'd been enjoying sloshed uncomfortably around the knots growing in her stomach.

"Fucking Ted," she mumbled under her breath, and Lena shot her a strange look. *Nothing*, she mouthed back to Lena.

Drews stood at a podium in the middle of the stage and began speaking about the convention center staff as a loving and supportive family that would protect each other. Maggie ignored the flowery intro speech and searched the room for Ted.

He stood far off to the left side of the room, leaning against a wall with a few of the food service guys he'd been with at the Peppermint Pony. He looked relaxed and focused on Drews. One thing gamblers learned how to do was hide their emotions. If they weren't sitting at a poker table, they were lying to family and friends. In either situation, showing emotions was a liability.

Drews wrapped up his opening remarks and turned the floor over to Lieutenant Morris. Morris introduced himself and gave his rather impressive credentials.

"Omaha Police Department is taking this situation very seriously. A series of events have led us to believe that a group of criminals is targeting the show generally and the closing night gala specifically."

Disbelieving murmurs rippled through the crowd. Maggie watched Ted. He didn't show the slightest reaction, unlike almost every other employee. He stayed slouched against the wall staring at Morris. She wasn't sure what to make of that—stupid poker face.

"At the request of Mr. Drews, Omaha PD will be taking an active role in increasing security for the event. Our presence should not concern any of you. We are here for your safety. But we do ask that, like at the airport, if you see something, you say something.

"Other officers and I will be on-site from the moment the first valuable exhibits start arriving until they ship out after the closing gala. Enhanced electronic security will also be installed, and all exhibitors are being encouraged to increase their private security staff.

"I asked to speak with all of you today because your eyes and ears are more valuable than a million-dollar alarm system. You all know this building and each other. Trust your instincts. You see someone out of place, tell security. Tell a cop. Tell everyone.

"Now, William Ball, your head of security, is going to go over the nuts and bolts of the security improvements and how they might affect your jobs."

Maggie reeled, questioning everything. Ted appeared almost bored with the speech. But that could be a front. Morris sounded confident up there, but his whole TSA-inspired *see something say something* speech also felt like a hail Mary. She wondered if Omaha PD had a clue.

Hopefully, Rick could shed some light on all this when she got home. He had a way better understanding of law enforcement than she did.

"Here you go." Rick uncapped the beer in his hand. Maggie reached for it, and he paused, holding it just out of reach. She was seated in one of the two new rocking chairs he bought to stage the front porch if and when this place ever got remodeled.

She wore her skimpy cut-off shorts, and her long, bare legs looked honey-gold in the setting sun. He cupped her jaw and tipped her head up so he could kiss her. It started as a simple brush of the lips, but he couldn't stop himself from thrusting into her mouth and kissing her breathless.

He pulled back, and she blinked a few times before taking the beer from his hand. He liked the dazed look that a few good kisses could put on her face. She had come home stressed from work and asked to talk.

His first instinct was that it was about their arrangement, and he couldn't keep from kissing her to remind her how fucking good they were together. He didn't care that people, probably neighbors, were walking in the park across the street. He didn't care that Mrs. Firebaum was weeding her sunflowers. He had to kiss her.

As far as he knew, casual didn't mean secret. They were consenting adults, and he hadn't tasted her lips since he slipped out of her bed at near midnight last night. Leaving her sated and half asleep was getting harder every time he did it.

Their fling had rules, and he didn't love them. But he couldn't change that either.

After a long pull off the beer, she sighed and closed her eyes, leaning back in the chair. "I needed that." Her languid tone let him know she was thankful for more than the beer. The knot in the pit of his stomach eased. This wasn't a talk about them.

"Long day. You said you wanted to talk." He took his seat in the rocker next to her. His fingers grazed her arm as he pushed back with his feet.

"Ugh, Lieutenant Morris gave a speech to us at work today. I'm not sure if it scared the crap out of me or made me think OPD has the situation under control."

"Tell me everything." He stopped the rocking chair and leaned in to get all the gory details.

The emergency company-wide meeting was an interesting tactic. Not one Rick or the FBI would have used. The FBI kept everything close to the vest. Sometimes to their detriment. He couldn't figure out how telling the world that the show and the gala were a target gained Omaha PD the upper hand in catching the bad guys. But he was on the outside looking in.

"Ted wasn't bothered by it in the least. I fucking hate his poker face. And I think it's gotten better over the years. When we were married, he would stand there, me with our new baby on my hip, and straight-up lie about everything. And he was so good at it I'd believe him." She drained her beer. "Today, same thing. Morris tells the whole staff how they are more valuable than a million-dollar alarm in helping catch the robbers, and Ted doesn't blink. The words washed over him like nothing at all."

"I can check in with Morris. Try and get him on the phone. I might get some more information on the case, but it's an ongoing investigation. They aren't going to tell me much. The FBI kept everything on a need-to-know basis. I can't imagine OPD is much different."

Yeah, that need-to-know crap was a big part of how he ended up shot in a room full of other agents. It was total bullshit, and the FBI culture was to blame.

"The whole meeting felt like a farce. When I got back to my office and thought about it, nothing that Bill, our head of security, talked about was new. The security improvements he discussed are the ones that the jewelry show people demanded before they would consider our venue." She rubbed her temples.

"I wish I had all the answers for you."

She gave him a weak smile. "I'll settle for a second beer now and an orgasm later?"

"I can make that deal." He stood to get the beer but paused halfway to the front door. "Can you get me a ticket to that gala?"

"Probably. It's a huge party. All the exhibitors and buyers from the show plus VIPs from across the country are coming. Proceeds from the ticket sales go to charity. It's the party of the year."

"The party of the year?" He raised an eyebrow. He got the feeling that Maggie wasn't exaggerating, unlike in Miami, where every third event claimed to be the party of the year.

"This is the biggest thing to happen in Omaha in forever. Why do you want to come?"

"Omaha PD is looking to protect a bunch of sparkly rocks. And catch some bad guys. I need—er, I want to have your back. Just in case." There was no way he would sit at home and pray OPD had it under control. There were too many ways he was responsible to and for her. Casual might mean temporary, but he would keep her safe until what they were doing ended. It was the right thing to do.

"Just in case?" She squinted at him like he was a puzzle piece that didn't want to fit where she expected.

"Mona would kick my ass if I didn't."

Twenty-Six

MAGGIE WAS ON EDGE. She had her phone out and was one hundred percent focused on it. Rick didn't mind. She was running the biggest event of her career—she should be kicking ass. He followed her through employee offices toward the convention center floor. She'd met him at the back entrance to the venue to avoid any parking headaches.

She muttered a few curses under her breath and jabbed the elevator button to call the car. She was in full professional event planner mode. She wore a simple navy evening gown, minimal jewelry, and swept-up hair.

As they waited for the car, she looked him up and down. "In case I forget to tell you later, you look hot."

Internally, he applauded his forethought to have his mother send his Tom Ford tux from Miami. He'd bought it for Ava's Palm Beach wedding. It fit like a glove and was James Bond cool.

"You look sophisticated and in charge. It's sexy as hell." He ghosted a polite kiss over her cheek. But he wanted to crush her to his chest and get her the hell out of there. Omaha PD's setup had too many echoes of the night he was shot for him to be comfortable.

"Thank you. I'm going to be swamped all night. I won't have time to be with you. You understand, right?" She walked into the elevator and pressed the button for the main level.

"I'm a big boy. I can be on my own. Promise me that we meet either at these elevators or your office if anything goes wrong. If they evacuate the building, head for the hotel across the street. Got it?"

She nodded.

"Remember, I'm here just in case. I'm not trying to freak you out, but I want us to have a plan. And keep your phone on and with you. I want to be able to use that find my phone app we installed if this gets ugly."

The ringtone from her cell reverberated inside the elevator. "I'm going to be so busy when I step out of this elevator. I won't have time to freak out. This event has to be perfect. And my phone is going to be glued to me all night." She pressed her cell to her ear. "This is Maggie."

Rick trailed behind her through the cavernous lobby where the last setup was being completed on a few bars and food stations. Massive flower arrangements were everywhere, and on the far end of the room, a press area was set up with a step and repeat backdrop for PR photos. It was like a high-end wedding combined with a news conference and a trade show.

Maggie slammed through a set of closed doors into the exhibit hall. "I have to deal with this. You should check it all out. Guests will be arriving any minute." Her stride lengthened into almost a run as she took off, her phone still pressed to her ear. She was rushing and stressed, but she kept her cool and managed her responsibilities with an unflappable efficiency. She handled a work crisis with the same impressive abilities as she handled being a single mom.

The displays were extraordinary. No expense was spared. Each vendor's booth was more elaborate than the next. He wandered around the exhibit hall, learning the layout and cataloging the security and police personnel. Soon other guests started to flood the building.

He checked his cell. Nothing from Maggie, not that he expected anything. He shook off the unease that had settled in the pit of his stomach. Tonight wasn't going to be anything like the night at Vizcaya.

On his right was the booth for Tiffany's. Looking for a distraction, he strolled inside the building-sized replica of the company's signature aqua blue box, complete with a huge bow. Rows of jewelry cases sparkled under crystal chandeliers. Behind each case, an employee waited to show off their wares.

He stopped at the first case in the front center of the room. The display's centerpiece was a pink diamond ring that had a center stone bigger than an egg yolk.

"Isn't she lovely? That's the Delphi Pink Jubilee diamond, 33.4 carts," the saleswoman behind the counter told him. "It was once part of the crown jewels of France and has been owned by Tiffany's for a decade."

She made no move to open the case.

"Is it for sale?"

"This is a jewelry show. Everything is for sale." She folded her hands in front of her.

"Let me rephrase my question. Do you plan on it selling? Or is it only for publicity?"

The saleswoman shrugged and glanced behind him. Her smile grew in wattage enough to rival the sparkle of the diamonds.

"Why Rick Cabrera, you have excellent taste." An elegant, bejeweled hand touched his forearm, and he turned to find Sylvia Barton and her husband Mark were the VIPs that excited the saleswoman. "Ava mentioned you were rusticating in Omaha. I never expected to see you tonight." She leaned in to kiss his cheek.

"Long way from Florida." Mark Barton stuck out his hand to shake. The older man's grip was firm, and he sported calluses from his years of building his company with his own hands.

"Yes, sir. A very long way." He and the Bartons began a circuit around the shop.

The Bartons, Ava King's parents, were wonderful people. He'd made billions in construction in South Florida but never lost touch with reality. And Sylvia was class personified.

"Ava and Jackson wanted to join us, but she's in the middle of a huge case, and Jackson is putting out fires for Mark at the company." Sylvia perused the jewelry cases as she talked. Her fingers danced over the pristine glass. Every time she would linger over an item, a staff member would pull it from the display to give her a better look.

"To be honest, I don't think they could find a dog sitter for Rodie." Mark elbowed Rick in the ribs, and they shared a chuckle. Ava and Jackson treated that dog like it was their child.

Sylvia completed her loop around the shop, stopping in front of the Delphi Pink Jubilee diamond.

"Good evening, Mrs. Barton." The saleswoman reached for the key at her waist and opened the case. "Would you like to try her? She was a gift from Louis XIV for his mistress, the Princess of Monaco. Lost tragically during the French Revolution and rediscovered a hundred years later in England."

Sylvia let the white-gloved saleswoman slide the massive stone on her finger as she recited its history. Sylvia cocked her head and tipped her hand this way and that, considering. The stone was so large it dwarfed her hand. "A bit much for me, I'm afraid."

Mark patted Rick on the back. "I've been taking her to this show since it started in Houston. She tries on all these pieces, one more over the top than the next. The salespeople know us by name. She's giving them false hope. But before her birthday, a list will appear in my email inbox of all the smaller pieces she never touched but adored so I can buy her something. I'm not sure how she remembers which was what."

"Women?" Rick shrugged. He glanced at the jewelry Sylvia was wearing. He was sure it was worth more than most people's houses. But it wasn't anything like the ostentatious Delphi Pink Jubilee diamond.

"Can't live without them." Mark smiled fondly at his wife, who still lingered over the massive pink diamond.

Before he'd been shot, before reconnecting with Maggie, he would have been quick to chime in with the expected *can't live with them* reply. But tonight, it got stuck somewhere in his chest.

Mark raised an eyebrow, a knowing grin on his lips. "It happens to us all if we're lucky. So don't screw it up."

"I'm not... She's not..." He didn't know what to say.

Mark laughed. "I suggest doing some ring shopping. You're in the perfect place. I think your days as Miami's favorite bachelor are over."

Rick shook his head. If only his life were as easy to transform as Barton made it seem. He and Maggie were the old story of the wrong place at the wrong time.

"Mark, darling," Sylvia joined the men, "I think I'd like to head for Graff next. They have a sapphire that was owned by a deposed Shaw. I have to see that." She sounded like a tourist plotting her exploration of a foreign city. "Rick, lovely to see you as always. If we weren't flying out tonight, we'd have loved to take you for dinner."

He took her hands in his and gave her a kiss on each cheek. "Next time, we will all plan better."

"Damn right. The best steak I ever had was here in Omaha." Barton gave him another firm handshake before escorting his wife toward her next stop.

Rick watched the older couple move through the crowd, stopping to say hello to acquaintances as they walked. Mark's hand rested on the small of his wife's back, and something about the way she would lean in to talk with him spoke of the long-lasting bond between them.

He pulled his cell out and flicked open the find my phone application. A few clicks, and he had a green dot on the screen that showed Maggie was on the other side of the convention center. He decided to see if he could catch sight of her.

He wove around the edges of the exhibit hall to stay away from the worst of the crowd. He passed at least ten well-armed private security guards leaning on back walls of booths. Their sharp glares and muscled builds screamed ex-military. In addition to the guards, there were security cameras and motion detectors.

There was no good way to rob this place. Not tonight. If a criminal wanted to steal something like the Delphi Pink Jubilee diamond, the worst time to try and take it would be tonight. During setup, tear down, or transport were all better options. There was no way unless Earl planned on a hostage situation or a bomb threat. Hell, stealing a pack of gum from the gift shop wasn't even an option tonight.

Ahead a uniformed custodian worked emptying one of the many discreetly placed garbage cans. It was fucking Ted. The guy looked bored out of his mind. A pair of earbuds hung from his ears, and he casually bopped his head to whatever he was listening to while slowly shoving a new bag into the can.

Rick had to remind himself not to stare, but poker face or not, nothing about Ted said he was biding his time until shit went down. Every inch of his body language read apathetic employee doing barely enough to avoid getting fired.

"Hey, FBI." Ted tugged an earbud out. "Thanks for the help."

"Excuse me?" Helping Ted was the last thing on earth he would ever do.

"You know what? Never mind. But be sure and tell your cop buddy Morris I said all this extra security was very impressive." Cool as a cucumber, Ted shouldered the trash bag and pushed through a nearby door marked employees only.

The guy was like an emotional sinkhole, not a single facial twitch or tell to help Rick figure out what the hell the cryptic comment about the event security meant. He'd relay the incident to Morris if and when he saw him tonight. Maybe the cop could make sense of it.

He thought about going after Ted and pressing him for an explanation, but it wasn't worth it. The only person he had allegiance to tonight was Maggie. He glanced at his phone and adjusted his course toward the green dot. Maggie appeared to be near the champagne bar in the center of the exhibit hall.

Maggie stood at the end of the long glowing white bar with Lena. They raised their glasses for a toast as Rick joined them.

"Ladies, celebrating?"

"Yes." They clinked their glasses and took a sip.

"Everything is under control." Lena waved at the bartender for another glass for Rick.

"The toast is a tradition. An hour after an event of this size has started, if we aren't panicking, then we have succeeded." Maggie's smile lit up her face. The waves of accomplishment rolling offer her were unmistakable.

"Succeeded. Huh, from where I'm standing, you two kicked ass." He accepted the glass from the bartender and saluted them before he took a small sip.

"Thank you," Maggie answered, sparing a moment to smile at him before she looked at the text message flashing on her phone. Damn, he was proud of all her hard work. "The VIP lounge is out of martini glasses. You got this, Lena."

Lena slammed her last ounce of wine before she took off at a brisk but still dignified walk. "On it!"

"I saw Ted. He looked totally unaffected by all this." Rick squeezed Maggie's arm and leaned close.

"Yeah, I saw him and thought the same thing. Maybe Evan was wrong about what he saw." She turned back to her cell, and her fingers flew over the screen.

"Could be."

"Thank you for coming." She leaned close and kissed his cheek. "Duty calls." She tipped back the last of her champagne before rushing off to handle the next crisis.

She was gone before he could say goodbye.

He leaned on the bar and watched the flow of people meandering from display to display. A Super Bowl winning quarterback with his pop star girlfriend passed a group of Middle Easterners in traditional dress. And on the other side of the bar, an Asian woman with a dagger-like stare sipped a martini. Wealth was the only common denominator in this eclectic crowd.

Evan wasn't a dumb kid, and Rick believed the kid's instincts were good. Planning a heist took brains and patience. Often, the best robbers, the ones that were the hardest to catch, were the ones that knew when to walk away from a job. This event was a case of too much risk, even for nearly infinite rewards.

He had a hundred dollars that said Earl Whitestone realized that and had walked away.

Maggie carried her low-heeled navy pumps in one hand and her dying cell phone in the other. It was almost two A.M. She'd gotten a text from the loading dock that the last armored truck full of jewels had left the premises. It was done.

She turned toward the champagne bar. Rick and Lieutenant Morris sat on stools with forgotten beers in front of them. They were in the midst of a deep conversation. Around them, crews worked to dismantle the elaborate booths. It would take some vendors over twenty-four hours to fully move out of the convention center.

"Gentlemen." She scooted her tired ass onto the stool Rick offered. Her flip-flops dangled from her tired toes.

"You look like you could use this for medicinal reasons." He pushed his nearly full beer toward her and moved behind her. The way he kneaded the tight muscles in her shoulders was heavenly.

Gratefully, she took a long pull off the beer. So good.

"Well, Lieutenant, looks like that was a big nothing. The loading dock confirmed the last of the valuables have shipped out." She leaned into Rick's massage. The man's hands were magic.

"Not at all. Nothing was stolen. No one was injured. Omaha PD counts it as a win." Morris nodded. Case closed.

"You didn't arrest anyone?" She was grateful nothing happened but also confused.

"In a situation like this, deterrence is a win. We outsmarted them." Morris looked pleased.

"Or outgunned," Rick added. Maggie heard a healthy dose of sarcasm in his tone.

"Yeah, there was enough private security here tonight to overthrow a dictator. And the firepower..." Morris whistled, impressed by the hardware the for-hire soldiers had brought.

"I saw a lot of your guys, too. Especially out front and near the loading dock." Maggie gestured toward the back of the convention center.

"A handful of uniformed cops make people feel safer."

"Maggie!" A shrill voice cut through the noise of the crews working around them.

They all turned to see Cheryl, still dressed in the magenta pink suit she wore for her TV spot with the Delphi Pink Jubilee diamond, picking her way around the men and debris. For the life of her, Maggie couldn't figure out why she would still be here. Rick's hands tightened on her shoulders like he was bracing for the worst.

"Cheryl, what are you doing here this late? Wasn't your broadcast at eleven?" Maggie asked as she accepted a hug and kiss from the reporter. Rick had stepped back as soon as Cheryl swept in, and she missed his touch.

"Why, yes, it was. But my date with Hendrik and his private plane starts when his booth is taken down. He's a diamond dealer from South Africa. Can you believe it?" She gushed and clapped her hands.

"Only you, Cheryl." Maggie started to introduce Morris to Cheryl, but it was unnecessary; the lieutenant was a fan.

Rick resumed his place behind her stool, his dexterous fingers stroking her neck and shoulders. Morris and Cheryl were chatting happily, but Maggie had a hard time following the conversation between her yawns.

"It's late. You're exhausted. Let's go home." Rick's lips grazed her ear as he spoke.

Home sounded like an excellent idea.

"Cheryl, I'm dead on my feet." Maggie interrupted her and Morris to hug her new friend goodbye. She had managed to catch part of Cheryl's broadcast earlier. Under the lights and in front of the camera, Cheryl's personality grew to epic proportions. No wonder she was rapidly becoming one of the most popular local reporters in the city.

Cheryl pulled her in tight and whispered, "Nice work, cowgirl, bringing that stallion to heel."

Maggie, sure she was blushing and yawning at the same time, stepped back enough to look Cheryl in the eye. "I'm calling you for wine and details on Hendrik next week."

"Absolutely. I want to hear all about hot Rick." She gave Maggie a super exaggerated wink.

Morris thanked her and Rick for their assistance and congratulated Maggie on her successful event before she and Rick escaped the exhibit hall.

As soon as they were in one of the deserted staff-only hallways, Rick stopped walking. He turned her to face him.

"I know nothing bad happened. But I worried all night." He wrapped an arm around her waist and buried the other in her updo; hairpins tugged free and fell to the ground. His mouth brushed hers softly—a tease of his lips on hers. He breathed her name, and her heart froze at the emotions layered in that one word.

She arched up into his mouth for more. They stumbled back until she bumped into the rough concrete wall. Fire engulfed them. His kiss turned to a claiming—a branding.

She melted. Her world narrowed. His mouth. His hands. He filled every corner of her mind. She met his tongue thrust for thrust. Gripping at the satin lapel of his black jacket, she let the raw need pouring off Rick sweep her away. She was dizzy with it.

When he finally tore his mouth from hers, they were both breathing hard. He crushed her against his chest, and the beat of his heart resonated through her.

She lifted her head and traced his jawline with a shaky finger. "Stay with me tonight. All night."

His answer was another searing kiss.

Twenty-Seven

"I CAN'T PROMISE ANYTHING, but you should try some." Maggie squeezed a dollop of arnica and chamomile muscle balm into the older woman's hands. The crowds along Eleventh Street were some of the biggest Maggie had seen this summer. The green market was buzzing.

"Even if it doesn't help my arthritis, it smells lovely. Clean, not too flowery." The older woman rubbed the cream over her knobby knuckles.

"I developed it to be a universally appealing scent for men or women." She glanced over at Rick, who was restocking a shelf of bar soaps, her guinea pig for the cream. He swore it worked on his sore muscles. It might help this nice lady as well.

The customer followed Maggie's gaze toward Rick and Evan. "You have a beautiful family."

"I—ah, thank you." She didn't want to explain her not so casual relationship to a grandma that seemed like the type to bake cookies and knit afghans. She couldn't even explain it to herself at this point.

"It's good to see a family support a wife and mother in her endeavors."

Evan swept up some spilled bath salts near the entrance. He shot an angelic gaze toward them, looking for praise of his diligent labor. Like she wasn't bribing him with extra video game time to get him out here helping.

"My son may look supportive now, but at five this morning, when I had to drag him out of bed, he was something else entirely." She poked her tongue out at Evan, and he went back to his sweeping.

"Yes, boys do like to sleep. It's all the growing. It wears them out at that age." She flexed her hands experimentally. "Is there menthol in it?"

"No, it's peppermint. It was Rick's idea to make it feel tingly. Do you like it?"

"Yes. Refreshing...no, not the right word."

"Therapeutic?" Rick offered. The booth wasn't that big, so he'd probably been listening to the conversation from the start. Maggie met his gaze, and he winked.

"Yes, exactly." The lady beamed at Rick. "Handsome and supportive. Reminds me of my Harold. I'll take four of the cream. I'm going to give them to the gals I play bridge with. They'll love it."

As Maggie wrapped up the arnica cream in gift bags, the customer continued to praise her beautiful family. Inside, Maggie couldn't decide if she wanted to cry or wince. She dared a glance at Rick. He didn't look annoyed or concerned about the woman's misconception.

He'd stopped working on the stock and was listening intently, a wrinkle on his normally smooth forehead. He wasn't shying away, running for the hills. Could he be considering more? A flicker of something like hope bloomed in her chest. The same hope she had been careful to snuff out viciously since they began their casual arrangement.

"The love of a good man gives us wings. Don't you agree, dear?" The customer patted Maggie's hand.

Maggie froze and looked at Rick. Their gazes locked. Her heartbeat felt like a bass drum pounding in her ears. The lady's words hung heavy in the air between them. That sentence was a tantalizing dream. The combination of love and support would be magical. A whoop of a police siren caught Rick's attention, and he turned, breaking the spell.

"Wings are lovely," she replied, wondering if she might ever have a pair that wasn't of her own making.

She passed the customer her bags and wished her good luck at bridge that afternoon as she escorted her out of the booth. She stared after the lady's disappearing back for a moment, letting her mind go blank.

"Hey, girl, you look a little funny. You okay?" Lena's one-armed hug startled Maggie out of her thoughts.

"All good. Up way too early this morning is all." Maggie shook off the odd feeling the older lady's comments had left her with and ruthlessly crushed the spark of hope for more with Rick. Lena's visit was a good distraction from her heavy thoughts.

"I bring you the elixir of life." Lena took a mocha latte from the tray she carried and presented it to Maggie with proper pomp and circumstance.

"You are my hero." Maggie savored the first sip, the familiar hit of sweetness drowning the last of her uncomfortable feelings.

"But what if I want to be your hero?" Hector jogged the last few steps to join her and Lena in the booth. He lifted a bag from the French patisserie at the other end of the green market. "I brought baguette sandwiches."

"Okay, you're both heroes. Those sandwiches are awesome." Maggie kissed Hector on the cheek.

"And you are...?" Lena looked Hector up and down like he was a tasty treat. Hector looked good, with a bit of scruff, a well-fitted T-shirt, and cargo shorts that showed off his tan, well-muscled legs.

"Hector. Rick's PT guy. And you must be Lena, the best friend. I've been waiting to meet you." He offered his hand. Lena accepted the friendly gesture with a wide smile.

"Is this a setup?" Lena asked Maggie as soon as she let go of Hector's hand.

Maggie couldn't help but laugh and almost snorted mocha out her nose. It was never a necessity to set up Lena. The woman could hunt down a single man like a bloodhound.

Rick pulled Hector in for a bro hug. The two chatted in Spanish for a moment.

"No. That's uncool, guys." Lena's hands on her hips glared at them. "You guys can't do that. My C-plus in high school Spanish was a really long time ago."

"Ah, chica, hang with me today, and I'll tell you all Rick's secrets. No need to brush up on your Spanish." Hector passed the bag of sandwiches to Rick and tucked Lena under his arm after she gave Rick his coffee. "We're going shopping. See you all later."

Hector paused to high-five Evan and tell him there was a brownie in the sandwich bag for him as he towed a very willing Lena out of the booth.

"I think that might not be a good thing," Rick told her as he watched the new couple walk away.

"I'm not sure who to feel bad for. Us, Hector, or Lena." Maggie moved to help a young couple smelling some of her soaps.

"How was the shopping?" Rick looked at the two bulging bags Hector carried.

"Love this market. I can't believe I've never come here before." Hector began to stroll away from the Lone Tree booth, and Rick followed him into the stream of people on Eleventh Street.

The day was getting hotter, and the crowd was thinning out. Maggie had everything under control with Lena and Evan's help. He glanced back at the booth to be sure. She and Lena were laughing and straightening inventory.

"We should tell the guys at the Latin Caribbean food truck about it. They could rock breakfast out here."

"I'm sure. I hear you and Maggie are rocking it, too." Hector bumped Rick's shoulder with his as they walked.

Rick groaned. Lena probably only got six steps out of earshot before pumping Hector for information.

"Keeping it casual... Yeah, I'm sure the casual thing you've got going is why your mood is better. Regular sex will do that for a guy. Endorphins." Hector shrugged. The careless gesture picked at an invisible wound Rick wasn't sure how to protect.

"It's— Fuck." Rick rubbed his eyes with the heels of his hands. Frustrated, so frustrated.

"It's not casual? Or you don't want it to be? You know what, don't answer that." Hector motioned him toward a small bench next to a flower stand.

Rick sat and consciously relaxed his tight shoulders. If there was ever a moment he could use some Zen advice from his physical therapist guru, it was now. This morning, the little old lady in the booth had painted an idyllic picture of him, Maggie, and Evan as a family. It had messed with his head.

"Stop playing the long game." Hector looked ready to slug him.

"Excuse me?" He shifted on the uncomfortable bench to watch the crowd stream past. Hector's earnest intensity was hard to confront eye to eye.

"You're looking so far into the future you're forgetting to live now, today." Hector jabbed his index finger into his opposite palm, emphasizing the present.

"I need a plan." A plan. A path. A track. Otherwise, he was just floating, bobbing up and down in the sea of life with no direction.

"No, you want a plan. Two different things. It might be time to stop and look around, see what you're missing."

Rick chuckled. "You get that off a fortune cookie?"

Hector rolled his eyes. "No, it's from Ferris Bueller, asshole. But it doesn't mean it's not profound. We all get caught running forward so hard and fast, we miss a lot of opportunities. Take the time to reevaluate."

"But I'm leaving."

"Are you one hundred percent sure there is no version of your future where you stay in Omaha?"

Rick deflated. He could envision that future. God, he could see it. He craved it. But how he could make it a reality was the issue. He had no fucking clue how to leave Miami and all his connections there permanently. And he'd be jobless, too. Not exactly a win-win situation.

"Start with something small and stay in the moment. Tonight, you and Maggie are having a date. A real one. Everything but the flowers are in this bag. Cook, laugh, and forget the future. Lena is going to take Evan for a sleepover."

"I'm not sure I should." He didn't need a *date* with Maggie to know they fit together perfectly, and it felt cruel stringing her along but couldn't stop himself from indulging in her at every opportunity.

"You have to have real things in your life. Your body is healed, but what good is it if you don't have things that give you hope and passion?" Hector stood and gave him a last pat on the back. "Tell Maggie and Lena goodbye. I've got a client this afternoon. I've got to bolt."

Rick picked up the bag Hector had left behind. He wrapped the cloth handles around his fist. Images bombarded him. Mona's house restored.

Maggie cooking barefoot in the kitchen for him and Evan. Her hair spread over his pillow in the morning light.

The pop of one of the canvas straps ripping from the bag pulled him from his thoughts. He rubbed at the red line on his skin where it had abraded his hand.

After the jewelry show, when she'd invited him to sleep over, everything changed. They had gone home and slept tangled together. No sex until the next morning. The slow, soft morning joining of two people barely awake, fumbling and languid, was a stark contrast to the fiery, almost desperate bouts they shared in the past. And the rest of that morning had played out so easy, nothing like that first time when he bolted out of her apartment, forgetting his shoes.

With a sigh, he stood. A huge bunch of sunflowers at the flower stand caught his eye. They would look perfect on the patio table by the barn. He decided to follow Hector's advice and paid for the flowers.

It was dinner. A date. Not him reinventing his entire existence for a woman. Not yet, at least.

A pang of longing rippled through him for what might be. If tonight wasn't about a nice, casual non-relationship with Maggie, then what the hell was it?

He loved a plan, but maybe it was time to toss the plan in the trash and take the opportunity to reevaluate.

Twenty-Eight

"RICK, THIS IS AWESOME. Thank you." Evan could barely stand still waiting for the ticket takers to check their tickets.

"I'm sure your mom would have brought you." Rick passed the stack of tickets for their group to a convention center staff member. The lobby looked completely different today. There were college mascots and balloon arches in place of fresh flowers and white-gloved waiters. The national college swimming championships had arrived in Omaha.

"Maybe. She's not a big fan of coming to work on her day off. And now we have someone to cheer for." Evan looked at his lanyard with athlete family credentials on it like the golden ticket.

"That we do. I've been watching Raul swim since he was younger than you. He's always been fast." Rick glanced nervously over his shoulder. Aunt Irma was ushering Maggie along like a mother hen with a chick. So far, neither one looked traumatized. He hoped that lasted through the day.

"What race is he in?"

"Today, the preliminary heats for the one-hundred-meter and two-hundred-meter fly." Daniel, Raul's father, filled in when Rick couldn't answer.

"Cool. Did you know it took over two weeks and two hundred people to build the two temporary pools?" Evan was fascinated more by the massive temporary swimming pools than the sport. Maggie had already brought him over twice to see the construction.

"Two weeks. That's impressive." Daniel put a hand on Evan's shoulder, steering him around a concrete post he almost slammed into while turned around talking.

It made Rick feel all kinds of weird when Evan had proudly announced he wanted to hang out with the men today. The kid didn't have many male role models in his life. Aunt Irma latched onto the request, using it to foist Evan off on Rick and Daniel. His aunt wanted Maggie all to herself. Shit.

He glanced back at Maggie and caught her eye. She shrugged. He couldn't tell if it was a good shrug or a bad shrug. His family rarely met the women he dated. And what he and Maggie were doing was...complicated.

He'd told Maggie she didn't have to come, but oh no, Maggie had been waiting for them in the lobby when they stepped into the convention center. He wondered if she regretted it...yet. His mother's youngest sister was excellent at prying information out of people. She should have gone to work at the CIA instead of owning a high-end boutique in Bal Harbour.

"Do you swim, Evan?" Daniel asked, checking his ticket against a sign to ensure they were in the right section.

"No. I math."

Daniel raised an eyebrow at Rick, looking for an explanation.

"Evan is a math genius. But he's also got some potential on the soccer field. He and I started working on skills this summer."

"Nice. That was your sport, right?"

"Soccer and debate. One for the body. One for the brain." Rick took Hector's approach when helping Evan learn soccer, balancing mental and physical. For a ten-year-old, he learned strategy incredibly fast. The footwork and ball-handling had a way to go. Nothing practice wouldn't fix if Evan was into it.

"What else does Raul do? You know, for his brain?" Evan asked.

"He starts law school in a few weeks at the University of Miami. So, then he will study." Daniel scooted down a row of seats, and Evan followed on his heels with a million questions about law school.

Rick hung back, indicating that the ladies should go ahead of him, but his aunt would have none of it. She gave him one long look, telegraphing her thoughts on the matter. Aunt Irma was only a little more than ten years older than him but somehow attained the same power his mother had to make all the grown men in their family do her bidding. With a sigh, he left Maggie to her fate and took the seat next to Evan.

"There are over 1.7 million gallons of water in the two pools. The fire department helped the engineers fill them from city hydrants." Evan peered down at the pools. "The decks weren't fully built when I was here last time. They look good."

Over Evan's head, Daniel asked, "How are the house renovations going? Someone in the family mentioned Carlos was helping."

Of course, someone mentioned he needed help from his little cousin. He loved his family, but he forgot how in everything they were—all the damn time.

"He is helping me with a bit of financing and some advice." He launched into a long explanation of the difficulties in getting good labor in Omaha, the lead paint problems, and his plans to sell the old home for top dollar.

"That's a lot of work to put into something to sell it." Daniel stood and waved to Raul who had come out on the pool deck and was doing stretches.

When Raul didn't notice his father, Rick stood. "Evan, cover your ears." Rick put two fingers in his mouth and let an insanely loud whistle fly. It did the trick. Raul shot a pair of thumbs up toward their section. Irma and Daniel waved excitedly to their son. Evan's jaw hung open in shock at Rick's whistle.

Rick ducked behind his aunt to see Maggie. "All good? You surviving?"

She nodded. "When I want a break, I'll take Evan to the concession stand. Until then, I'm loving stories of you as a kid." She reached behind Irma to squeeze his hand.

Maybe he'd take Evan and Maggie to the concession stand and never return.

"Rick, can you teach me to whistle like that?" Evan had two fingers in his mouth trying to make a sound but only managed an odd-sounding raspberry.

"I can try."

Maggie and Irma polished off the last of their popcorn before Raul took his place in the pool for the two-hundred-meter race. In the earlier one-hundred-meter, he finished well within the time for tomorrow's finals.

"This race is harder for him. The longer distance." Irma stood and pulled Maggie and Rick to their feet.

Evan and Daniel were already up. Three. Two. One. Bang. The race started in a flurry of white water. The butterfly was an insane stroke, and the swimmers in the pool below were all incredible athletes. They pounded down the length of the pool and flipped.

"Third, I think he's in third." Irma was holding onto Maggie's arm and jumping up and down.

Nearby, someone was ringing a cowbell for all they were worth.

Irma was a small woman with rich dark hair much like Rick's. She wore a sophisticated emerald-green jumpsuit with an orange sash. Her nod to the University of Miami colors, she had explained. Maggie liked her. She was funny and smart. Watching her stare down Rick over the seating order had been priceless.

With a family like this, no wonder he wanted to stay in Miami. Her family had pretty much written her off after the divorce. Divorce was not acceptable in the Stewart household. Her father was a strict Presbyterian minister, and her failings reflected badly on him. In her least charitable moments, she wondered if he might have told his parishioners she was dead.

Raul was holding his place in third, and they were clapping for him. Irma had a hold of Rick and Maggie, squeezing hard and yelling as Raul kicked it into overdrive for the last quarter of the race.

"He's going to win—he's going to win— He did!" Irma practically crawled over Rick and Evan to hug her husband.

Rick high-fived Evan and stepped over to Maggie. "Are you— Is she— Fuck." He ran a hand down his face.

"Relax, Rick. I like Irma. And she knows all about me and Evan from talking with Mona over the years and vice versa. It's nice to see a family that's so close."

"As long as you're cool with the, ah—"

"Interrogation?"

"Ugh, that bad?" He looked ready to grab her and Evan and run.

"You mother mailed you a tux so you could go to an event with me. Your cousins had a bet going we were eloping to Las Vegas."

Now he looked ready to faint.

"Don't worry. I explained it was an event here at the convention center. She already texted Carlos and the others to pay the winners."

"Carlos thought we were eloping to Vegas." He mumbled a few curses under his breath in Spanish.

"Apparently, you're taking too long fixing up the house. You should slap up some paint and list it already. The only reason he can see you're still here is love." She folded her hands together under her chin and batted her eyelashes up at him like a smitten cartoon character.

"I need a beer."

She straight-up laughed at him. It was fun seeing him squirm. Obviously, his fear of commitment ran deep, and his family must have been pushing him at every eligible woman in South Florida for years. He told his family they were friends, but she didn't think Irma was buying that platonic explanation.

Irma elbowed Rick in the ribs and pushed him back to his original seat with a few terse comments in Spanish. Seeing a woman nearly a foot shorter than Rick push him around was hilarious.

"Now we wait a bit. Raul will text when we can all go down to say hello and leave for dinner. We are on the coach's schedule now. You are joining us for dinner?"

Maggie nodded as she sat back down with Irma. She planned to meet them at the restaurant since she'd worked a half-day and her car was in the employee lot.

"He looks good."

"Raul?" Maggie was confused. Of course her son looked good; he was an elite twenty-year-old athlete. The guy could have been on the cover of a men's fitness magazine with his rippling abs and huge pecs.

"No, Ricardo. When he left Miami, he wasn't good. Body or soul. My sister was sick over it. He survived the bullets, but then he collapsed into himself, ignoring family and friends."

"His healing has been remarkable. His physical therapist, Hector, is incredible."

"Pfft, no, this is more than hours in a gym." Irma turned in her seat and took both of Maggie's hands. "He is almost whole again. Thank you." Irma squeezed her eyes shut and bowed her head a moment.

"No, no, no. I can't take any credit. We're just friends." She pulled her hands back and folded them in her lap.

"Life is complicated, I understand. But whatever part you have played, friend, lover..." She shrugged. "We are grateful. It will be good to have him home again."

Maggie felt her throat close around an almost sob. Irma's thank you was the end of her stupid, crazy delusion that he might stay in Omaha for her. He had all of his people back in Florida and a career. It was time to start pulling back. She wasn't sure how, but soon, she needed to take a big, painful step back from Rick before she couldn't do it with dignity.

She forced a garbled sound that might have been either you're welcome or a thank you from her lips before she turned and pretended to watch the next race start.

Twenty-Nine

SHE'D GIVEN HERSELF A firm talking to and decided that getting either mad or sad about Rick in front of Evan and his aunt was an immature move and beneath her. She was going to dinner with everyone and would have a great time. Laugh, relax, and forget that it was time to disrupt the status quo because she was both an adult and incredibly good at lying to herself about emotional things. Hell, that last fact explained her entire marriage to Ted.

She waved her key fob over the sensor and gained access to the administrative office area. She would only be five or ten minutes behind Rick and the others arriving at the restaurant.

She stopped by Lena's office first and knocked lightly on the door before popping her head inside. "I'm heading out. Dinner with Rick's family is tonight."

"Good luck with that." The sarcasm was thick like pea soup.

Lena managed the swimming event and would be at the convention center until the last of the spectators and competitors left for the night. Most of the rest of the office staff was long gone.

"I like them. And his uncle is Evan's new bestie."

"You and Rick are a train wreck waiting to happen." Lena was possibly more frustrated with the whole casual relationship than Maggie. And true to form, her friend thought the answer was to pressure Rick. Not something Maggie would ever do.

"Night, Lena." Ignoring Lena's comment, she closed the door and headed for her office where her purse, laptop bag, and coffee mug were waiting on her desk. Stepping back was the right answer.

Her office door was cracked open. Odd. She rarely left her door ajar. She pushed it open the rest of the way.

"Where the fuck are your keys?" Ted had every drawer on her desk open, and he'd dumped office supplies and files all over the floor in his frantic search.

"Ted? Why are you in my office? In my desk?" She marched toward her ex, ready to kick his ass.

"Why couldn't you leave your keyring in your purse or desk like a normal human? Where are they?"

"Like hell, I'm giving you my keys." Her shitty car might have been shitty, but it was hers.

He stalked around the desk and, without warning, backhanded her hard enough she tasted blood. The side of her face felt like it was on fire. When she reached up to cradle her injured cheek, he grabbed her right hand and cruelly twisted the keyring from her index finger with a grip so hard she worried it might break her wrist. Her cell phone dropped to the carpet at her feet.

Ted was a liar and asshole, but he had never been violent like this. She brought up her knee, hoping to catch him in the balls. He shoved her back and put his other hand around her throat, pinning her to the wall.

"You bitch, sleeping with an FBI agent, trying to take my kid. You thought I'd let it happen. Fuck you. It all changes today." His eyes were bloodshot, and she could smell booze on his breath.

"Take my car. I don't care. Take it." She tried to wiggle free of his hold, but his fingers tightened at her throat, trapping her breath. No air. She couldn't scream. Panicked, she raked her nails over his wrists and tried to pry his fingers away.

"Bring her and her keys." The sharp command cut through the blood pounding in her ears.

Ted loosened his grip, and she gulped in a shaky breath.

The older man from the Peppermint Pony stood inside her office wearing a blue convention center staff polo shirt. The guy Rick said was the real owner of the pawnshop. Maggie yanked away from Ted; she wasn't going anywhere with them.

She edged toward her desk. If she could push two buttons on her office phone, she'd have the security desk on the line.

"Earl, I got her." Ted grabbed her upper arm. She fought against him, and he pinned her to his chest, one hand covering her mouth. She tried to scream anyway. The pathetic muffled sound wasn't enough to draw anyone's attention.

"Enough." Earl calmly pulled a sleek black gun and pressed it under her chin. The touch of the cold steel sent shivers racing over her skin. "I need your palm print, not you. You walk quietly with him, or I get that paper cutter in the copy room, and I'll take what I need. Your choice, lady."

Terror made her nod. Earl's dead eyes and flat tone made her sure he wasn't bluffing. Earl took her keys from Ted and opened the office door.

Her office was one of the last in the hallway. Ted half dragged, half carried her the ten or fifteen steps to the emergency stairwell. No alarm sounded when Earl pressed the door open. It must have been disabled.

The stairwell was brightly lit, cavernous, and rarely used. The convention center installed the door alarms after too many employees had been caught using the roof for smoke breaks during the day. No one would be stumbling in to save her accidentally.

Maggie tripped, and Ted let her fall. Her desperate grab for the handrail saved her from falling down the entire flight of stairs. Pain shot up her legs from her skinned knees.

"Watch your step." Ted's cruel laugh filled the stairwell. He grabbed her arm and pulled her to her feet. Fear froze her in place.

"Keep moving. Or next time, I'll tell him to give you a push." Earl pointed down the stairs with the gun.

Trembling, she picked her way down the concrete steps. It was like navigating in a dream. Her limbs were wooden and time totally distorted. Her mind flashed through a million scenarios, trying to understand what was happening. Earl wanted her palm print for access. Somewhere she could get that a janitor couldn't.

Somewhere with something valuable. Money. Cash.

The concession stand revenue... The vault. Shit.

Every dollar spent on food and drinks during the championships went into locked cash register drawers That were transferred to the cash room before going in the vault to await pickup by an armored truck. Hundreds of thousands of dollars in cash. Untraceable cash.

When they reached the bottom of the stairs, Ted grabbed her and slapped his hand over her mouth. Earl eased the door open and looked out. Maggie tried to twist free, but Ted's grip was unforgiving.

"All clear. Bring her." Earl pulled a ball cap from his back pocket and tugged it on.

The stairs ended in a seldom-used service hall not far from the vault. Earl's gun as much as Ted's rough handling kept her walking. She desperately needed a plan of her own if she wanted to get out of this. The sound of their footsteps echoed through the quiet part of the building.

A pair of men dressed in convention center security guard uniforms leaned on a wall next to a door that required a key fob for entry. Maggie didn't recognize either man. It was now her against four men.

"Any problems grabbing her?" one of the guards asked.

"None." Earl waved her fob over the sensor and sent the two guards ahead. A few moments later, they returned.

"The security cameras are adjusted like you told us to point at the ceiling." The guard with the prominent gold tooth waved them into the room.

"Perfect." Earl and Ted dragged her forward. The room they were in was a secondary security office. It was used occasionally during larger events when they wanted a command center closer to the arena floor. The swimming championships weren't an event that called for that kind of security, so the room was empty.

The office had a few desks with chairs, and at the back was another door that Maggie knew led to the cash room...and then the vault.

Her palm would open the cash room but not the vault. The vault was on a time lock. Drawers could be put into the vault, like a night deposit at any bank. But the vault only opened at a scheduled time when the Brinks truck arrived to pick up the money.

"Time to get changed." Earl dropped his backpack on the ground and took out a pale blue shirt that looked like the Brinks security guards' uniforms. "Tie her to a chair or something. Until we need her hand."

Ted's grip loosened as he glanced around the room, deciding where to restrain her.

This was her only chance. Once she was tied up, she would be totally at their mercy. She yanked violently to the left and rushed toward the emergency fire alarm pull on the wall. The red handle called her like a beacon of hope.

"Stop her," Earl barked.

The guard with the gold tooth was first to react. His hand landed between her shoulder blades, propelling her forward with all his body weight. The last thing she saw before her head smashed into the cinder block wall was the fire alarm pull just out of her reach. Pain and blackness engulfed her as she crumpled to the floor.

Rick had called and texted Maggie. No reply. The tracking app on her phone showed it was at the convention center. Thankfully, Evan knew Lena's cell number and rattled it off for him when asked.

Rick excused himself from the table to call Lena. He didn't want to worry Evan, especially if it was something as simple as car trouble. Maggie's shitty car was the simplest explanation for why she hadn't shown up at the restaurant yet. Car trouble... and cell phone trouble. What were the odds?

He had a bad feeling about this.

"Lena, are you still at work? It's Rick."

"Maggie's casual friend Rick?" A thick layer of snark coated every syllable.

"Are you still there?" He didn't have time to unruffle Lena's ruffled feathers. Not if the bad feeling he was having was prophetic.

"Yeah."

"Can you go see if Maggie is in her office?"

"She shouldn't be. She left a while ago. Let me double-check." Her aggrieved sigh came through the phone loud and clear.

Rick cursed under his breath as he waited for Lena to make her way to Maggie's office.

"She isn't here at the restaurant. I have Evan, and she's not answering her cell," he explained.

"Shit." Lena's breathing changed. She must have started jogging toward Maggie's office after Rick clarified the situation. "Oh, God, Rick! Her office is a disaster. Her purse and cell are on the ground, and papers are flung everywhere."

"Do you have a window? Can you see the employee parking lot?" He whispered a silent prayer that Lena would see Maggie next to her old Honda kicking a flat tire.

"Hold on."

Again, he heard Lena's loud breathing as she jogged through the office. It felt like it was taking her forever to find a fucking window.

"Her car is out there, but she's not. Shit. What do we do now?" Lena's voice was shrill with panic.

"You call security. I'm coming. I'll call when I get there so you can let me in the employee entrance."

He ended the call and raced through the restaurant, nearly taking out a waiter with a full tray. He needed to get out of there, but first, he had to explain what was going on without freaking out Evan. At the table, he switched to Spanish to talk with his aunt, uncle, and Raul.

"I have to go. Maggie's car is still at the convention center, but her office has been ransacked. Please have dinner and take Evan with you to the hotel if you don't hear from me. I don't want to scare him if there is a reasonable explanation for all this." It was a shitty way to keep Evan in the dark but efficient.

After a beat, Irma gave him a nod. "We have him. Go find her."

Daniel clapped him on the back.

"Evan, your mom's got a problem at work. I'm going to see if I can help her with it. You cool with staying with my family?" Rick tried to keep his expression and tone mild.

"Ah, sure. Is it her car?"

"Maybe, I think so." Rick hated lying, but time was of the essence.

"After dinner, we can check out the hotel pool," Raul offered to distract Evan. "I'll give you a few pointers so you can swim extra fast."

Rick was already headed for the door when Evan replied, "Awesome."

The drive to the convention center was a total blur. He broke every speed limit and traffic law and didn't give a shit about it. His used SUV's brakes were practically smoking by the time he pulled up to the twelve-foot-tall razor-wire fence around the employee parking area and back of the convention center.

He parked his SUV in the fire lane and leaped out as he called Lena to meet him.

"Lena, I'm here. Come let me in."

"On my way." She sounded breathless but more in control.

Rick started pacing the length of the fence. At the corner, he glanced down the well-lit alley behind the convention center. A few hundred feet away, a Brinks armored truck idled at the loading dock. Two men stood guard while others loaded the truck with rolling metal carts. The kind banks and casinos used to move trays of cash.

Rick ducked back around the corner so the guards couldn't see him. Something about the situation looked off. It was the guards with the rifles watching the alley. They were wearing convention center uniforms. Not once at the jewelry Show had he seen a convention center guard with a firearm. And definitely not with something like an AR-15 assault rifle.

The two men who had been rolling the cash carts into the truck made another trip, but the second man carried an unconscious woman. Despite the odd yellow glow of the security lights, he knew that dirty blond hair was Maggie's.

The fake convention center security guards jumped into the truck's cab, and one of the other men started closing the back doors getting ready to pull away. Rick bolted for his SUV in the fire lane.

"Rick?" Lena shouted from the employee entrance as he ran past.

"It's an armored truck robbery. They took Maggie." He didn't slow down. He yanked open his car door and slammed the SUV into drive. He jumped the curb, whipping a U-turn, and took off toward the loading dock exit on Meca Drive. He could see the Brinks truck making the turn ahead of him.

He fumbled for his cell phone and dialed 9-1-1. As it rang, he reminded himself to relax, detach. Do his job. They didn't know he was following them, and for Maggie's safety, it had to stay that way.

"What is the nature of your emergency?"

"I've witnessed a robbery at the convention center—a Brinks armored truck. The suspects are well armed and have at least one potential hostage. I'm following them on Cass Street going west."

"Sir, don't attempt to be a hero. Stay well back. Omaha PD will handle this." The dispatcher's voice was firm and controlled.

"No offense, but I'm an FBI agent. Please connect me to officers en route." Talking to a 9-1-1 dispatcher was not efficient. It would end up like the law enforcement version of the telephone operator game kids played with her trying to relay messages to him.

"Sir, I'm not sure I can do that. Hold."

The line crackled in his ear. He flipped on the speakerphone and dropped the cell in the cupholder. The Brinks truck lumbered through the city traffic, obeying every law. The truck angled for the on-ramp to the interstate. Shit.

He followed onto the highway, careful to keep a few cars between him and the truck. His fingers ached where he gripped the steering wheel, and he wouldn't let himself think about Maggie. Dead and unconscious looked pretty damn similar from a few hundred feet away.

"This is officer Staub. Who am I speaking to?"

"Agent Rick Cabrera. I'm FBI in Miami. I witnessed a robbery at—"

"The convention center. Brinks and convention center security have called it in. You're following the truck?" The cop on the line sounded like a veteran. Solid and experienced.

"Yeah, I just got on Interstate 480. Doesn't Brinks have GPS on this fucking thing?" He needed backup and a fucking plan. He didn't even have a gun in the car. Why would he? He was at a swim meet.

"The GPS has been disabled."

"We're merging to go south."

"Understood. Units are scrambling to you. Give me the exit and mile marker numbers as you pass them."

Rick relayed each number, then waited as Staub communicated it to the other officers. It felt like it was taking hours for the cops to get close. With every mile, he worried more about Maggie.

"Staub, they're changing lanes. Signal on. Exiting here."

Rick followed, thankfully managing to keep another car between him and the truck on the off-ramp. The unfamiliar neighborhood was mostly older commercial buildings with few streetlights.

"Update?" Staub demanded details. His voice on the speakerphone was loud enough to make Rick jump.

"It's a quiet industrial area. I won't be able to tail them long. There's no traffic to hide behind."

The truck rolled down the narrow street. Two and three-story brick warehouses lined both sides of the road. The truck turned and stopped in front of a roll-up garage door that looked about a hundred years old—rusty and graffiti-covered.

"They're stopping at a warehouse with a vehicle entrance." Rick rattled off the building number and rolled past. Craning his neck, he saw the passenger in the Brinks truck hop out to open the roll-up door.

"Units are one minute out."

Rick turned left and cruised around the other side of the building, checking out the warehouse. Despite the rusty door and graffiti, it was a solid structure. Getting in would be a problem. It was a fortress. He turned left again, following the perimeter of the building.

In the distance, he could hear police sirens. "Staub, are they coming in with lights and sirens? There's a hostage." Un-fucking-believable.

It was too late. The sirens were everywhere. The shrill screams bounced off the brick buildings and seemed to amplify in the narrow, deserted streets.

He slammed on the brakes. Camouflaged to match the orange-red brick of the building was a second garage door. This one was likely directly across from the one the truck entered through. And at that moment, he knew. It was the escape hatch.

Rick whipped the car into reverse and hopped the curb so he could block the second door before the rats trapped inside scurried out. Staub's cursing became indistinct white noise that he ignored while maneuvering into place.

Two cruisers pulled to a stop in the road and killed their sirens. Rick scooped up his phone and got out of the SUV nice and slow. Hands up. The red and blue glow of their police lights flicked across his white shirt.

"Staub, I'm on the backside of the building. I have two units here. Please advise them not to shoot me. I just got out of my SUV." Rick shouted toward the phone he held above his head.

The officers were still in their cars, but that didn't stop nervous sweat from breaking out across his body at the idea they could have guns drawn. He resisted the urge to rub a hand over his chest. His scar burned and tingled.

"Copy that." Staub's voice came to him from far away, barely audible over his pounding pulse.

Rick had taken half a dozen steps when an enormous crash and the sound of twisting metal and breaking glass came from behind him. He spun to see his SUV T-boned by the Brinks truck. Son of a bitch. The adrenaline already flooding his veins short-circuited his brain.

He felt like he was experiencing the events from outside his body. His training, situational awareness, and focus disappeared. Basic animal instinct took over. He wasn't the cool, seasoned agent he'd trained to be.

Four cops, guns drawn, rushed past him toward the truck, yelling for the robbers to surrender. Rick stumbled, then followed them. No gun. No vest.

"Now!" Staub shouted over and over. Not to Rick but to his officers.

Seconds later, Rick heard a battering ram take out the other roll-up door. The truck was surrounded on all sides. He moved closer, following in the cop's footsteps. The front axle on the vehicle looked broken, and smoke billowed from the cracked engine block.

He circled back around the wreck, closer than was smart. The cops with guns drawn were on edge, ready to fire.

He desperately wanted a look inside that truck. He needed to know Maggie was alright. He put Staub on mute. The officer wasn't talking to him anyway.

An entrance door to the right of the smashed garage door swung open. Two uniformed cops rushed out. Rick bolted for the door. It was a way inside and that much closer to Maggie.

The interior of the warehouse was filled with the smell of smoke from the smoldering truck. In the dimly lit space, more than a dozen cops, guns drawn, waited to see if the smoke would be enough to drive the robbers out of the truck.

Rick edged closer, and an officer grabbed his arm. "Far enough, Agent Cabrera."

"Staub?" He blinked. The stern and familiar voice cut through his single-minded determination to find Maggie at any cost.

The cop nodded. "You need to stay back."

"The hostage—" Rick started forward, but at Staub's signal, two younger officers grabbed his arms. He pulled against their hold but knew he wasn't going to win this battle. His rash behavior could get him killed. He was a complete idiot. He'd been trained to know better than to rush into this type of situation.

The seconds ticked by, each one slower than the one before.

"I've got movement," someone on the other side of the truck shouted.

Then the back and driver's side doors popped open. Smoke billowed out. Ted, wearing a Brinks uniform, fell out the back coughing. The cops swept in to collect the bad guys. Rick shrugged off his keepers and rushed for the truck.

An officer was already pulling Maggie from the back of the vehicle. She was pale and not moving. Blood stained the side of her face. Rick helped carry her from the vehicle and gently lay her on the warehouse floor. She was still, so still. It made him want to pummel Ted and the others.

He stroked her hair back from her face and leaned closer. A puff of her breath feathered over his cheek. He pressed his fingers to her throat and found a pulse. It was strong and steady. Thank God.

She gasped and coughed softly. It was the sweetest sound he'd ever heard.

"She needs an ambulance. And oxygen." He looked at the cop who helped carry her out of the truck.

"Already on the way," the officer told him.

He threaded his fingers through hers and lifted her hand to his lips for a kiss. He could feel the rush of adrenaline ebbing now that she was safe.

The cops had the three robbers lined up in handcuffs. It was Ted and the two lackeys from the pawnshop: Jameson Green and Nelson Myer. Earl

Whitestone was missing. That slippery son of a bitch.

Thirty

GRATEFUL FOR THE MOMENT to relax, Maggie took the cup of tea Rick offered. On her day off, she had spent the morning talking to the District Attorney. She was the key witness in the convention center robbery.

"How bad was it?" Rick slid a plate of her chocolate chip cookies across Mona's kitchen table toward her. She'd made them last week, before the robbery. It seemed like a lifetime ago.

"The DA is nice enough. Persistent. She asked about a million questions and most of them twice. Earl Whitestone must have some kind of control over Ted and the two other guys because they aren't talking. So I'm it. I'm the key to the entire case." She sighed and took a huge bite of the cookie. Comfort in carbohydrate form. It wasn't even stale.

"Did they say anything about arresting Whitestone soon?"

"No, but they did say without me, they wouldn't have identified him from the tapes. The guy did an excellent job hiding from the security cameras and has some kind of alibi."

"A guy that dirty only stays out of jail because he's smart. Too smart." Rick reached over and squeezed her forearm gently.

He'd been doing more incidental touching since the robbery. And he'd spent every night since sleeping in her bed. Casual had transformed into something that looked like a relationship. Not that they'd talked about it. Nor had she tried pulling back as she planned.

"I hate that this thing is going to drag on for like a year. On TV, it's crime, arrest, and trial all in one hour."

"Trust me; real life is nothing like television. I could tell you horror stories from the FBI. Judges and courts are nothing but delays and frustrations." His forehead wrinkled at the memory.

"Okay, enough about the robbery for today. I can already tell it's going to suck up more hours of my life than I have to give." She had no problem testifying and wanted to see all these guys in jail. Even her ex. But her role as the star witness was another weighty responsibility added to her busy life.

"You sure you're up for this today? It can wait." Rick pulled a calculator and a few files from a bag on the seat next to him as he talked.

"Bring it on. I'm all for a distraction." She reached toward the pile of home improvement and design magazines stacked in the middle of the table.

"This is what I like." He passed her a folder.

She opened it and flipped through the magazine pages that he'd torn out and saved. His choices had a chic modern farmhouse aesthetic sure to appeal to high-end buyers.

"Here is my budget and what Kevin says I can afford. You were so great at picking the paint color. I wanted your help."

She looked at the economics. Damn, that was a lot of zeros. And not anything close to the total reno Rick envisioned. She reached for a home improvement magazine with a title article about remodeling for less. Because that was what the house needed. When she flipped it open, a hand-drawn floor plan fell out.

The drawing was of the kitchen, completely reimagined. Two walls were gone, the sink was relocated to an oversized island, and a huge pantry spanned the far wall. It was a hell of a good use of space. It would be gorgeous.

"Is this yours or Kevin's?" She turned the drawing so Rick could see it.

"Mine. I switched to home improvement shows from food ones. And that is the dream, the wholly unaffordable dream. Instead, we're going to put some lipstick on this pig and sell her on down the road like my cousin Carlos keeps saying."

Move on down the road, like Rick would do as soon as he sold Mona's house. The soulless assessment of the situation struck a painful chord.

"Alright. So no walls get ripped out. No plumbing gets moved."

"Exactly." Rick looked totally unhappy with the compromise that he needed to make.

She went back to the suggested plan from Kevin. It was a minor facelift. Giving the house a mild update from top to bottom. Being on a budget sucked—she would know.

"What if you skipped the basement? Just do the lead paint removal and nothing else down there. Look how much you can save." She pointed to a dollar figure for the renovation of her apartment on the estimate. It was a big number. There were two bathrooms and a kitchen down there.

"Your apartment? No." He stood up and paced the length of the kitchen a few times. "I'm not going to leave you living in the past when the new owners won't care to fix it up. You deserve to get your space remodeled. It's the least I can do."

He was agitated, pacing and running a hand through his hair. It was like he had a visceral desire to fix up her part of the house. Poor, misguided man.

She caught his arm as he passed by her, stopping him in his tracks. "Once the garden is ripped out, I can't stay here. I've already started looking for another place. I might have to go farther out of town, but I'll figure it out. You wouldn't be fixing up the apartment for me."

"You can't move out of this neighborhood. You love it here. And Evan has friends. The park across the way is so great."

He wasn't telling her anything she didn't already know.

"I'll find a new neighborhood. Evan will make new friends." She shrugged.

He was back pacing the room, his fist clenched at his side.

"Rick, forget about the basement. Make this kitchen a showplace, and it will sell the house." She had to fight back tears at the end of her statement.

This house shouldn't belong to some yuppies too lazy to do their own renovation. Why couldn't he see that? He should understand this house had been in Mona's family, his family, since it was built. He was throwing away a legacy for money. It didn't need lipstick and a half-ass renovation; it needed love.

He moved to her side and crouched down. He cupped her jaw and smoothed his thumb over her flushed cheek. "I thought... I wanted to give you something for when I'm gone. If I don't do the basement for you, what can I do when I leave?"

His eyes searched her face, practically begging her for an answer.

She couldn't do this anymore. She wanted to scream at him, *don't leave*. Tell him to stay and build a life with her in this house. This was her last chance at stepping back with dignity. It was now or never. She squashed her angry, frustrated words back down and sucked in an unsteady breath. It was time.

"When you leave, I'll manage like I always have, Rick. Me and Evan." She turned away from his beautiful face and his confused eyes. She found the dream kitchen floorplan and put it on top of all the papers spread across the scarred table.

"Do this, and you'll be rid of this place in no time." She wiped away the tears that rolled down her cheeks.

She stood and stepped back so he couldn't touch her. She might crumble if he did. And all the things she shouldn't say would come flying out. She would tell him all of it, and most of all, she would beg him to stay. And begging was something she would never, ever do. No matter how much she wanted him in her life.

She gathered up her dignity and fled the house.

The sound of the front door slamming reverberated through the empty house. In a trance, he plopped into the chair Maggie had been using. He swept all the papers and magazines off the table and onto the floor.

Life sucked.

He'd healed up, but what fucking good was it when he didn't have what it took to be a field agent? The way he behaved at the warehouse after the robbery proved that. He couldn't go back to the FBI. It wasn't part of him anymore.

He dropped his head onto the tabletop. The wood warmed instantly under his cheek, and the smell of his grandmother's wood polish filled his nose. He stroked the wood; his fingers found one of the hundreds of small nicks that gave the table its character.

He hated that he didn't have the money to give the house the renovation it deserved.

Deserves. It's a house, an investment. One that hasn't earned him a dime. Yet he felt guilty that he wasn't the proper steward of its future. That guilt kept him from firing Kevin and finding a cheap, low-quality contractor to do the work. Every time his cousin Carlos reminded him the house was a flip, he cringed.

And Maggie... God, he'd fucked that up. She hadn't just walked out of the house. No, she closed the door on whatever they'd been doing. It was over.

He should never have touched her. If he'd stayed away, all this would have been less whatever the fuck it was. Confusing. Painful. Debilitating.

He should have stayed the heartless dick of a landlord that didn't care about her or Evan. He should have dropped off eviction papers and hired some half-ass reno team and gone directly back to Miami where he belonged.

The house, Omaha, the people in this stupid charming neighborhood, they had all grown on him. They wormed their way into his heart—the best, nicest fungus in the world. For God's sake, he smiled every time he went up the stairs and the sixth step creaked under his foot.

It was pathetic. In love with a house he was selling and a woman he was...he was—fuck, he didn't even know.

He picked the dream kitchen design up off the ground. Maybe if he left the sink where it was and only took out one wall, he could afford it.

He laughed. Pathetic. Fixing this kitchen wouldn't fix his life.

The idea of not fixing up the basement for Maggie and Evan hurt. If she ripped out her garden as she promised, she would move. He wanted to think about her here in this house when he was gone. Making sure the lavender bushes were trimmed and the front porch parties kept happening.

Shit. He'd counted on her being here, staying in this house to ease his guilt about selling it to strangers.

Guilt was the only thing he had in excess. He had enough to drown under the weight of it.

He laid his hand in the center of the kitchen plan and crunched it up into a wad in his fist. Anger at all of it bled through him. Anger like he hadn't felt since leaving Miami.

A chime on his phone turned his head. Thank you, technology, a distraction. His run-tracking app notified him that he was behind on his weekly goal. Perfect. That he could handle. He shoved out of the chair and went to find his running shoes. A punishing workout might get his head sorted out.

Thirty-One

"HEY, KEVIN, GOOD TO see you." Rick shook his contractor's hand.

"Good to see you too. We're all ready to get the lead handled. Thanks for emailing over the paint choices. Although getting Maggie's help last time was fun." Kevin gave Rick one of those smirks that said he liked checking out Maggie's ass in her shorts, not that he gave a fuck about paint colors.

"Speaking of, let me go tell her your team is ready to get started." Rick wanted to put some space between him and Kevin before he did something stupid. Maggie wasn't his and never had been, but he still itched to punch Kevin for thinking about her like that. Hell, he should try and set them up. Kevin was good-looking, made great money, and wasn't leaving Omaha.

Rick wiped his hands on his jeans before he knocked on the apartment door. While he waited for her to answer, he tried to school his features into something calm, relaxed, and normal when he felt none of those things. Since she left him sitting at the kitchen table surrounded by home improvement magazines a few days ago, they had been avoiding each other.

No accidental on-purpose meetings on the front porch. No sharing a drink while watching Evan play with the neighborhood kids across the way in the park. No invites to dinner. And definitely no nights tangled together in her bed. He ached to feel her under him one more time or to wake up with her cuddled into his chest.

Logically, he knew their time together would be finite. That was the agreement, but the jarring way she ended it sent him into a tailspin of regret. He hadn't been prepared for the emptiness left behind.

The door opened, and he thought she might have been happy to see him for a split second. But then the light in her eyes dimmed, and her lips thinned.

"Kevin's guys are ready to get started. I thought you might want to hear what he has to say." He shoved his hands into his pockets.

She nodded and slipped out the door, careful not to accidentally brush against his chest as she passed. All the same, he caught a whiff of her distinctive smell. And all he could think about was burying his face in her neck and pulling her close.

He followed her to the front porch where Kevin leaned on the rail, waiting for them

Kevin made a big deal of shaking her hand and kissing her cheek. And Rick ground his teeth, watching them smile at each other and exchange pleasantries. Why did the one honest contractor in Omaha have to be so good looking?

"You are both lucky. The lead is only in the original sections of the house that weren't renovated in the last fifty years. That's most of the basement apartment and the formal sitting room, dining room, and living room in the main house. Not too bad." He shrugged. "It will take the crew three or four days to get the work done."

On the front lawn, his guys were donning hazmat suits and unloading equipment.

Evan trooped around the corner from the apartment dragging a rolling suitcase. Rick rushed to help him.

"Hi, Rick." Evan smiled and held up a fist for a bump. It was their thing.

"Evan, did you watch the MLS game last night?" Rick bumped his knuckles against Evan's. He had turned Evan on to major league soccer to teach him some skills.

"The Dallas midfielder is amazing!"

Rick nodded and sat the suitcase down at the base of the front porch steps. Maggie and Kevin were still talking.

"You've met Kevin, right?" he asked Evan.

"Yep, when they did the roof."

"Cool, I'm going to see if he needs anything before we all head out."

Evan nodded and took a seat on the last step after Rick climbed up.

"I moved all our stuff and the small furniture to the barn. Your guys are doing the big stuff, right?" Maggie had one hand on her hip and her head cocked. The pale skin of her exposed neck called to him. He wanted to drag his lips over the soft skin, catch it between his teeth, taste her one more time.

"Absolutely. When you get back, your place will be all freshly painted and like we were never here." Kevin smiled and patted Maggie on the shoulder, his hand lingering longer than Rick liked.

"That's great. I'm glad I never got around to taking down that old wallpaper in the hall. I had no idea there was lead paint under it."

"Lead paint is always a concern in these old homes. Breathing in the dust is a real hazard." Kevin touched Maggie's arm...again. His concern about her respiratory health seemed excessive in Rick's opinion.

"It must be." Maggie pointed at the workers putting on hazmat suits next to a panel van parked in the street.

"We take all the precautions."

"That's great. I'm sure your employees are thankful." Rick interjected before turning to Maggie. Kevin got the hint, and with a nod, headed toward his crew.

"You're sure Lena is cool with you staying at her place? I can call my hotel and book extra rooms for you and Evan."

Maybe they could have dinner together and work out the mess between them. If he could find the words to explain how his life was in shambles and what she meant to him, he could fix some of this weirdness.

"It's fine. We'll be close to Evan's school."

Nothing was fine when a woman told you it was fine. Even a dumbass like him knew that.

"Lena has a big old house a lot like this one. And Evan is with his dad for the weekend." She looked down at her son, her worry easy to see and understand.

"Are you kidding me?" Ted just got out of jail. Rick wanted to pull her close and tell her it would be okay. But he had lost that privilege.

"The family court judge said he's innocent until proven guilty and said I had to obey the visitation agreement. I still can't believe his parents put up bail money for him." Her shoulders sagged with defeat.

He wished he could do something, anything to help.

Thirty-Two

HIS HOTEL ROOM WAS fine. He'd stayed in worse and better. Rick reached for his red tie lying on the cheap faux-wood dresser and looped it around his neck. He wasn't sure how formal lawyers in Omaha were, but a suit and tie were always a better choice than jeans in this kind of situation.

The feel of the silk sliding through his fingers reminded him of blindfolding Maggie, how she'd trusted him and offered up her vulnerability to cope with his insecurity. He might never put on a tie again without thinking about that afternoon. Fuck, he had it bad. He looped one end of the tie over the other and started on the knot.

He was meeting with Mona's lawyer, Jacob Hansen. Hansen's office had called him yesterday to make the appointment right after he'd checked in to the hotel. He had a vague memory of Hansen telling him to stop by the office, but it had been a while ago. Before all the crazy shit with the robbery. And before he and Maggie had started their, er—fling. He wasn't sure what else to call it other than over.

The suit and tie looked good, felt good. He wore one to work every day in Miami when he had a job. And a purpose.

The beep of an incoming call on his cell pulled him away from the depressing thoughts of his future.

"This is Cabrera."

"Rick, it's Lena. Is Maggie with you?"

An awful sense of déjà vu filled him hearing the anxiety in Lena's voice.

"No, she's with you."

"Shit. She went to drop Evan off at Ted's and hasn't come back."

"So you called me?" He bit back the curse that was on the tip of his tongue. Maggie shouldn't have been anywhere near Ted.

"I thought—I hoped..." Lena sighed. "She was pissed at you, Ted, and the family court judge. Oh, hell, men in general. She left to drop off Evan and told me to open a bottle of wine and have Kill Bill ready on Netflix when she got back. I kind of hoped she had called you to chew you out, and you pulled your head out of your ass and apologized. That you told our girl how much she meant to you and that you were going to figure out a way to have a real relationship with her. And the make-up sex was why she had her phone off."

"Her phone is off, and Ted has Evan? No way. She never turns her phone off when Evan is with his dad." Rick's blood chilled in his veins. Maggie was careful to never leave Evan without a way to contact her when he was with Ted.

"Should we call 9-1-1?"

"I'll call the lieutenant I know. He might be more helpful than 9-1-1. How long has she been gone?"

"Just over an hour."

That was the only good news so far.

"Do you know where Ted lives?"

"Unfortunately. I'll text you the address."

Rick hung up and moved to the small safe under the television. He keyed in the combination and pulled out his M&P and half a box of ammo. He closed his hand around the gun still in the holster and pushed down the fear that tried to immobilize him.

He straightened his tie and rushed from the room.

In his new rental car, he dialed Lieutenant Morris as he drove toward Ted's apartment.

"Morris." The curt greeting made Rick think he caught Morris at a bad time. Oh well.

"It's Rick Cabrera. Maggie, your star witness, is missing and last seen with Ted Kurtz, one of the suspects in the convention center robbery."

"She's not my anything. I didn't catch that case. But tell me what's going on."

Rick ran through what Lena told him but had little hope based on Morris's attitude.

"An hour? You want a missing person report on a responsible adult who's only been out of contact for an hour. Look, I'll go find the detective on the Brinks truck robbery and get him to call you, but we're going to need more."

Rick let Morris keep talking, but he didn't listen. The sniveling, puffed-up bureaucrat wasn't going to help. Morris and the other detective would still be eating doughnuts and scratching their balls while he handled this on his own.

"Yeah, I'll wait for that call from the detective." Rick clicked off the phone. He pulled into Ted's apartment complex and started searching for building numbers. It was one of those complexes where every building looked like the one next to it. All beige paint and brown trim.

He found a visitors spot right in front of Ted's ground-floor unit. He shut off the engine and reached for the M&P in the glove box. The expected wave of discomfort at touching the gun came with a sense of resolve. He opened the action and checked the chamber. He was loaded and ready.

If Ted had hurt Maggie or Evan, he wouldn't hesitate to act.

Ted yanked open his front door before Rick had the chance to knock. He stepped across the threshold and closed the door behind him. Never a slick dresser, Ted looked worse than usual in an old T-shirt with holes and bleach stains. It hung over the waistband of his ratty jeans. He hadn't shaved in days.

"I'm here to see Maggie and Evan." Rick stood his ground, hands hanging at his side.

"Yeah, bet you are, Mister F-B-I. Ain't happening." Ted rocked back and forth on his heels, giddy he got to tell Rick to fuck off.

"Are they both here?"

"My son is inside, and we're going fishing tomorrow. He's a great kid."

The offhand comment about the fishing trip was odd. Rick wondered if Ted was drunk or high.

"Maggie?" He flexed his fingers, the urge to grab Ted and rough him up growing with every moment.

"That bitch isn't here. She's gone...long gone." He cackled with disturbing glee.

That was it. Rick grabbed the stretched-out shirt with both hands and shoved Ted against the brick building, making sure his skull thumped hard on the wall.

"Gone where, Ted?" Rick leaned in close to intimidate the smaller man. He took a whiff, and while Ted did need a shower, he didn't smell like booze.

"Where she can't cause any more problems. It was unnatural how she always kept me from my boy."

"Where?!" Rick shook Ted, trying to rattle some useful information out of him.

"Fuck you, FBI. She's gone. And I'm going to walk free. Thanks again, making sure the cops heard about our jewelry show plan in advance."

"That was a setup?"

"A little misdirection so we could test the security." Ted laughed in his face.

Rick let go of Ted before he did something regrettable, like choking him to death with his bare hands.

"Give me Evan." He hated the idea of leaving Evan with Ted.

"Not happening. My son, the court says so. Back the fuck off. Or I'm calling the cops. Now get off my property."

Rick took two steps back, rigid with impotent fury. He couldn't force Ted to give him Evan. But he had an idea.

He spun on his heel and headed to the car. As soon as he got behind the wheel, he dialed Lena.

As it rang, he drove toward Council Bluffs and the person with the most riding on Maggie's testimony. Earl Whitestone.

"Lena. I want you to call 9-1-1. Ask for a welfare check on Evan at Ted's place. Tell them you think Ted is on drugs. Talking crazy and out on bail with nothing to lose. Scare the shit out of the 9-1-1 operator."

"Jesus, Rick. Is it that bad?"

"It's not good. And I want to make sure we keep Evan safe." He wanted law enforcement so far up Ted's ass that he could taste their badges in the back of this throat. Rick might not be able to pull Evan out of that apartment, but he could get some cops inside.

He would be at the Jokers Wild pawnshop in ten minutes. And any help Omaha PD offered might as well be a million miles away since he would be out of their jurisdiction there.

The sudden flood of light blinded Maggie. She blinked a few times and struggled against the silver tape binding her wrists. Earl Whitestone's face came into focus, one hand holding her car's trunk partly open. She kicked out but missed her abductor's face. She wouldn't go down without a fight.

Earl had attacked her as soon as Ted and Evan had gone inside Ted's apartment. He grabbed her from behind and shoved a taser into her side. The shock took her down to her knees. The pain had flooded her body, incapacitating her. He snatched her keys and dumped her in the trunk of her own car before she recovered.

Trapped, she'd had too much time to think about how this car ride was going to end. Her fear had grown with each mile as she huddled in the fetal position in the dark, tugging at the tape on her wrists with her teeth to no avail.

She blinked again and tried to look around. Behind Earl, all she could see was the corner of a small building and blue sky.

"Bitch," the older man hissed as he dodged her second kick. His dead eyes showed no mercy. He spit his half-chewed toothpick at her and slammed the lid shut. He pounded on the trunk after it was closed. The hollow thumps made Maggie think of the sound the first few shovels of dirt made landing on top of a coffin.

She went a little crazy forced back into the dark. She kicked at the seatbacks and punched at the trunk lid, screaming until her throat was raw and her side burned. Her heels and knees ached from striking the hard walls of the trunk. In the silence, her ears rang with the echoes of her screams. Tears slid down her face, falling on the scratchy carpet under her head. The stale air in the car seemed to grow hotter by the second.

A sob grew from deep in her chest, and she curled into herself, shaking and nearly hysterical. She made a life-ending mistake agreeing to drop Evan off at Ted's place. What a fool she'd been. She walked into the arms of her kidnapper... murderer. She had little doubt that was going to be her fate.

Poor Evan would end up paying a huge price. One parent dead, the other undoubtedly going to jail.

Thirty-Three

RICK PARKED IN ONE of the bays at the old coin-operated car wash next to the Jokers Wild pawnshop. He could see Maggie's car parked behind the shop from his vantage point.

The car quaked, moving back and forth on its tires. She was in the fucking trunk. The realization lanced painfully through his heart as he reached for the door handle. She was alive. He was going for her. His foot crunched on some broken glass as he stepped out of the car, and he froze.

His FBI training kicked in, stopping him from rushing in without thinking. He couldn't fuck this up, acting like he did at the warehouse. He didn't have a guy like Staub here to save his ass. He exhaled and let his training take over.

He scanned the pawnshop parking lot. He counted four security cameras posted to give 360-degree views of the lot, and he recalled the way Earl stared at the CCTV monitors when he'd been in the shop. The cameras weren't just for show.

After a few more violent shudders, the car stopped moving. He closed his eyes and tipped his head back, cursing Ted, Earl, this situation: two states sharing criminals but not cops. Fuck. He pounded his fist on the roof of his car. She was so close but entirely out of reach.

Earl and his guys were sitting on an armory. He was out manned and out gunned. He needed backup.

He sat back in the car and dialed 9-1-1. He gripped the armrest so hard that the plastic trim cut into his palm.

"Nine-one-one, what is your emergency?"

"I believe there is someone in the trunk of a car parked behind the Jokers Wild pawnshop." He forced his voice into some semblance of calm. But saying the words out loud hurt almost like being shot.

"Do you feel safe rendering assistance?"

"Not alone." Was Iowa the state of do-it-yourself police work? It was crazy. He confirmed the details of the situation and the pawnshop's address with the operator.

"I'm dispatching units now. Would you like to stay on the line until they arrive?"

"No." Rick hung up and again got out of the car. Now that he had backup on the way, it was time to get Maggie out of that trunk. It might have been early October, but a lingering summer heat wave had the temperatures feeling more like Florida. In the direct sun, she could die of heatstroke long before Earl decided what he would do with her. Or the cops arrived.

His resources were limited. He popped the trunk of the rental, dug the tire iron out from under the spare, and pulled the tool kit free from the Velcro tabs holding it in place. Inside the kit, there was a wrench and a screwdriver-like tool to remove the covers on the hub caps. He could work with this.

He jogged across the cracked pavement between the car wash and the back of the pawnshop. Potholes and weeds offered little cover from the security cameras. He wouldn't have long.

He reached the back of Maggie's Honda and wedged the screwdriver-like tool under the gap in the trunk lid near the latch. Using all his weight, he leaned on the tool. The car shifted, but the latch didn't give. He swore he heard Maggie whimper from inside.

Fuck this.

He walked around to the driver's side window and took a swing with the tire iron. The impact glass crazed under the force of the blow. Two more punches, and it gave way. He reached inside and flicked the trunk release.

"Maggie." He flew around to the back of the car.

"Rick, thank God." Tears streamed down her face. She was bright red, and sweat dripped down her chest. She never looked better. She was alive.

He scooped her out of the car, his hands under her knees and around her shoulders. She clung to him as best she could with her bound hands. He relished the feel of her fingers clutching his shirt. He pressed his lips to her hair for the briefest kiss.

"We got to go—" His last word was cut off by a gunshot.

He rushed behind the car and dropped to the ground. That was even faster than he expected. A hail of bullets pinged off the car. They were pinned down until the cops got there.

He untangled himself from Maggie and pushed her back against the front tire. He knelt and looked over the hood toward the back of the shop. It wasn't good. Earl and his two minions were armed to the teeth.

"Son of a bitch." He slid the M&P out of the holster. He had a full clip, seventeen rounds, and a handful more bullets in his pants pocket. He squeezed off a couple of poorly aimed shots at the three men. He didn't dare pop his head up. Playing whack-a-mole against a guy with a modified assault rifle was deadly.

"What?" Maggie stayed huddled behind the tire, cringing at the loud report from his gun.

Despite it all, he dared another glance over the hood. And the barrage of return fire confirmed what he already knew—bad idea. If he didn't want a bullet in the skull, his head stayed down. "I'm pretty sure one of them has a modified AR-15 rifle with a bump stock."

She shook her head, not understanding.

"It's like a machine gun. An illegal and very dangerous machine gun." His 9mm wasn't going to hold them back for long.

Another flurry of bullets thunked into the far side of Maggie's car. Glass from the shot-out windows cascaded over them as he unwound the tape on Maggie's wrists.

"The way I see it, you two are trapped. Come on out. Let's end this now, before someone gets dead," Earl shouted.

"We'd rather not." Rick got low to the ground and snuck a peek around the end of the car. Earl Whitestone, Myer, and Green had taken cover behind the metal dumpster behind the pawnshop.

"Don't make me come get that bitch."

"Try it!"

"Rick..." Maggie looked horrified. He cupped her tear-stained cheek for a moment.

"Stay down. I've called the cops already. We only need to keep Earl and his goons back until the police get here." He held her gaze, willing her to stay strong.

"Okay." Her reply was barely more than a whisper.

More shots pinged off the Honda.

On his belly, he looked beneath the car toward the men. He could only see their feet. One of them had stepped away from the dumpster. Rick tracked the black work boots, step by step, as they moved toward the trunk side of the car.

For the first time since getting shot, it felt natural when Rick tightened his grip on his gun. His M&P was his last and only option to keep him and Maggie alive.

He leaned close to her ear and whispered, "Stay low and quiet. If anything goes wrong, roll under the car." And pray the Council Bluffs cops would get there in time. Even in a neighborhood like this, gunfire had to draw attention.

She grabbed his left arm and squeezed once before ducking her head into her hands. Rick clambered over her toward the back of the car. The gunman was close enough for Rick to hear the gravel crunch under the soles of his boots.

In a single movement honed by years of practice, Rick pivoted from behind the car in a low crouch and held his gun out in front of him. He came face to face with Earl Whitestone holding a huge chrome semi-automatic. Earl's big body shielded Rick from whoever had the AR-15 back by the dumpster.

Rick closed his index finger around the trigger. Three shots. Earl pitched forward, and his handgun tumbled from his slack grip, clattering to the pavement. Rick ducked back behind the Honda as another wave of bullets from the AR-15 tore across the parking lot.

Rick was sure he'd killed Earl. His heart pounded violently against his ribs, and the gun suddenly felt heavy in his grip. He could taste bile and had to force himself to breathe. There hadn't been another way. Staring down the barrel of Earl's hand cannon, he knew there was no other choice. Kill or be killed.

Maggie's hand on his arm pulled him from the grim downward spiral of his thoughts. "Is he dead?"

Rick nodded and pulled her against his chest. He pressed his face into her hair, and the familiar scent of her herb-infused shampoo helped keep him in the moment. Maggie burrowed harder into his body, and he leaned his head back on the side of the car as another dozen or so bullets hit the far side of the Honda.

"The police should be here any minute." He stroked her back, trying to reassure her. She'd managed to be brave and strong until now, but he could feel her beginning to unravel.

She nodded, but her hold on him didn't relax. A slight tremor shook her.

"Just give us the girl!" Myer or Green shouted.

Rick didn't bother to reply. The cavalry had arrived. He'd never been so happy to see a few black and whites in his life.

"Weapons down! Hands up! This is the police." The commands crackled through a speaker on one of the squad cars that ripped into the parking lot. Gravel and dust trailed behind it.

Thirty-Four

RICK HELD OPEN THE door of his rental car for Maggie. A nurse helped her up from the wheelchair.

Earl had done a number on her. The doctors couldn't tell if her bruised ribs were from Earl's rough handling while unconscious or the initial hit with the taser. Either way, once her adrenaline waned, Maggie had realized she was in pain.

"Easy does it," the nurse told Maggie as she helped her swing her legs into the car. The nurse closed the car door and looked at Rick. "She is on some pretty decent meds right now. She should take it easy for a few days, but she'll be good as new soon."

"Thank you for the help." Rick shook the nurse's hand. The kind woman had been helping Maggie since she arrived in the ambulance from the pawnshop. Much to the annoyance of the cops in Iowa, he had insisted on following Maggie to the hospital. While she underwent medical tests, he was interviewed by a detective in the waiting room regarding everything else that had gone on that day, including the death of Earl Whitestone.

Night had fallen while they were in the hospital. The breeze held the promise of rain. Rick took a deep breath, and the hot, humid air reminded him of Florida.

He was taking Maggie back to Lena's house. Evan was there waiting. Lena's 9-1-1 call had triggered an extensive welfare check, and his second call to Morris from the hospital waiting room got Evan safely delivered to Lena's house.

Rick slid behind the wheel and glanced at Maggie. She was out. When the car moved, her eyes fluttered open, and she smiled at him. He threaded his fingers through hers. He wasn't going to let go.

"Lena said I need to pull my head out of my ass."

"Sounds like Lena." Her voice had that soft sing-song quality that only pain meds and exhaustion could cause.

"She's right." He lifted her hand and placed a kiss on the back.

"What is she right about?" Her eyes were closed again, and her hand was limp in his hold.

"Nothing for you to worry about right now. But when you're feeling better, we need to talk."

"Okay."

He drove to Lena's house, holding her hand while she slept. He traced small circles on her skin with his thumb as he drove. The delicate bones reminded him of how fragile life was, and he'd be damned if he gave up one more minute of a life with her because of guilt. Or family. Or a job he knew he wasn't cut out for any longer.

He pulled his car into a small side driveway like the one at his house. Lena's farmhouse was similar to his, but 1970s ranch houses flanked it closely on either side. Her lot was a postage stamp compared to his.

He slowly unwound their fingers before getting out of the car.

He opened the passenger door and knelt to talk to her. "Mi corazón, you are going to turn my world upside down." Who was he kidding? She already had. It just took him some time and a gunfight to figure it out.

He leaned in and pressed a gentle kiss to her cheek. "Time to wake up."

She started to turn and hissed. "Ouch."

"We'll get you inside where you're more comfortable. Okay?" He wished he could take away all her pain but was grateful she only suffered a minor injury.

"Thank you." She cupped his jaw in her hand. "You saved my life."

"For you, anything." She didn't know it, but she had saved his life months ago.

Getting Maggie into Lena's house wasn't too difficult. They had barely stepped inside when Evan came rushing down the stairs.

"Easy." Rick caught him before he could hug-tackle Maggie. "Mom's ribs are bruised."

"Mom? Are you going to be okay?" Evan stopped short. His eyes were big and filled with worry.

She beckoned him to her uninjured side and pulled him into a tight one-armed hug. "I'm going to be perfect." She smiled at Rick over Evan's head.

Rick cleared his throat. Emotion made it feel tight as he watched the reunion of mother and son. The word *mine* welled up from deep in his soul. They were his. The staggering weight of the realization didn't send him to his knees. Instead, it calmed a restlessness that had been plaguing him for too long.

"Mom, what happened?" Evan looked up at her without letting go.

He and Maggie shared a look. After the Brinks truck robbery, they had glossed over parts of the story, not wanting to give Evan nightmares. Today they would do the same, walking a thin line between the truth and lies. His father's involvement in both crimes made the situation incredibly delicate.

"The bad men your father foolishly got involved with were angry that I talked to the police. But it's

all fine now. The men are going back to jail."
Maggie smoothed a wayward lock of her son's hair.

"What about Dad?"

Maggie looked to Rick to answer the question.
She hadn't spent the day with the police as he had.

"Yes, he's going back to jail. His association with
those men means he has broken the law." Rick kept
his tone even. He and Maggie knew Ted was
almost as bad as Earl and the others, but they
didn't need to ruin Evan's perception of his father.
The prison sentence would most likely do that.

"To serve justice like we talked about before?
Like in the comic books?"

"Exactly." Thank you, Captain America.

"Could Mom get hurt by them again?" Evan
chewed the corner of a fingernail, and concern put
wrinkles on his normally smooth forehead.

"No worries, Evan. I'll be here to make sure she
doesn't." Rick's vow to protect Maggie satisfied
Evan.

"Mom, you look tired. You should lay down." He
took her hand and led her toward the stairs very
slowly.

"Get some rest, Maggie. We'll talk soon." Rick
wished he could come up with a reason to stay, but
Maggie should rest.

"Thank you again." She smiled, and his heart
warmed. She was spectacular.

He turned away from the stairs, happy in a way
he hadn't been in ages.

"Looks like you've pulled your head out of your
ass." Lena leaned on a door frame between the
living room and the kitchen, a self-satisfied smirk
on her lips.

"Yeah. I have to figure out the logistics, but I'm
staying. After all this, I can't walk away." He rubbed
the back of his neck and chuckled. "Hell, I can't
even run away. She's part of me now. She, Evan,
and that money pit of a house. I need a plan to
make it all work. And convince her to give me
another chance."

Lena straightened away from the wall and gave him a light punch in the upper arm. "Love will find a way."

"Did you quote song lyrics to me like a 1980s DJ?" A platitude from a pop song. He was having an existential crisis upending his life, and that was all Lena had to offer.

"There are only like six songs with that title, so it's got to be good advice." A ridiculous smile curved her lips.

Rick groaned. "I guess if it's good enough for YES and Lionel Richie."

"Don't forget my favorite Pablo Cruise." She laughed. "I'll take good care of her."

"Thank you." He passed her the small bottle of pain meds and explained the doctor's orders. "I'm going to get going. Please tell her to call when she wakes up. I don't care what time."

He walked out to his car. He needed a shower. His suit pants were stained with dirt, and his dress shoes were scuffed. He'd taken off his tie and jacket hours ago. His missed meeting with Jacob Hansen felt like ten years ago, not that afternoon. He would have to call and reschedule it on Monday.

On his drive back to the hotel, he tried to ignore how much he missed being with Maggie. Soon enough, they'd be back on the front porch of the house, sharing a drink and watching Evan and the other neighborhood kids in the park. His new goal: a plan to fix the house and a new job to finance the dream.

Thirty-Five

"RICK, I'M FINE. I can carry a suitcase." Maggie started to reach into the open trunk, but he brushed her aside.

"I didn't say you couldn't. The doctor did." He took her bag out of the back of his rental car. Since the kidnapping, Rick had been attentive, compassionate, concerned, and all in her business. He stopped by Lena's and sent texts. But he hadn't brought up the future.

Physically she felt a ton better. Her bruised ribs were tender but fading to yellow and green from black and blue. A few more days and everything would look normal again. She would like a big heaping dose of normal for a few months. Her brain and her body both needed it.

Rick had stopped at Lena's and picked up her and Evan after checking out of his hotel. What was left of her car was in a police impound lot. It was evidence. So that would be interesting to explain to her insurance company.

Kevin, the contractor, trotted around from the front of the house. "You're back. That's great. My guys are finishing the cleanup in the main house. We should be out of there in thirty minutes. Want to check out the apartment?"

Kevin led them to the door, unlocked it, and pushed it open. He hung back, letting her, Evan and Rick walk ahead. The smell of fresh paint wasn't overwhelming, but it was intense. She would need to open some windows.

At Rick's insistence, she had chosen the paint. It was the palest almond white, making the rooms feel bigger and brighter. It was lovely, and she would miss it when she moved. The last of the 1970s wallpaper was a distant memory.

"It looks great. And no more lead paint." All her furniture was back where it started, and her things from the barn had been moved back in.

"Nice work, Kevin." Rick clapped him on the back.

"Thanks. I'll leave the final bill on the table in the main house. I'm going to help the guys wrap it up." Kevin gave her another of his flirty, lingering smiles. The guy was incorrigible. But harmless.

"I'm going to unpack." Evan rolled his suitcase toward his room, leaving her and Rick alone.

Like really alone for the first time since everything happened. Other than a car ride home from the hospital when she was drugged out of her mind on pain meds. She rubbed her bare arms and looked anywhere but at him. What the fuck was up with the nerves?

"Invite me to stay for a while?" Rick stood behind her; his breath tickled her neck, and one hand rested on her hip. The heat from his touch unfurled in her belly. She resisted the urge to lean against his chest.

"Okay." Her breathless reply had nothing to do with her bruised ribs and everything to do with Rick. "Want some tea?"

"Sure." He removed his hand from her hip and followed her to the kitchen.

She fumbled with the teapot, intensely aware he was watching her every move. When she dropped a teaspoon, he moved behind her and caught her wrist. "Sit. Let me do this."

She sank into the kitchen chair. He moved like a man comfortable in his skin now, unlike when he arrived months ago. His dark wash jeans fit him like a glove, and when he bent forward to fill the kettle, she bit her lip. God, that ass. He finished getting the water on to boil and set out the honey she liked along with two mugs.

He sat across from her while the water heated.

Their gazes met across the table. He reached for her hand and threaded their fingers together. His thumb stroked the back of her knuckles. A shiver raced up her arm at his delicate touch.

"Maggie..." He took a deep breath like he was building up his courage. "I want you. And this life. I want this house and to stay in this city. I want to coach Evan at soccer or at least let him beat me at every video game made. And I want to wake up with you every morning."

"You do?" It wasn't that she didn't believe him. She knew how good they were together, but she wanted him to tell her because he'd fought it for too long and had been so willfully blind to her emotions. A tiny, nervous part of her needed him to spill his big messy feelings out on the floor for her to examine.

"When I realized you were in that trunk, it finally ripped through all the excuses I've been building up in my mind. All the ways I'd been undermining what we could have." He shook his head slowly. "Change scares the shit out of me. And falling in love with you is the biggest change I've ever faced. Casual was an excuse. Nothing I've ever done with you wasn't meaningful. Can I have another chance?"

He stood and moved next to her chair. When he kissed her lips with infinite care, the gentle caress felt like a promise.

"I love you, Maggie."

She wrapped her arms around him and pressed her lips to the pulse pounding at the base of his throat. "I love you, too."

"I want to pull you into my arms, but I'm sure I'd hurt you." He cradled her gently, his arms barely closing around her. "Forgive me for not being there when you needed me. I should have been with you when Earl grabbed you. I could have stopped it." His deep regret hurt her to hear.

"None of this was your fault." She rested her head on his chest and listened to his heartbeat under her ear.

He stroked her hair and bent to take her lips for another soft, slow, drugging kiss. She pressed her open mouth to his, feasting on his lips and tongue. She shifted in the chair, wanting more, but a twinge across her ribs pulled her back to reality.

She stiffened and reached for her side.

He pulled back. "You okay?"

"I will be." A smile curved her lips, and a tear slid down her cheek. Today, in the last few moments, Rick shifted from what might have been, to her future. She would treasure the memory forever. "You're staying."

The kettle shrieked, and he turned to move it off the heat.

"Finally!" Evan strolled into the room, king of all he surveyed.

"What?" She looked at her son. Her eavesdropping son.

"Took you guys long enough. I'm ten, and I've seen every Disney movie. I knew you and Rick were like the princesses and their prince charmings since the first time he stood up to Dad." Evan pulled a cookie out of the jar on the counter. "Mom, you needed saving, not because you were weak or sad, but because you're amazing, and you deserved it. Just like a real Disney princess." He emphasized his points with a thrust of the cookie in her direction.

"So, I guess you're cool with me dating your mom?" Rick asked while he made their tea.

"Duh." Evan reached for the milk in the fridge to go with his cookie.

Maggie wiped away a few more happy tears, watching Rick and Evan rub elbows in the tiny kitchen. She wasn't sure what she had done to deserve two wonderful men in her life, but she was grateful.

Rick put her mug down on the table and leaned close to her ear. "And they lived happily ever after."

"Yes. Let's do that."

Thirty-Six

"SORRY I MISSED OUR first appointment." Rick settled into the wingback chair across from Jacob Hansen's oversized walnut desk. It was good he'd put on a suit. The man's office looked like something from an episode of Perry Mason—dark leather and gold-trimmed law books.

"Not a problem. The local gossip mill kept me up to date. We're forever grateful for you rescuing our Maggie a second time. That appears to be your new hobby." Hansen closed a folder on his desk and added it to a neat stack in a tray.

"I'd rather that was the last time she was in danger. And I'm sure she would agree. She's still nursing some bruised ribs. It was awful to see Evan upset."

"You care about them?"

"Yes." Hell yes. They were the reason he was figuring out a new life halfway across the country from Miami. It was more than caring. They were the center of his life.

"Good show."

A soft knock at the door behind him preceded the entrance of Hansen's administrative assistant. "Your coffees."

She bustled in, placing cups in front of him and Hansen. The white china cups with gold trim felt like they were from another era.

When they each had a sip, Hansen sat back in his chair and steepled his hands in front of him. The pause grew, and tension filled the office. Rick felt a tingle of unease. He'd come to this meeting unsure why it was warranted. If this kept up much longer, he would freak out.

"I knew Mona long before she up and married your grandfather." Hansen sat back in his chair. He gazed off into the distance as he reminisced. "Our families have been close for generations. When Mona concocted this plan, I was the only one she trusted to execute it."

"What plan?" Oh, fuck.

Hansen spun his big leather chair around to reach into a filing cabinet. He pulled out a thick stack of manila folders and put them on the edge of the desk.

"Your grandmother was an incredible woman. If I had been a little older and a lot smarter, I would have married her before your grandfather stole her heart."

"Thank you. I loved her dearly."

"She was also an incredible businesswoman." Hansen delivered the comment with a surety that took Rick back.

"Excuse me?" He was sure he'd misunderstood. Business? Mona was a loving mother, grandmother, and excellent cook. She was everyone's favorite neighbor, but not once had he heard her called a businesswoman.

"Your grandmother was a pillar of her community. And as part of her support for her neighborhood, she invested in the people she knew and loved. She invested in their dreams. Her husband left her a rather impressive nest egg."

According to family legend, Rick's grandfather had been an important man in the Florida sugarcane business. Rick had only the vaguest memory of him as Mona's bigger-than-life personality had always blotted out her husband in his youthful memories. His family had wondered about the money he'd left to Mona when it didn't show up in the will.

"At first, she helped cover some expenses for families with kids at college. Books and such. But as those kids graduated, some came to her and asked her to be part of their business ventures. Her original investments were small things, like a florist shop." Hansen reached for a file from the stack at his elbow and tossed it in the center of his desk.

"Then a neighborhood auto mechanic who wanted to buy the building he rented." A second file landed on top of the first.

"A young veterinarian that wanted to set up practice back home in Omaha." A third file.

Rick plucked the first file off the top and flipped it open. He scanned the partnership agreement and balance sheet. His grandmother owned twenty percent of a thriving veterinary practice. In the next folder, he found a loan agreement between Mona and Steven Dawes, the military veteran and auto mechanic from the neighborhood. The monthly payments were a sizable sum, but the rate was probably lower than what many banks would offer.

He wasn't sure what the hell was going on. He looked at the stack still on Hansen's side of the desk; there were at least a dozen more folders. Mona was a tycoon. He smiled at the idea. Only she would be able to surprise him from beyond the grave.

"Not everything she invested in was a success. But most were. She knew the people and the city. It made her extremely good at picking winners." Hansen pushed the rest of the folders toward Rick.

He turned them to read the company names on the tabs. He recognized many of the businesses from around Omaha. The second to last folder was labeled Lone Tree Botanicals.

Maggie had said something about legal papers filed with Hansen, but he'd forgotten to follow up.

He remembered worrying that Maggie had taken advantage of Mona. Now he itched to read the documents in the folder and make sure the opposite hadn't happened. Wow, overprotective much? He took the Lone Tree file and set it aside. He would want to take that one home and read it with Maggie. Keep himself from doing or saying something dumb. Mona and Maggie were obviously more than capable of making a fair deal.

"But none of this was in her will?" Rick replaced the folders on the desk.

"That's where I come in." Hansen chuckled. "Mona was a meddler who liked to see people happy and successful. Years ago, she decided Miami wasn't the right place for you. And she dreamed up a plan. I tweaked it."

"You tweaked it?" Rick sat back in his chair, arms crossed defensively. He wasn't so sure he liked Hansen at this moment. Secrets weren't a good way to make friends.

"The will had a codicil that stipulated you wouldn't get any of this unless you resided in Omaha for ninety days. Your mother let slip about your injury when I called a few months after the funereal looking for you. So, I sent that letter urging you to come up here and stay in our fair city to 'sell' the house."

The old man was nuts. Or crazy like a fox. Rick had no idea which.

"Seriously?"

"I wanted you to spend those ninety days getting to know Mona's world, not just counting the days until your payday. I think Mona would have approved of the plan, and as executor, it was within my purview to make that choice. Take the risk." Hansen shrugged and sipped his coffee like playing God wasn't a big deal.

"Risk my inheritance, you mean?" Suddenly, the deferred maintenance on the house made sense. Mona was investing in the future of her city, not her home.

"Yes, well, it worked out, so no reason to hold a grudge. I'm an old man. Playing matchmaker is good for me. It keeps me young."

"Matchmaker?" Rick had a hard time saying the word.

"Please, Maggie was made for you. I knew that back when you were kids catching frogs and climbing trees. Mona agreed." The self-satisfied smile on Hansen's face was a lot to take.

Rick rubbed a hand over his jaw and loosened his tie. "Well, Mr. Hansen, since you're now my attorney, why don't we go over these files, and you can explain to me what the hell I inherited."

"Son, you're a wealthy man in your own right. The monthly income from these investments is nothing to sneeze at. Every penny they've earned since Mona's passing has been held in trust for you. When you see that dollar figure, paying to remodel your house is going to get easier. A lot easier."

The money. The business investments. Mona's grand plan for his life. It was a lot to absorb in one sitting. Damn, he missed his grandmother. After hearing everything Hansen had to say, he wanted to give Mona a hug and a high five. His grandma, the businesswoman—what a crazy revelation.

***

Maggie hopped out of Lena's car in front of the house. Rick sat in one of the rocking chairs on the front porch in the dark. He was staring at a streetlight in the park like it held the answers to the universe. A beer bottle dangled from the fingers of his right hand.

She jogged in his direction as Lena pulled away.

"Earth to Rick. Come in, Rick." She nudged his shoulder.

He startled. She caught the beer bottle before it slipped from his slack fingers. It was warm. He'd been out here a long while.

"A lot on my mind."

"Spill?" It was late, and she was exhausted. Her event at the convention center had ended after ten P.M. But sleep could wait, especially since she wanted to sleep in Rick's bed. Evan was with his babysitter, Suzie, and she wanted to take advantage of a night alone with her boyfriend. Damn, she liked thinking Rick and boyfriend in the same thought.

"I met with Hansen today. It was a revelation." He held up a familiar manila file with her company's name on it.

"What do you mean?"

"Mona was some kind of tycoon. Bankrolling businesses across Omaha. I had no idea." He shook his head.

Maggie laughed. "She just helped a few of us get started, nothing big."

"No, it was, or rather, is big. I spent the afternoon learning how big. My grandma was a big-time small investor. I don't understand how Hansen kept you all from telling me or looking for answers."

"He said it was tied up in probate. Wasn't that the delay?" Maggie had taken Jacob's word for what was going on. Her agreement with Mona was for a small share of profits to be paid at the end of the summer as rent. She hadn't worried much about it.

Rick gestured to the other chair. "You're going to want to sit down for this one."

His detailed play-by-play of his meeting and the extensive nature of sweet little Mona's business empire was eye-opening.

"Matchmaker? You're kidding me? He said that." Maggie couldn't believe Jacob and Mona planned setting up her and Rick into Mona's will.

"Yep."

"Hold on. I'll be right back. We need one thing to finish this conversation properly." Maggie rushed into Rick's house. She knew exactly where to look for what she wanted. She grabbed up everything and went back out on the porch.

She balanced two heavy crystal snifters on the porch railing and tugged the stopper out of the bottle. Rick stood and watched her, a knowing grin on his face.

"Mona's favorite orange blossom brandy?" he asked as he reached for one of the glasses.

"What else would we toast her with?" The heady scent of the brandy reminded Maggie of quiet winter nights spent talking with Mona near a roaring fire.

"I can see her and my grandfather up there somewhere, laughing at pulling one over on us kids. We thought we chose our destiny, but all along, she had a plan for us."

"She did a damn fine job, too." Maggie lifted her glass. "To Mona."

"To Mona, a life well lived. We hope to follow in your footsteps." Rick touched his snifter against Maggie's and then took a sip. She watched as he fought the urge to cough as the orange liquor burned down his throat. "Good Lord, that's orange-flavored kerosene."

"I know. It's painfully good." Maggie wiped a tear from her eye. She wasn't sure if it was from the deceptively strong booze or bittersweet memories.

Rick pulled her back against his chest, and she relaxed into his arms. A few more sips of brandy and a wonderful warmth spread through her veins. She pressed a kiss on the underside of his jaw.

"Maggie." His breath caught on the second syllable of her name when she nipped his skin. He dug his fingers into her hips and shifted so she could feel his cock lengthen against her ass.

"Rick." Everything about this man made her want him.

He turned her in his arms and took her mouth in a sweet kiss. He tasted of oranges. Desire unfurled deep inside her, and she took control of the kiss. She trapped his face in her hands and ravaged his mouth. Since her bruised ribs, Rick had been so careful and delicate when he touched her. Tonight, she wanted him to stop it.

Her hand slid between them, and she cupped him through his slacks. He was already thick and hard. She squeezed, and he groaned. The primal sound made her ache. She pushed him back, and he stumbled toward the house.

He yanked open the screen and front doors, pulling her along. As soon as they crossed the threshold and the door snicked closed, Maggie pulled off her blouse and removed her bra. Her pale skin glowed in the well-lit foyer. She caught Rick's shoulder and pushed him back toward the wall, undoing his shirt buttons as they walked.

He buried his hand in her hair and ravaged her mouth with another searing kiss. His new habit of delicately handling her body faded fast. She slipped from his hold and dropped down to her knees. Her insides were molten. She squeezed her thighs together as she undid his pants and freed his erection.

She closed her mouth over him, sliding down. She took his shaft as deep as she could.

"Fuck, Maggie." His head thumped on the wall. He widened his stance, bracing for her onslaught.

She worked him in and out of her mouth, stroking his length with one hand and pushing up her skirt with the other until her fingers brushed over her panties. They were damp, and she tugged the fabric away so she could touch her needy clit.

The first brush against her aching flesh sent a jolt through her. She groaned around his length, and he flexed his hips, begging her to take more of his cock. She plunged her mouth down until he nudged the back of her throat.

Over and over, she stroked and sucked him, her hips rising and falling in the same rhythm. Desire sang in her veins as she worked her fingers between her thighs. She felt overwhelmed, possessed as she lavished pleasure on them both.

"I love watching you." He tangled a hand in her hair, and she tipped her head back to meet his gaze. Her heart swelled with emotions from lust to love; it all rushed through her. And his eyes burned with the same powerful emotions.

Her nipples hardened, goosebumps raced across her skin, and she clenched her thighs as the first pulse of her release washed over her. She tore her mouth away from him and cried out. Pleasure ripped through her in waves.

Rick stripped off his shirt and helped her to her feet. She trembled as he bent her across a small table next to the front door.

"Hold on." He fumbled for something, and she heard the sound of a condom wrapper. He ripped her panties down and kicked her legs wide.

As he filled her from behind, his teeth sank into her shoulder. Her gasp echoed in the foyer, and she looked into the mirror over the table. Their eyes met in the glass and held. He cupped her breast with one hand. The other slid down her hip and under her skirt. He strummed her clit in the same rhythm he fucked her. His lips skimmed the shell of her ear as he whispered sexy, broken Spanish endearments to her.

Sex with him was everything sex with other men wasn't. It was passionate and hot, but it was also making love. The intensity of the emotion made every caress that much more incendiary.

"Come for me, mi corazón." He worked her clit between his fingers harder and harder, and she came apart under his touch. The orgasm swept her up higher and crashed over her with more force than her first. She bent her elbows and sagged down, gripping the edge of the table. Rick's touch was magic.

In the mirror, she watched him. His eyes focused intently on where he plunged into her. His chest glistened with a fine sheen of sweat. Any concern he might have once had about his scars seemed long forgotten.

He held her hips steady, and he moaned her name over and over. She felt him shudder before his body stiffened, and he ground into her, coming hard.

"Please tell me I didn't hurt you." He peppered light kisses along her spine between gasping breaths. His hand skated over her ribs where only the smallest remnants of her bruises remained.

"Pain was the furthest thing from my mind."

Epilogue

RICK AND HECTOR SHARED a high five as they crossed the finish line. He'd done what Hector had promised—finished the Thanksgiving 5K turkey trot. He would have said something profound about how he couldn't have done it alone, but he was breathing too hard. And Hector was doubled over with his hands on his knees.

He glanced at his watch to check his time. A new personal best. Faster than any 5K he ever ran, even before getting shot. The combination of a cold Nebraska morning and extra time devoted to speed training had paid off.

Hector straightened. "I told you...you could...do it!"

Rick nodded, worried that if he spoke, he might barf. Their sprint to the finish had been an asinine show of machismo. Vomit was the way you ended Thanksgiving Day, not started it.

"I think you guys came first and second for your age group." Maggie bounced up to them, a steaming cup grasped in her gloved hands. She passed him a lightweight jacket. "Here, Florida boy, we can't have you freezing to death."

He took the jacket and draped it over his shoulders before grabbing her for a sweaty kiss. She squealed and grabbed his ass. His girlfriend was sassy, and he loved it.

Next to him, Hector was giving Lena the same treatment. Maggie's best friend and his physical therapist were an odd couple, but it worked. They had been dating for a month now, and it appeared to be getting serious.

"You guys are gross," Evan grumbled.

Rick was sure the kid was sleeping standing up. The race had kicked off at five-thirty in the morning, way too early for Evan. Dragging him to the last few green markets before the season ended, Rick had learned all about how sloth-like a prepubescent boy could be.

Maggie's Lone Tree Botanicals wasn't the only one of Mona's investments he had put some sweat equity into. Mona had offered emotional support and business advice to her partners. Rick knew that wasn't his strong suit, so he decided to physically step up and offer his time when needed. In the last few months, he'd done it all from filling in at Steven Dawes's auto shop, changing tires when Steven had Army Reserve duty, to answering phones at the vet clinic when the whole office got strep throat.

He was making a name for himself in Omaha and building a new reputation. Here, he wasn't the FBI agent playboy who hopped from club to club at night. He was an up-and-coming local businessman. For his first solo venture, he planned on helping his favorite Latin Caribbean food truck start a brick-and-mortar restaurant. The chance to reinvent himself with Maggie at his side was a dream come true.

"Morning, Maggie!" They all turned at the cheery greeting—Cheryl from channel seven, with a camera crew in tow, headed in their direction.

"Cheryl!" Maggie and the reporter exchanged hugs.

"Can I grab these two gorgeous men for a second? Nothing says Happy Thanksgiving like hot men dripping in sweat." She signaled her cameraman to set up so the finish line balloon arch was behind Rick and Hector.

"Tell the camera your first name and wish your family back home happy Thanksgiving. Got it?" She pulled his jacket off his shoulders and groped his bicep. "Sex sells, big guy." Rick was sure he was blushing, and next to him, Hector's shoulders shook with laughter.

She counted down and gave them their cue. He and Hector pulled it together as the camera started rolling.

"Morning, and happy Thanksgiving, Omaha! I'm Rick, and I'm thankful for all my family back home in Miami, Florida, even if I won't be joining them for dinner today." A bittersweet feeling tugged at his heart. It was the first Thanksgiving he spent away from home in decades, but he was excited to start making new memories with Maggie and Evan.

"I'm Hector, and I want to wish my family in New York City feliz día de acción de gracias from beautiful Omaha."

"That was perfect, guys. Maggie, we still must get together for a glass of wine. I never got to tell you about my date after the diamond show. You will die!" With a finger wave, Cheryl and her camera crew moved to interview another race finisher.

"I love her on TV," Lena said. "We are so doing happy hour. I want to hear about that date."

"If Cheryl and Lena ever manage to get me out for happy hour, you might have to come pick us up." Maggie draped his jacket back over his cold arms. "I'm sure it will involve way more than a glass of wine."

Rick laughed and started herding the group toward their parked cars. They had a giant ass turkey waiting to get shoved into an oven back at the house and a parade to watch.

"Maggie, what's up with all the cars? Did the neighbors say anything about a big Thanksgiving Day party?"

"Ah, must be?" Shit, just park the car, Rick. Stupid FBI training—the guy couldn't roll with it and ignore the cars lining the street. It was a holiday; cars were normal.

He parked her new car in the drive, leaving room for Hector and Lena behind him. Her ten-year-old Honda Bertha had been totaled after the day at the pawnshop, riddled with bullets through and through. And since she and Evan had moved in with Rick, she put some of her rent money toward payments on a nice new SUV.

Rick came around to open her door. "Ready to cook?"

"Absolutely. Come on, Evan." Her son was bundled in the back seat, half asleep, but at hearing his name, he rubbed his eyes and fumbled for the door.

"Nice." Rick ogled a black Charger parked across the street from the house. "Looks like mine."

"Oh, the car. Yeah, very fancy." Maggie pushed him toward the front porch before he could walk toward the car. She'd gotten this far, damn it. She would be pissed if her big surprise was ruined in the last moments.

"Rick, a game of Mario Kart before the parade?" Evan asked.

"I'll play winner!" Hector shouted, heading toward the house with Lena and a cooler full of side dishes.

Maggie was thankful for their help getting Rick to forget about the car.

Rick wrapped an arm around her, talking trash with Evan and Hector as they all headed toward the front door. She knew the moment he realized something was up. He gripped her shoulders tight and stopped walking. So much for a surprise. Apparently keeping quiet wasn't a Cabrera family trait.

"Maggie, what's all that noise?"

"Just open the front door." She gave him an encouraging smile.

He stepped inside before her.

"Shit, Mom, they're back," a good-looking man about Rick's age shouted toward the kitchen.

"Michael!" Rick pointed at the guy before he spun and kissed Maggie. "Thank you for this."

Then all hell broke loose. At least twenty people rushed toward the front of the house, speaking in Spanish and English interchangeably. All of them tried to hug Rick and Maggie. Even Evan, Hector, and Lena got caught up in the colossal holiday welcome from the Cabreras.

One of the younger family members took Hector's cooler and passed him a beer. It was barely eight A.M. Maggie suddenly realized this was going to be an epic day. She accepted a mimosa from another Cabrera and welcomed the liquid courage.

Evan and a few kids his age ducked out of the chaos, heading for the Xbox. She hoped she had enough food for everyone, and maybe she could get Hector to snag a few more chairs from the barn. She would figure it out.

The sea of people swallowed up Rick. Maggie hung back, sipping her drink and letting him enjoy the love of his family. When she formed this plan, she thought maybe his parents and a sibling or two might make it out for the holiday. But looking at the crowd, it looked like the entire family was here in Omaha for Rick. Her heart swelled. She was so thrilled that she'd been able to arrange this for him.

Aunt Irma fought her way to Maggie. "This is so perfect. I can't believe you did it. Come, you must meet Rick's mother, Anna." Irma pulled Maggie into the thick of the family. The crowd had moved into the new open-concept living area.

Thanks to Mona's investments, the house remodel went from penny-pinching to living a dream. Maggie and Rick had worked with Kevin to make the old house into a modern home that functioned for a family and looked beautiful. The dream kitchen Rick had planned out on paper was now a reality. She had two sinks. It was incredible. And her old apartment had gotten a facelift, and while Rick didn't know it, his parents would be using it for the next few days.

Anna and her husband were chatting with Rick. He caught her eye and waved her over. Irma kept close, and Maggie was thankful for her support. She and Anna had communicated via email, but this was the first time they had spoken.

"Mom, Dad, this is Maggie." Rick took her hand, pulled her next to him, and kissed her temple.

She held out her hand to shake and tried for a friendly, confident smile. Hopefully, she didn't look like a lunatic. "Mr. and Mrs. Cabr—"

"We're practically family. I'm Anna, and this is Luis," Anna interrupted. She pulled Maggie in for a hug and a kiss on each cheek. Luis did the same; his smile reminded her of Mona.

"It's wonderful to meet you both." The warm welcome helped her relax. The mimosa might have also contributed. But as far as a first impression, so far, so good.

"I can't believe you got them all here." Rick looked down at her. The love and gratitude shining in his eyes made all the secret planning worth it. She had so much to be thankful for this year.

"Irma and your mom did the real work of organizing your family. I just made the offer."

"It's amazing. Thank you." He squeezed her waist and left his hand curled around her back.

"Hey, Ricky. You so fine I'm going to blow your mind!" A young guy that looked like Rick's carbon copy slapped him on the back.

"Carlos!"

"Forget your mom and dad. I'm the real hero. Come on." Carlos turned toward the front door, pointing with his beer.

"Man, give me five. I need to shower and change." Rick was still wearing his running clothes.

"No way. You want to see this. Trust me." Carlos held up a keyring.

"No shit! I'll be back." Rick snatched the keys for his Charger from Carlos.

"I'm not going to miss this. I might see my grown son cry." Luis kissed his wife and followed the others out, leaving Maggie with Anna. She wiped her palms on her jeans and smoothed her hair. Shit, she should have grabbed another mimosa.

"Boys and their cars. My Luis is the same." Anna nodded at the men, laughing under her breath.

Maggie nodded. She was lost at sea and desperate for a conversation life raft to grab onto before she drowned.

"I have mimosas." Irma pressed glasses into Maggie's and Anna's hands. Bless her.

"Come, sit. I want to chat." Anna pointed to a pair of chairs in the window overlooking the barn and what remained of her garden. Winter had come early, and her plants were long gone.

"Sure. Yes." She sat and took a fortifying sip of the cocktail.

"Did you know Mona talked to me about you and your son Evan all the time? I know everything about your life from the moment you moved into her basement."

"Really?" She cringed internally. When she first moved in, she'd been a wreck. Newly divorced with a young son and overwhelmed by everything.

"Yes. I think Mona had been getting me ready to lose Rick to you long before you two reconnected. She told me once that you were his girl. Only geography was keeping you apart." Anna looked out the window, a faraway look in her eyes. She took a sip of her drink and refocused on Maggie.

"Has Rick told you about the will?" Family politics could be deadly. Maggie didn't want to tread on any dangerous ground.

Anna laughed. "My mother-in-law couldn't help herself. Given the opportunity to orchestrate another person's happiness, or what she perceived as such, she would take it. The shenanigans with the will were typical Mona."

"Mona was incredible. She wanted everyone to be happy. She seemed to know the times I was having the biggest problems in life. And I'd come home from work with Evan and find a casserole waiting for me so I didn't have to cook. A million of those small gestures from her over the years kept me going."

"That was Mona. When she talked about you and Rick together, I thought she was crazy. But as I watched Rick never find the right girl, I started to wonder if she had a point. When Rick said he was coming here, it killed me. He wasn't in a good place. But another part of me hoped Mona's prediction would come true. And you two would find your way together."

Maggie dashed a tear away. "We really have."

"Wonderful. I hate him being so far away, but this place and you are good for him."

"Thank you." Maggie sagged with relief at the warm acceptance from Rick's mother.

"No, thank you. His leaving the FBI is a dream come true to a worried mother. When he was shot, it nearly killed me. I hated seeing his pain. Now he's happy and has a chance at a whole new kind of life." Anna reached out and covered Maggie's hand with hers. "Enough serious talk. Let's get in the kitchen and rescue Tom Turkey. Lord only knows what Irma has been up to."

"That was a crazy day. I loved every moment. Thank you." Rick swung his legs into bed and pulled Maggie into his chest. His mind was still reeling. Maggie had orchestrated everything from his car's delivery to the dinner for thirty. He loved her so hard it hurt.

"I think you were more excited that Carlos drove your car up than to see your family."

"She is my pride and joy." He nuzzled his nose into Maggie's hair, enjoying the familiar scent of her shampoo. He needed to focus on what he had impulsively decided to do tonight. No plan. He was going on instinct. He wanted something big to show her how much she and today meant to him. He'd already gotten Evan's blessing.

"Should I be jealous of your car?" She turned in his arms to look at his face in the low light of the bedroom. After the extensive renovation on the second floor, he and Maggie had moved into the master bedroom. Very little remained to remind him it was Mona's old room other than the lady's vanity in the corner that Maggie had decided to keep and use.

"No. Never. But know if the house is burning down, I will load you and Evan into the Charger to escape so everyone I love is far from the flames."

She pinched his side. He laughed and batted her hand away.

"Hey. Easy. I ate too much. Don't pinch the food baby."

"I feel you." She rubbed her belly in sympathy.

"It was an epic day." He folded her back into his embrace. His mind far from calm, he was doing it. Now was the time.

"My thoughts exactly."

"I have one more memory I'd like to add to the experience." Rick sat up and opened the bedside table drawer. His heart thumped hard in his chest as he closed his fingers around the velvet box. Planning for the future and living in the moment, it all came down to a single question.

"Maggie," he tugged her up to sitting so they faced each other. "Will you marry me?"

He started to open the box and show her the ring but never got the chance. She flung her arms around him and tackled him into the pillows. His nervousness evaporated like it had never been at her excited response.

"Yes. A million times yes." With her face buried against his chest, she kept repeating that one word. Yes. And it echoed deep within him, filling up his heart until it felt like it might burst from his chest.

He pulled back and tipped her head up. He swiped away a tear on her cheek. "Happy tears?"

She nodded, her eyes so full of joy he knew he'd made the right decision asking her tonight.

He dipped his head and kissed her. He teased her lips open and cradled her jaw in his hand, savoring the feel of her, soft and yielding. He let the kiss unfurl, building from tender to hungry. His hand slipped around the nape of her neck. He pulled her down into him. Heat grew and blossomed out of control. This woman was his, and the rightness of their life together was his everything. Her, Evan, their house, and a new city he was happy to call home. It was the beginning of a journey he couldn't wait to take, and he never wanted it to end. She really was his heart.

He broke the kiss for the barest moment. "I love you, Maggie."

"I love you, Rick."

He swallowed her words as he took her mouth for another epic kiss.

THE END...or is it?

Do you want to salsa the night away under the Miami sky? Join Rick and Maggie for a tropical winter wedding.
Scan the QR code below to read a bonus chapter and get a few recipes inspired by Omaha Heat.

SCAN ME

Also By Michelle Donn

The Protecting Love Series
Savannah Run
Chicago By Chance
Palm Beach Bodyguard
Las Vegas Risk
Miami Reignited
Omaha Heat
Lone Star Revenge (Novella)

New Series Starting in 2022
Miami Private Security

About The Author

Michelle Donn lives in South Florida with her real-life prince charming, two dogs, three horses, a cat, and Daisy the donkey. Most evenings, you will find her floating in the pool, enjoying a cocktail, and working out the plot of her next book with her husband. If you want to see her silly side find her TikTok!

facebook.com/michelledonnauthor

TikTok: @michelledonnauthor

Instagram: @michelledonnauthor

Printed in Great Britain
by Amazon